THE FELSHAM AFFAIR

Jacqueline Beard

The Lawrence Harpham Mysteries are published by Dornica Press

The author can be contacted on her website
https://jacquelinebeardwriter.com/

While there, why not sign up for her FREE newsletter.

ISBN: 1-91-605064-6

ISBN-13: 978-1-91-605064-8

First Printing 2020

Dornica Press

Dedicated to:
My sisters Caroline & Jo

Also, by this author:

Lawrence Harpham Murder Mysteries:

The Fressingfield Witch
The Ripper Deception
The Scole Confession

Novels:

Vote for Murder

Short Stories:

The Montpellier Mystery

PROLOGUE

Prologue

They call me Ratman, a name which has haunted me in one guise or another all my life. But they are the vermin, not I. They whisper to each other when I draw near – spiteful mouths uttering monstrous jibes, their barbed words piercing arrow-like with cruel intent. Innocents, you say. They know not what they do? Damn their eyes, but they understand. They may be young, but they know how much the words sting. Why must I tolerate it, just because I am fully grown, and they are yet to mature? Perhaps.

What they see on the surface does not represent the man beneath. He is disguised by the manner of his dress, the odour of his toil, whether he smiles or frowns. They look upon him and judge those external trappings without considering how he feels inside, how I feel. Whether I am happy or sad, and who I have loved and lost.

Who have I lost you may ask? No one important, as it happens. I care less about what I have lost and more about what I should have had in the first place. I should have had a loving family. I should have had a happy home. Somebody should have cared for me, but they did not.

I went to school with a boy called Johnny Curtis. Johnny spent his formative years in an orphanage before an aunt of his scraped together enough money to support him. They lived in abject poverty in the ground-floor room of a crowded house. The mildewed walls were bare, the room icy cold, and how they were able to cook and sleep, I cannot imagine. But Johnny was content. The orphanage clothed and fed him better than his impoverished aunt, but she made him feel worthy. In the orphanage, Johnny was merely another mouth to feed, cared for but unloved, a problem to resolve – a number, not a name. But his aunt's love was all he needed, and he went to bed happy with a rumbling stomach. Johnny is dead now. He died of typhoid thirty years ago and is dust in an unmarked grave. Why does Johnny matter? In short, he does not, but the circumstances of his childhood illustrate the darkness of my own, for I was jealous of Johnny. Jealous that he was warm and fed, jealous of his aunt's love – jealous, even, that he died young and did not have to endure years of nightmares. I wish I had grown up in an orphanage.

I did not know my father. I doubt my mother knew him either. She was probably drunk when he impregnated her. A small miracle had she been sober as she was rarely without alcohol. Gin, ale – it did not matter. And if alcohol was unavailable, then opiates would do. You may wonder where she obtained opiates so readily. After all, we were poor. Her fault – she worked but drank away whatever money she made. And she had a ready supply of opiates because she charred in a squalid club in Limehouse. A low opium den. And when I say charred, that was what she told people. In reality, she sold her drug-addled body to whoever was desperate enough to pay for it.

I could have endured this if I'd had a real home. Our filthy rooms off Amoy Place were squeezed between Pearl Gordon's laundry house and a food store owned by a Chinaman. The laundry was always full of red-skinned women bellowing to each other above the thud of the washing dollies. They despised my mother for reasons unknown to me. I expect she uttered some nonsense in one of her alcohol-fuelled diatribes, but I was not there and do not know what she said. Mother would scuttle past when the weather was warm and the laundry door was open, to avoid the catcalls that invariably followed. Mother likewise avoided Mr Chan's food emporium, refusing to eat anything handled by foreigners. Quite ridiculous considering the varied nationalities of the men from whom she took money in the course of her work. No, it wasn't that she hated strangers. It was that she hated me. And Mr Chan was one of the very few adults in my life who had time for an unloved, unwanted child.

5

I found this out one cold day in February when I was about five years old. Mother had shut me out – something she often did, but this time, she refused to let me take my coat. I sat shivering at the bottom of the stairs, as was customary under these circumstances. I could not get warm and decided that walking in the sleeting rain was preferable to the boredom and discomfort of the damp hallway. As I walked outside, steam billowed from a window in the laundry. The shop was open, and I remember wishing that my mother was on better terms with the laundry girls. Then, they might have offered me shelter, but it wasn't only my mother that they taunted. They did not spare their venomous words on me either. So, I turned right instead and loitered outside Mr Chan's shop gazing at the spiky writing on the wall and wondering what it meant.

Despite the cold weather, the door to the shop was ajar, and I pushed it with a pale finger, numb with cold. I peered around the door and into the brightly painted room, and my jaw dropped in wonderment. The walls were lurid yellow save for one painted scarlet. Paper lanterns hung from hooks on the ceiling, and the L-shaped shop counter was full of wondrous, colourful foodstuffs that smelled of the East. I reached for a spiky star-shaped object in a jar and held it to my nose, inhaling the aromatic scent. It was like nothing I had ever known, and I stood entranced until a snuffling at my ankles caught my attention. I looked down to see a small hairy dog with a flat face, panting as it licked at my legs.

I stepped back in alarm, and at the same moment, a soft voice spoke in a language I did not understand. I spun around to see a short, thin man clad in a shiny jacket with gold braid. I stood stock-still in fear, expecting a tongue-lashing at best and a beating at worst for daring to enter his shop. But the man spoke softly and pointed towards the dog. He mimed a stroking gesture and, biting my lip, I knelt and touched the dog's ears. It wagged its tail, then placed a paw on my knee. Screwing up my courage, I stroked its back and tickled its ear. It did not bite or growl but sat benignly panting with something close to a grin upon its face. I looked up at the man, and he smiled benevolently before offering a jar containing round objects that looked like nuts. I took one and opened my mouth, but the man waved his finger and touched his nose, so I smelled it instead. Like the star-shaped object, it conjured warm, unfamiliar scents and my fear vanished, replaced with a childish

6

curiosity. The man pointed to my hand and then to the threadbare pocket of my jersey, and I placed the two objects inside. He smiled at me and pointed to himself. "I Mr Chan," he said in broken English. I repeated his name, and he nodded.

Mr Chan's food emporium became my only place of refuge. Somewhere I could escape from the horrors of my home. And there were horrors aplenty. It wasn't only the alcohol that made my mother a bad parent. It was her loathing of me that made my childhood so miserable.

My mother bore two children. I came first then Noel arrived a few years later. Noel, the favoured child, was born in December and was, if not loved, then at least tolerated by Mother. The treatment meted out to me by her was callous and unfeeling. Being left in the cold was the kindest of her punishments. More often, she beat me, but at least that was bearable. I can hardly bring myself to remember the other punishment, the one in the cellar, in the dark. The one with a wooden board drilled with holes for straps. The one where Mother dragged me to the basement by my hair, strapped me to the wood and left me standing for hours and hours staring at the chink of light above the basement window. The hairs would rise on the back of my neck, and I would screw my eyes tight. I remember watching the window as the light faded away, waiting for Mother to release me, listening for the dread scrabbles of the basement rats. I longed for her to set me free, but the rats always got there first, slinking towards me, beady eyes fixed on their captive audience. I would scream and shout and sing and cry, bawl and yell – anything to scare them away. But as the hours crawled past, the rats grew bolder. The dark was their domain, and they were the masters. They waited as tiredness sapped my purpose, and I became quiet and terrified. Then, they would surge towards me, whiskers brushing at my legs, teeth like needles nipping at my ankles. I would wake and kick out, and they would flee for a while before the whole nightmare began again. By dawn, I would be a shivering, terrified wreck, and when Mother finally remembered me, she would sneer with disgust at my soiled trousers and urine-soaked shoes.

I tried to be good, tried to recall what I had done to deserve the cellar punishment so I could avoid it, but the rules changed every time. Eventually, I realised that there were no rules. Mother didn't like me, and she enjoyed torturing me. It was as simple as that. I don't recall her ever leaving Noel in the cellar, but then I doubt we had the same father. Perhaps that was why Mother treated us so differently.

Every night I spent in the cellar was worse than the last. Fear turned to boredom, and boredom turned to self-loathing as I grew older. But the worst incident happened during the day. I was about seven by then. Mother had marched me to the basement for some invented reason, and I had gone more willingly than usual as it was mid-morning and I hoped she might release me before the evening. I was all compliance and even helped when she dropped a strap. Then she left without a backward glance, and I was alone.

There is only one way to look when tied to an upright piece of wood, and that is dead ahead. And the small cellar window was fortuitously positioned directly in front of me. Outside the window, was a recess the size of a packing crate about half a foot down from road height. If I was lucky, a bird might find its way down, and I could occupy my time watching it go about its business, and sometimes a cat might find its way to my prison. But on this particular day, a much bigger creature appeared.

A thud precipitated its arrival. There had been an unusual amount of noise from the street that day. I could hear laughing and shrieking and came to realise that children were playing outside. They sounded happy and carefree, and I thanked God that they could not see me shackled to a miserable piece of rotting board. But then it happened. The thud heralded the arrival of a tightly wadded cloth. It bumped against the recess and settled shadowed against the window. I froze, my heart thudding harder than it did when I had fallen asleep one night and woke to find a rat with a mouthful of my blood and a hole in my leg. I held my breath, hoping that whoever had dropped the makeshift ball, did not care for its return, but it was not to be. I heard a clatter of stones and a boy vaulted into the recess and picked up the cloth ball. I stared through the grimy window in silence. It had been many years, if ever since the glass was cleaned, and he might not be able to see through. But I had not accounted for the curiosity of small boys. He spat on his palm and wiped the pane, then stared at me with round eyes as I gazed upon his familiar features. It was Billy Nugent. He was in my class at school.

Billy's mouth opened in shock, then he turned and scrambled up the recess. I closed my eyes, willing him to get on with his game and leave me in peace. But within moments, he had returned with two other boys,

8

both known to me. The three of them squeezed into the tiny space, and Joe McGuiness jabbed a podgy finger towards me. "Look at 'im, trapped like a rat in a cage," he shrieked, and I closed my eyes and wished them all away. They were still there when I opened them again; noses pressed to the window like three ugly monkeys. "Rat in a cage, a rat in a cage," they chanted over and over until they grew bored with the game and left me there, alone. Never once did it occur to them to offer help to a fellow human being.

By the time I arrived at school the next day, I had a new name. They called me Ratty, that day and every day after. I grew to hate those boys, the school, the teachers, just as I grew to hate the children that taunt me now. I learned my letters and numbers and took care of myself and Noel for a while when my mother died. But it's taken me until now to understand my condition. Some people are born to be unloved, never evoking compassion or empathy, always rejected. I am in no better a position now than I was then. An object of ridicule. A small boy tormented by an adult or an adult tormented by children. Either way, the common factor is me. And if I was born for the world to despise, then I may as well do something despicable. Why pretend? I was born bad. Somehow, the acknowledgement of this thing that I have always known brings a rare glimmer of peace.

CHAPTER ONE

Missing

Monday, September 7, 1896

Lawrence Harpham opened his desk drawer and extracted a brown envelope. He removed a single sheet of paper and placed it on his desk, before turning to face his business partner who was sitting to his right. "How about this one?" he asked, brandishing the paper.

Violet Smith sighed. "I haven't finished checking Mr Baldry's accounts yet," she said.

"I know, but it's clear your heart's not in it. I can finish the accounts if you want to take something more interesting."

"I don't," said Violet. "I'm perfectly happy with this."

Silence settled over the office and Lawrence bit his lip as he considered the change in Violet since her return from Cornwall earlier in the year. It had been her second visit to her aunt since the unfortunate appearance of Loveday in their office the previous June. Upon sight of Loveday, Violet had left without a word, reappearing two weeks later with no explanation about where she had been. Lawrence had tried to explain his entanglement with Loveday during his time in Liverpool, but even as the words left his lips, he had to admit that his account sounded lame. Violet listened, impervious to his pleas. "How you spend your leisure time is none of my business," she'd said impassively, pursing her lips as she tallied three months' worth of accounts. Moments later, her face had darkened, and Lawrence winced as he heard the snap of a breaking pencil lead. He'd cringed with embarrassment as he remembered the money from the company bank account that he'd borrowed to pay for Loveday's expensive dinner.

Not long after that, Violet left again, this time for an extended visit to her ailing aunt. She was away for more than six months, during which time Lawrence handled their caseload alone. He'd ploughed on, perplexed and baffled at her insistence on placing family duty first. It was a lonely six months, giving him an insight into how it must have been for Violet when he was too ill to work. When Violet walked in unannounced through the door of Harpham and Smith Private Investigators at the end of May, Lawrence had breathed a sigh of relief, hoping that things would soon return to normal. They had not. Violet was back in body, but not in spirit. She seemed distracted, aloof, and burdened. Their easy discourse was a distant memory. Lawrence had hoped for the opportunity to express his regard for her, but a serious barrier threatened their friendship. Lawrence had somehow drifted into an engagement with Loveday Graham from which it was impossible to extricate himself without embarrassment. And he was no longer sure that he wanted to. Loveday was bright and beautiful – a golden-haired, glamorous young woman with a warm personality and friendly approach. And better still, Loveday wasn't bound by family duties and had given Lawrence a month of rapturous devotion while Violet was away before she'd returned to India. Lawrence had assumed he wouldn't see her again, but in the meantime, Loveday's father had died, and her mother returned to Cheltenham to rent a house in Pittville. In the last two months before Violet's return, Lawrence had visited Loveday and she had come to Bury. Her bright personality cut through his loneliness in the way that Violet's used to when she was there. Lawrence hadn't been sure when Violet would return, or even if she would return, although she wrote from time to time.

He looked up at the clock and sneaked a glance at Violet again as she leaned over Baldry's ledger. Her face was gaunt, and she'd pinned her hair into a tight bun. Her neat, black dress with the lace cuffs and collar was starkly formal. Violet was starkly formal – not a stray hair

11

or curl, not a loose button or thread. All bound up tightly – expressionless. Violet must know about Loveday by now. Lawrence hadn't told her, but she'd seen both Michael and Francis and they knew. On hearing the news, Francis had shaken Lawrence's hand and offered his congratulations. Michael barely acknowledged it, which indicated his disapproval. Francis, bolder and more curious than his brother, had asked Lawrence for details of the engagement. Lawrence hadn't embellished. He couldn't easily explain. He hadn't exactly asked Loveday to marry him in the first place. She had taken it for granted and on learning of her cousin's impending marriage, had told her mother of her intentions regarding Lawrence. Mrs Graham, though far from keen on Lawrence's less solid social status, had nevertheless placed an announcement in the *Cheltenham Examiner*. Now the engagement was formal, and unless one of them changed their minds, a marriage would take place in December.

The clock ticked loudly, in time with the rhythmic scratch of Violet's pen. Lawrence sighed. Violet ignored him, and Lawrence sighed again. Violet stopped writing, pursed her lips and placed the pen onto the inkstand. "What is it?" she asked.

"Nothing much," said Lawrence.

"Then I'll return to my work, if I may?"

"Of course. It's just that…"

"What?"

"Don't you think we should talk about it?"

"Talk about what?" Violet hissed the word, and her eyes narrowed.

Lawrence gulped. "About the old cases," he said, changing tack. He removed a second brown envelope.

Violet raised an eyebrow.

"The ones that came in while you were away. I didn't get to them. There wasn't time."

"How old are they?"

"Anything from a few weeks to almost a year," said Lawrence.

"Is there any point? Won't the clients have gone elsewhere after all this time?"

"I don't know. Do you want to look through the files? You've all but finished with Baldry. You'll get bored if you keep this up."

Violet shook her head but held out her hand for the envelope. She peered inside and removed a sheaf of papers, silently sorting them into three piles before handing the largest set to Lawrence. "They're not worth our time," she said. "We should write and refuse."

Lawrence nodded, happy to indulge her if it meant breaking the unsettling silence between them.

Violet continued. "These might be worthwhile if the fee is good enough. Have you discussed a price with them?"

Lawrence shook his head. "I've been too busy."

Violet sighed. "And this one – well. I don't know what to say. If it wasn't for the money, I would dismiss it out of hand. How on earth are we expected to investigate something that happened over three decades ago? I don't know if it's possible."

"We managed it in Fressingfield," said Lawrence. "And that mystery began hundreds of years before. If we can do that, we can do this."

"I'm surprised you have even contemplated it," said Violet. "It's not the sort of matter that usually interests you."

"It doesn't. I kept it because I thought you might want to look into it."

"Well, I don't."

"Why?"

"I just don't want to."

"Is there a reason?"

Violet picked up the paper again and scanned the page. "I told when we left Scole that I wouldn't be dealing with children's deaths again."

"I remember," said Lawrence. "And I'm sorry. It was that boy in the barrel, wasn't it?"

Violet closed her eyes and winced. "Please, don't," she said.

Lawrence stood and instinctively reached towards her. She recoiled, and he stared aghast, shocked by her unconcealed antipathy. The doorbell interrupted the discomfiting moment, and Francis Farrow entered, with a worried expression on his face.

"Francis," said Lawrence, recovering himself. He walked towards the door and offered his hand. Francis shook it and smiled.

"What are you doing here?" asked Lawrence. "Aren't you due in court today?"

"No. That's next week, and it's dashed inconvenient. It's bad enough having your possessions pinched without having to turn up to court as a witness. I wish I hadn't bothered reporting it."

"Even you can't afford to lose a carriage," said Lawrence.

"I know." Francis sighed as he sat down opposite. "Anyway, how are you keeping, Violet?"

"Well," said Violet, unconvincingly.

Francis raised a knowing eyebrow and smiled sympathetically.

"What can we do for you?" asked Lawrence. "Or are you here for a chat?"

"A chat? No, not at all. I need your help, Lawrence. I am here in an official capacity. I want you to act for me."

"But they've found the thief. I'm not sure what else I can do."

"It's not that," said Francis. "And strictly speaking, you wouldn't be acting for me. I'm asking for your help on behalf of a young lady."

"Who?" asked Lawrence.

"I'll tell you later. It's easier if I introduce her. Come for tea this afternoon, and we can talk it through. You too, Violet."

"I have other plans," said Violet.

"Can't you change them? This matter requires a woman's touch. Please join us."

"Very well," said Violet reluctantly. "But I'll meet you there." She stood, cleared her desk and left the office.

"Things a little frosty still?" asked Francis.

"I assume so, but she won't talk about it."

"It's hardly surprising. From what Michael tells me, she didn't have much time for Loveday when they lived together in Fressingfield."

"I don't know why. Loveday was always perfectly agreeable."

"I daresay. But it must have been a shock to Violet to return and find you on the cusp of marriage."

"If it gets that far."

Francis raised an eyebrow. "What do you mean?"

"Nothing," said Lawrence moodily.

"Having second thoughts?"

"No. She's a lovely girl, but I can't help wondering what would have happened if she hadn't returned to England. Violet and I were such good friends…" Lawrence stared wistfully into the distance.

"Less of that," boomed Francis. "It's pre-wedding nerves. You're a gentleman and must do the right thing by Loveday. Let's hear no more about it. Now, be at Netherwood for four-thirty. Don't be late."

#

Lawrence approached the entrance to Netherwood House to see Violet entering the door. He strode down the drive, but she disappeared before he reached the doorway. He glanced towards the covered, doorless outbuilding that had formerly housed Francis Farrow's Brougham carriage and wondered who had taken it. Granted the building was unsecured but coming onto a man's land in broad daylight and harnessing horses to his carriage to steal it, was breathtakingly audacious. The theft must have been carefully planned. Five years ago, the Brougham had been Francis' pride and joy, but familiarity had tarnished its appeal, and the furore surrounding the loss had become an inconvenience. Had Francis less money, he might have cared more, but he could comfortably buy another three carriages without financial difficulty. Though now in a similar position, old habits died hard and Lawrence would never have taken such a cavalier attitude.

He rang the doorbell and waited for a few minutes, knowing that it would take a while as Albert Floss the butler, would be showing Violet into the drawing room. But Albert must have returned immediately and opened the door while Lawrence was idly removing mud from his shoe with the boot scraper.

"Mr Lawrence, come inside," said Albert, with a weak smile.

"Thank you. It's good to see you again, Albert. Are you keeping well?"

"For the most," said Albert, quietly. He gestured towards the drawing room. "Please join Mr Farrow and Miss Smith. I will be with you shortly."

Violet and Francis were earnestly whispering when Lawrence entered. They looked up at the sound of his footsteps and immediately stopped talking. Francis stood and offered his hand. "Glad you could make it, old man," he said. "Do sit down."

Lawrence settled on a leather chair close to the fireplace and gazed around the room. It was still as he remembered it when he'd stayed last year after what Lawrence feared was a nervous breakdown. He'd recovered quickly, thanks to Violet's care and was able to resume his work far sooner than expected. It was hard to believe that it had been over a year ago. Francis had also been away, spending more than a few months abroad. He had left Netherwood House in the care of Albert Floss, who received no visitors while his master was away, all of which made Lawrence feel as if he had only popped out for a brief moment.

"Help yourself," said Francis, gesturing to a side table in the corner of the room upon which stood a three-tiered china stand filled with a variety of cakes and pastries. Beside it, lay a plate of sandwiches and a large pot of tea.

"I don't mind if I do," said Lawrence, approaching the table. His stomach rumbled as he helped himself to a large plate of food.

"What's it all about then?" he asked through a mouthful of sandwich.

Francis didn't have time to answer before Albert Floss returned to the drawing room, accompanied by a young lady dressed in a plain, black woollen dress with turned-up cuffs and a lace collar. She looked young – perhaps in her mid to late twenties. Her face was gaunt, and her eyes were puffy and red-rimmed.

"Sit down, my dear," said Francis, gesturing towards the settee. "You too, Albert."

Albert sat uncomfortably beside her with his hands on his knees and an upright back.

"Lawrence – may I present Miss Flora Johns. She is Albert's niece. Flora – meet Lawrence Harpham and Violet Smith."

"Pleased to meet you," said Violet while Lawrence nodded and smiled.

"Right," said Francis. "I'll get straight to it. Miss Johns is in trouble and needs your help. I'm quite prepared to meet your costs. What do you say?"

"That I'd like to know more before agreeing to anything," said Lawrence, frankly.

"What he means, is yes, we would love to help," said Violet, glaring at Lawrence.

"Capital," said Francis. "It's a complicated affair. Shall I tell them about it, or would you rather do it yourself?"

16

"I... I... Flora Johns opened her mouth to speak, but the words would not follow, and her eyes brimmed with tears. Albert patted her shoulder, solicitously. "There, there," he said.

Violet rose and approached Flora. "Do you mind?" she asked, turning to Albert.

"No, miss," he said, rising from his seat.

Violet sat next to Flora and took her hand. "What is it, my dear," she said kindly. "You look like you are carrying the worries of the world on your shoulders."

Flora burst into tears, removed a handkerchief from her sleeve and sobbed noisily into the delicate fabric.

"Cry it out," said Violet. "Take your time."

The girl continued weeping, and after a few moments, Violet clasped her wrist and gently stroked the back of her hand until the crying stopped. "I'm sorry," said Flora softly. "What must you think of me?"

"You mustn't worry," said Violet. "Tell me how we can help."

"It's Bertie," said the girl. "I've lost Bertie."

"And who is Bertie?"

"My son." Flora's voice wobbled as she said his name. She bit her lip and shut her eyes as if in pain.

"You poor girl." Violet could not conceal her shock. She was half expecting to hear that Bertie was an animal. In the five years since Harpham & Smith Private Investigators had been in existence, no one had ever asked them to locate a missing child.

"When did you last see him?" asked Violet.

"Three weeks ago," said Flora. "Though it seems longer now. I can barely remember his dear face already. He seemed to change every time I visited, but then he was – is – a young baby and they grow up so quickly."

"He didn't live with you?" asked Violet.

Flora shook her head. "I am a housemaid," said Flora. "He could not live with me. Oh, this is embarrassing. I have to tell you – that is I am mortified, ashamed, but..."

"What Flora is trying to say," said Albert, smiling at his niece, "is that she is unmarried. Her employer doesn't know she has a child and Flora's mother, my sister, is dead. But she is a good girl and is making the best of a difficult situation."

17

"You are so kind to me, Uncle," said Flora. "I would be utterly alone without you."

"I only wish I could do more."

"You did," said Francis. "You came to me, and I have passed this to Lawrence who will do his best to find your boy."

"Thank you," said Flora, breathlessly, choking down tears.

Lawrence grimaced. He wanted to help, but even without details, he knew the case would be complicated. "Where did you last see Bertie?" he asked.

"At a lodging house in Gideon Road," whispered Flora.

"What was he doing there?"

"I placed an advertisement in the newspaper for someone to mind him. I cannot keep him with me. My mistress does not know, and she would let me go if she ever found out. But I get a half-day every Thursday, and Gideon Road is not far from where I work in Battersea. I visited Bertie every week until three weeks ago."

"What happened then?" Violet's eyes were wide with concern. She stared at Flora intently.

"I went to the lodging house at the usual time, knocked on the door and asked to see Dorothy Jones. She was the lady who had been looking after Bertie. But the landlord said she had gone away unexpectedly. I asked where Bertie was, and he said he did not know. I returned every day for a week, knocking on all the nearby doors but nobody could tell me anything, and nobody had seen Bertie. The police were no use, and I didn't know what else to do, so I told my mistress that Uncle was gravely ill and came straight to Bury to ask his advice."

"I don't know what to say," said Violet. She was still stroking Flora's hand, and her face was white. "I cannot imagine how you must be feeling."

"I'm frightened," said Flora. "And I don't know where to begin. London is vast, and Bertie is so tiny. And I cannot think where she might have taken him, or why. It's utterly hopeless." She closed her eyes in abject misery as tears streamed down her face.

"There is hope," said Violet. "There is always hope. We will do everything we can to help, won't we, Lawrence?"

Lawrence nodded and swallowed a lump in his throat, touched by the young girl's love for her child."

18

"I'll need the full address of the lodging house and names of anyone connected to it. Do you know anything more about Dorothy Jones?"

"No," whispered Flora. "She answered the advertisement, and we arranged to meet in Battersea Park. I met her for a second time at the lodging house and then weekly when I visited Bertie."

"How old was she?"

"I'm not sure. Older than me, I think," she said, looking at Violet.

"And she hadn't mentioned she was going away? Could she have taken a break in the countryside?"

"Definitely not." Flora shook her head as she spoke. "I had made arrangements to see Bertie as usual on Thursday afternoon. Miss Jones had asked for some more clothes as he was growing so fast, and I said I would bring them with me."

"When are you returning to London?" Lawrence stood as he asked the question and helped himself to another sandwich.

Flora glanced at her uncle. "Tomorrow, I suppose."

"Are you sure?" asked Albert. "You've had very little time to rest."

"I should be close to Battersea," said Flora, "in case he's found. Anyway, I cannot take too much time away, or my mistress may suspect my story."

"I'm surprised you've been able to carry on with your work with all the worry you have suffered," said Violet, sympathetically.

"It hasn't been easy." Flora bit her lip. "But I feel a little better knowing that you're going to help."

"We'll travel down tomorrow," said Violet.

Lawrence glanced towards her with a surprised expression on his face. "We'll return to the office and make arrangements," he said, passing his open notebook and a pencil to her. "Write down the address of the lodging house, and I'll visit as soon as I get to London."

#

Violet arrived at the office first and was busy reading *The Bury and Norwich Post* when Lawrence opened the door. He'd called into the butchers on his way back and carried a brown paper parcel containing a couple of lamb chops which he intended to have for his dinner.

19

Violet looked up and glared as he entered the room. "You said, as soon as *I* get to London," she muttered, without waiting for him to speak.

Lawrence sighed. "There's a reason for that," he said.

Violet raised a cynical eyebrow.

"Annie's in Norwich. She's not due back for a week. Who will mind the office if we both go?"

"Oh." For a moment, Violet looked crestfallen, then she continued. "You don't normally care if the office is empty. We've left it unattended before."

"I didn't have much choice when you were in Cornwall," said Lawrence, "but Annie was marvellous, and we managed between us. It matters more now because we're busy and there's a backlog of cases."

"Not very worthwhile cases," said Violet.

"Come, now," said Lawrence. "The Felsham case will pay well."

Violet expelled a long breath. "So, you get to go to London, and you expect me to stay here and look into a trivial historical matter."

"If you would be so kind. And it's not trivial. Did you read the letter?"

"Not properly," Violet admitted. "I glanced at it."

"It's a poisoning," said Lawrence.

"The one with the dead child? I said I wouldn't do that."

"Yet you'd deal with the missing child in Battersea?"

"There's still hope of a happy outcome. The mother and child may be reunited."

"Or they may not," warned Lawrence. "The Felsham case is a known quantity. The child is dead and however hard that is, there is no room for false hope."

"You shouldn't go to Battersea if you don't think you'll find Bertie," said Violet. "You risk failing before you've even started."

"You ought to know me better than that," said Lawrence. His blue eyes looked downcast and sad. "If I take a case, I'll do my damnedest to see it through."

"I'm sure you will." Violet relented, registering his hurt expression. "But you don't sound very hopeful."

"I'm not," said Lawrence, frankly. "You've seen the news."

20

"I can't bear to think about it – that wretched woman. I don't like the idea of executions, let alone for a female, but she deserved it. How a mother can kill little children for profit defeats me. Thankfully, monsters like Amelia Dyer must be one of a kind. There could not be two such cruel women in the world."

Lawrence raised an eyebrow. "She didn't work alone," he said.

"I wouldn't know. I've taken care not to read any of the torrid newspaper accounts," said Violet. "You don't suppose that Flora's boy has met a similar fate?"

"No, of course not," Lawrence assured her. "But it's going to be difficult to find a small child in a city like London. It could be quite an ordeal."

Violet mellowed at the evident concern in his eyes. "I don't need protecting," she said.

"I know you don't. But please consider looking into the Felsham case while I travel to London," he said. "I'll only be there for a few days, and then I'll return. We can compare notes and work on the conclusions together. What do you say?"

"Tell me what I need to do."

Lawrence picked up the brown envelope from his desk where Violet had left it.

"Drucilla Brown is our client," said Lawrence. "She is the wife of a farmer in Felsham. Her sister-in-law Julia was accused of murder in 1864, but she was acquitted. Drucilla has come into some money and would like us to look into it."

"Whatever for? Doesn't she like Julia?"

"Yes, very much. That's why she's willing to pay. Julia's child was poisoned. Drucilla doesn't think that Julia hurt him, but someone did, and she wants us to find out who."

"I see. But after all this time…"

"It won't be easy, Violet. That's why I thought it might suit you."

"I suppose I could go to Felsham and also keep the office open for a few days this week."

"Exactly. That's settled then. I'll go to London, you go to Felsham, and we'll meet in a week."

CHAPTER TWO

In Search of the Truth

Wednesday, September 9, 1895

Violet walked along Guildhall Street on her way to the coach stop. She'd spent the previous day alone in the office while Lawrence had boarded the train for London. Violet had been both sad and relieved to see him go. Sorry because they'd always worked well together, and the life of a private investigator was often lonely, but relieved at not having to pretend to be happy when she wasn't. This unhappiness surpassed any doubts about working alone. Violet had been shocked when Loveday turned up in their office last year and the betrayal that she'd felt when it became clear that Lawrence had dallied with Loveday in Liverpool, sent her reeling. She'd gone straight to the station and taken a train to Diss, arriving without notice at Michael's cottage in Scole. He'd taken her in and looked after her for two weeks while Violet licked her wounds. Michael didn't ask questions but waited until she was ready to talk. Even then, Violet told him little of her feelings. Sharing personal information was not her way. Violet withheld far more than she gave and dealt stoically and rationally with her disappointment, returning to Bury and back to the occupation she had grown to enjoy. When Violet thought about it, she had spent more time investigating alone than she ever did with Lawrence, carrying their caseload solo for two years while he was ill. Splitting up to manage two cases had become a recent habit. A good habit. One that undoubtedly improved their profits.

A sudden blaring noise interrupted Violet's reverie. She spun to her left to see a shiny black and gold horseless carriage pulling up beside her. The driver waved, removed his hat and gestured. Violet returned a smile as Francis Farrow hopped confidently from the vehicle. "What do you think?" he asked.

"I don't know what to think," said Violet, honestly. "It's very handsome, but what exactly is it?"

"Ah, it's an Arnold Benz automobile," said Francis. "One of a very few. I had it driven up from Kent yesterday – a little treat to myself, don't you know? Would you like a ride?"

"I can't," said Violet. "I'm catching the coach to Felsham."

"Nonsense," said Francis. "Forget horsepower. I'll get you there much quicker in this."

Violet looked uncertainly at the overcast sky. "I don't want to get wet."

"It won't rain," said Francis confidently. "We'll be in Felsham in under an hour. Come on. Keep me company. I want to see what speed I can get out of the old girl."

Violet sighed, unhappy about the prospect of driving fast in a horseless carriage, but she didn't like to curtail Francis' enthusiasm. He seemed even more besotted with this motor than he had been with the Brougham when it was first purchased.

"Very well," she said.

"Excellent. Give me your luggage." Francis took her carpetbag and squashed it into a small box at the front of the automobile, then he reached for her hand and helped her aboard. She watched while he rotated the flywheel and the vehicle purred into life.

"Off we go," said Francis, manipulating a tall steering wheel. They pulled off slowly and drove through the centre of Bury, while Francis waved at the passers-by as if he was royalty.

"I can see why you weren't upset at the loss of your carriage," said Violet. "Why didn't you say something?"

"In case the purchase didn't happen," smiled Francis. "As I said, there were only a few available. I ended up in a bidding war with a chap from Southampton, as it was. I probably paid too much for it," he continued cheerfully.

23

They meandered towards the outskirts of Bury and onto Sicklesmere Road which stretched long and straight into the distance. "Now let's see what she can do," said Francis, activating the clutch. The car lurched forwards, gaining speed, and Violet's hair began to loosen from its pins as the breeze swept past.

"How fast are we going?" she asked, alarmed.

"About twelve miles an hour," said Francis with a grin. "Fun isn't it?"

By the time they reached The Fox and Hounds public house at Maypole Green, some two miles from Felsham, it had stopped being fun. The rhythmic throb of the engine turned to a juddering whine, and the automobile limped to a stop. Francis jumped from the vehicle and regarded it with his hands on his hips. "Hmmm," he said, removing his driving hat and gloves and placing them by the side of the road. "I'd better see what's wrong with the old girl."

He examined the area beneath the high seats, chewing his lip as he muttered under his breath. "The engine looks all right, and the pulley clutch seems fine. Ah, I know." He stood up and opened the box, rifling beneath Violet's carpetbag until he found a small container of oil.

"Oh. That will make my bag smell nice," said Violet, wrinkling her nose.

Francis ignored her, opened the can and oiled an exposed chain. "That should do it," he said uncertainly before spinning the flywheel again. The engine started after a couple of attempts, and they set off once more.

"Marvellous," said Francis, smiling. "That could have been a tricky moment. Thank goodness I thought to stow the oil before I left the house."

"Well done," said Violet, glad to humour him. Anything to get them to Felsham quicker. The wind had picked up, and she was sure she'd felt a drop of rain while they were stationary. Unlike a horse-drawn carriage, the automobile was not built for poor weather, and Violet couldn't see the appeal.

It was mid-morning when they finally arrived in Felsham. Attractive, well-built cottages sat snugly in the centre of the village, within sight of St Peter's Church. The cloud lifted, and the sun shone momentarily, dappling the thatched roofs of a row of cottages nestled along the green.

"Where shall I drop you?" asked Francis.

Violet pulled a notebook from her pocket and extracted a folded document. "Hill Farm Cottages," she said. "I suppose I'd better find someone to ask."

"You could try there," said Francis, gesturing towards a square, stone building with a sign reading 'The Six Bells'.

"It doesn't look as if it's open yet," said Violet, doubtfully.

"No matter," said Francis, striding towards the window. He rapped smartly upon the glass. Inside, a young woman looked up abruptly and clutched her chest.

"Francis," hissed Violet. "You startled her."

"Just as I intended," he said. Within a few short moments, the door opened to reveal a frowning, auburn-haired girl.

"What do you want," she said rudely.

"I'm so sorry," said Violet. "We didn't intend to alarm you."

"Well, you did."

"I really am sorry. Please can you tell me how to find Hill Farm?"

"It's about half a mile away from here," said the girl. "On the way to High Town Green." She reeled off directions while pointing to a substantial timber-framed building in the distance.

"I can drive you," said Francis.

"You won't get that thing there," said the girl disparagingly. "Better to walk or wait for the farm cart. It's up and down between here and there several times a day."

"I'll walk," said Violet. "And thank you for your help."

The girl went to close the door, but Francis raised his hand. "Hold on," he said. "Now, Violet. Are you staying here, or shall I wait for you?"

"Would you mind?"

"Not at all. I have plenty of time since I retired. You won't want me to come to the farm though?"

"No need," said Violet. "Why don't you stay here?"

"That's just what I was thinking," he continued, turning to the girl. "I say. Is there any chance of a drink?"

"We're shut," said the girl sullenly.

Francis extracted his wallet from his breast pocket, rifled through and emptied some coins into his palm.

"Sure?" he asked.

The girl sighed, opened the door, and waved him in.

"I'll see you later, Violet," he said, grinning triumphantly.

#

Violet's stomach rumbled as she left the public house. She hadn't felt like breakfast that morning, but the drive had given her an appetite, and she was hungry now. As she walked up Church Road, she spied a cottage beside the church. Boxes of pears and punnets of plums balanced on top of wooden crates in front of the window. As Violet walked up the pathway, she saw a painted sign on the brickwork. It read Felsham Post Office. Could be useful, she thought, remembering an invoice she had intended to post that morning. She felt for the envelope in her pocket and pulled it out.

Violet took two plums and a pear from the top of the crates and opened the door. She peered through the dark room beyond and into the bearded face of the postmaster.

"Good morning," she said. "I'll take these and a stamp, please."

"Right you are," said the man, removing a black postage stamp from a large bound register. "Anything else?"

"No, I don't think so."

"Just visiting?" asked the man.

"You could say that," Violet replied. "I've business to attend to at Hill Farm."

"You don't say. I'm heading that way myself," said the man. "George Godbold," he continued, holding out his hand. "Postmaster and grocer, for my sins. My pony and trap are outside, and I'm ready to go now if you would care for a ride."

Violet raised her eyebrows in surprise and gratitude at the gesture. Mr Godbold was a stranger to her, yet she'd been offered travel assistance for the second time that day. With this much help, the investigation would be over in no time.

"That's very kind of you," she said. "I'd be most grateful."

26

They left the cottage, and George Godbold assisted her into the small trap, tugged on the reins, and the pony trotted along Church Road and towards the outskirts of the village. After a few hundred yards and a little small talk, they saw another horse and cart approaching.

"God, it's him," said George Godbold, frowning. His previously pleasant expression darkened.

"Who?" asked Violet.

"Ayling," he replied, "Stephen Ayling. The man's a fool."

Violet stared at her companion, not knowing what to say. His demeanour was sour, and although she could not see beyond his full beard, she did not doubt that he was scowling.

As the cart drew closer, Violet noticed the same disgruntled expression on Stephen Ayling's face. Ayling raised his hand and made a rude gesture at Godbold, then seeing Violet, turned scarlet. The cart crossed with the trap, and the two men glared at each other. Ayling mumbled, "Excuse me, miss," as his horse plodded past.

"I'm sorry you had to see that," said George Godbold, looking embarrassed.

"Don't worry about me," said Violet. "I'm not easily offended. It's clear you don't get on though."

"No, well, that's his fault," said George moodily. "I've had a little shop in Felsham for over twenty years. Nothing fancy. I started selling groceries and then became the postmaster as well. And I've done alright out of it – or I did until Ayling came along. That man's a parasite."

"What's he done?" Violet blurted out the question before she considered the wisdom of it. Her inquisitiveness was obvious and indiscreet, but George Godbold wasn't shy of offering personal information.

"Interfered with my trade, that's what," said Godbold without hesitation. "Ayling's a johnny-come-lately. He's only been here for a year, not even a year, come to think of it. He arrived in the village early last summer, set up shop on the upper green and wandered down to my shop, bold as you like, writing down my prices. And what do you think he did next?"

"I can't imagine," said Violet, with a good idea of what was coming.

"He undercut me," said Godbold. "Every last blooming item I sold, he sold for less."

"Is he a grocer?" asked Violet.

"You could say that," said Godbold, darkly. "He's a grocer and druggist. But not a very good one if the only way he can get business is to steal mine."

"Surely your income is supported by the post office?"

"Of course, but it doesn't make up for the difference. Ayling's a blooming crook."

"Oh dear, I'm sorry," said Violet, sympathetically.

"I bet you think it doesn't happen much," said George Godbold.

"I wouldn't have thought so."

"Well, it does." He turned to Violet, pursed his lips and nodded. The pony slowed to a halt. "Move along," he said, tugging the reins. "Nobody told you to stop."

"You mean someone else is undercutting your prices?"

"Not mine. This was years ago."

"Really?"

"Yes. I bought this shop from Alf Chipperfield over twenty years ago. It was just a grocery store then – the post office came later. That was my doing. And I remember Alf telling me to be careful and watch out because he had the same problem with Jimmy Gladwell. The same Jimmy Gladwell who now delivers for Ayling. Can you believe it could happen twice?"

"If you say so," said Violet, not entirely convinced. Selling groceries in a village store was hardly going to make substantial sums of money. And if Godbold was telling the truth, there had been not one, but two generations of warring grocers.

"It makes you think, doesn't it?"

"Indeed. What will you do?"

"I'll have to drop my prices again," said Godbold. "And that's the devil of it. Nobody wins."

"It's a shame," said Violet. "It's hard enough to make ends meet without this sort of thing. Oh, are we here?"

The pony had slowed to a halt outside a large, yellow-painted timber-framed farmhouse. "This can't be the right place," said Violet. "I am here to see Mrs Drucilla Brown. She is the wife of a farm bailiff, not the master."

Godbold's face broke into a smile. "Don't you worry," he said, pointing to a row of farm cottages a small distance down the road. "She's in the middle cottage," he said. "My business is up at the farm. I'm taking the trap into the yard. Best you get out here. It's quicker and less messy."

"Thank you," said Violet, relieved to be in the right place, after all. She'd listened to a long and rambling story due to the generosity of Mr Godbold, which was worthwhile under the circumstance, but would have been intolerable under any other.

George Godbold tugged his forelock as the pony moved away, and Violet walked a few yards down the lane to the little row of pink cottages. The front door of Drucilla Brown's property stood ajar. Violet knocked out of politeness regardless, but nobody greeted her. After waiting a few moments, she peered around the door. "Hello, are you there, Drucilla?" But there was no reply. Violet wasn't prepared to hang around aimlessly any longer and tiptoed nervously through the dark hall, past a small parlour and into the kitchen at the rear. It was empty. Violet sighed, hoping it wasn't going to be a wasted journey. She really ought to have written and warned Mrs Brown of her impending visit. Drucilla's original letter was nine months old, but Lawrence had written a month or two previously to say that he would contact her soon. At least, he said he had. Knowing Lawrence and his not always scrupulous attention to detail, he may or may not have penned a letter. Violet approached the bottom of the stairs and shouted again but was not prepared to go upstairs. That was a step too far. She sighed and returned to the kitchen, pulled back the curtain and peered into the garden. A slender woman was pinning washing on the line. Relieved, Violet left through the back door.

#

"Hello, Mrs Brown? Sorry to intrude on you. I couldn't make myself heard."

"Who are you?" Drucilla Brown stared wide-eyed at Violet as if she was an apparition.

"My name's Violet Smith. You wrote to my business partner, Lawrence Harpham."

"Yes. That was some time ago. Your man finally deigned to reply last month, but I thought he was probably giving me the brush-off. Too important to investigate my silly little problem. Except that it isn't silly, and I was willing to pay good money – money I could easily use elsewhere."

"I'm sorry," said Violet. "It's not that at all. I was away looking after my sick aunt for many months, and Mr Harpham was too busy to take on new work."

"Oh." Drucilla shoved the rest of the pegs into the capacious pocket of her white apron and picked up a wicker basket, now empty of laundry. "That's a different matter. When they read me the letter, I assumed he wasn't interested."

"He is. We are," said Violet, "If you still want us to help."

"Oh, I do. Very much. If I could only be of use, I would do anything for Julia."

"Is there somewhere we can talk about it. I'd like to help, but I'll need to ask you a few questions to see if it's possible?"

"Yes. Come into the parlour, and I'll tell you all about it."

They returned through the kitchen door and into the front room. It was small but cosy, with pretty flowered curtains gracing the window. They looked new. Drucilla gestured to a comfortable chair, and Violet took a seat.

"I would offer you tea, but I have to go and collect my granddaughter, Eva, soon. She's staying with a relative."

"You don't look old enough to have a granddaughter," said Violet, genuinely surprised. Drucilla's face was largely unwrinkled and her hair still a rich chestnut brown with barely a trace of grey.

"Thank you," she smiled. "I come from good stock. My mother was the same."

Violet reached into her bag and pulled out the brown envelope Lawrence had given her. "I've read your letter a few times. What happened to poor Frederick was quite shocking."

"Yes, it was. It happened the year before William and I were married. William was still living at home, and the whole affair deeply unsettled him. I can't tell you how relieved he was when Julia was acquitted. He feared she would do herself harm, so distressed was she at the insinuations against her."

30

Violet nodded. "I quite understand. It is bad enough to lose a child without being accused of murder. What can you tell me about poor Frederick's death?"

"Not as much as Julia can," said Drucilla. "This investigation is for her, not me. The memories of her children still haunt her."

"There were others?"

Drucilla hesitated. "She will tell you herself if she wishes to. It is for her to say as much or as little as she will."

Violet chewed the pencil she had taken out at the same time as the envelope, wondering if there was any point in taking notes. So far, the conversation was not going to plan. There was a distinct lack of information coming from Drucilla Brown.

"I'm not trying to be obstructive," said Drucilla, as if she had overheard Violet's thoughts. "But I wasn't there, and others were. It is better that I tell you why we need your help and leave you to discover the facts."

"That's refreshing," smiled Violet. "Speculation is the enemy of good investigation. You are quite right only to offer what you know. Tell me about Julia then."

"Julia is a lovely woman," said Drucilla. "She's younger than me by the best part of a decade. When I married William, I married his family and Julia is the sister that I was closest to. She's warm and kind-natured, though it's fair to say that she is also naive."

"In what way?"

"Not in the ways of the world. Freddy was born out of wedlock as I'm sure you realise. But Julia would do anything for anyone. She wouldn't necessarily consider the consequences if she felt she was helping."

Violet considered her words. "Can I ask you a question without offending you?"

"Of course."

"If Julia was naive and eager to please, then isn't it possible that she could have harmed her son?"

"I understand why you've asked that, but no, not in my opinion. Julia wasn't capable."

"And may I ask why you've offered to pay our fees? And what you hope to gain from an investigation into a death that happened so long ago?"

"They're good questions," said Drucilla. "Julia's mother died a few years ago, and it hit Julia hard. Charlotte Brown lost her husband over a decade before. The other children left home or married, but Julia stayed. In the end, it was just the two of them. Julia was devoted to her mother and cared for her when she became poorly. That was enough to stop her fretting about Freddy, but when Charlotte died, grief finally consumed her."

"Poor thing," murmured Violet. "She must have felt it keenly."

"She did," said Drucilla. "But Julia and I were close, and she was always welcome here. She visited regularly, but she became skinny and anxious. There wasn't much money while they were growing up, and Julia was used to going hungry. But I soon realised it had gone beyond that. I hadn't seen her for a while and visited her lodgings one day to find her prone on the floor in a faint. She was all skin and bones, so William fetched a cart and brought her back here, and I fed and looked after her until she recovered."

"Was it the loss of her mother?" asked Violet.

Drucilla nodded. "Yes. But that loss opened other wounds. Julia could not settle for thinking about Freddy. You see, she knew she hadn't hurt him, which meant that somebody else had."

"Or it could have been an accident?"

"That's for you to decide," said Drucilla. "If you think you can help us."

"Was this Julia's idea?" asked Violet.

"No. It was mine. It took a lot of persuading."

"I thought she wanted a resolution?"

"She does. But she didn't want to be beholden to anyone for money."

"I don't understand."

"A relative died, and I unexpectedly came into a little inheritance. I used some of it to furnish our home, but my children have left now, and our needs are little. Julia has nothing. She has no home of her own and her job as a housekeeper covers her board and food with barely anything left. She is over fifty and has few prospects, but she has been a good sister-in-law to me, and I would like to help her."

"That's a very kind gesture."

"It's the least I can do."

Violet leaned forwards. "My concern is that so much time has passed that she may be none the wiser by the time we have concluded the investigation."

"I realise that. And some of the people who were there when Freddy died, are no longer with us. But I know Julia well. If she thinks that she's done everything possible to find his killer, then she will rest more easily. It is the feeling of having done nothing that torments her so."

"Wasn't there an attempt to find the real culprit at the time?"

"No. The authorities took Julia's guilt for granted. No thought was ever given to the prospect of anyone else, nor any other suspect named. They marked Julia guilty right at the start. All she wants is to find out what really happened to her son. Even now, some still doubt her innocence. If you could find out who killed Freddy, tongues might stop wagging. Will you help us, Miss Smith?"

Violet nodded, any misgivings about the complexity of investigating an old case forgotten. She couldn't abide unfairness and especially not to the helpless and vulnerable. Julia deserved a chance to clear her name, and Violet would do whatever it took to help her.

CHAPTER THREE

Gideon Road

Lawrence was loitering outside an end-terrace house in Gideon Road which stood in the lee of a large and imposing school. It was mid-morning, and the children were attending their lessons leaving the outside yard empty and the building exterior silent. A sudden gust whipped across the railed enclosure carrying fallen leaves and a single piece of paper which briefly rested against the iron railings, then fluttered down the path. More silence followed, of the kind too quiet for a suburban street. Lawrence surveyed the empty road feeling an uneasy calm before a possible storm.

He gathered his thoughts, then knocked on the blue door in front of him, thinking how smart it would have looked when freshly painted, no doubt a long time ago. Scratches and scrapes now covered the door, and an inferior washed-out, mid-blue paint obscured the original royal blue with no effort made to match – a sign of hardship, perhaps indicative of the need to take in lodgers.

Lawrence flinched as the door opened to the grind of wood on wood. The early autumn weather was still mild, and there hadn't been much rain, let alone enough to cause a swollen door. It wouldn't take much to plane the excess wood away, which suggested that the owner was not skilled in carpentry. And when Lawrence registered the jutting jaw of the towering, low-browed individual in front of him, he seemed barely human. A lack of carpentry skill was the least of his worries.

"Yes?" The man regarded Lawrence curiously.

"My name is Lawrence Harpham. I'm acting for Flora Johns. Are you the owner of the property?"

"You could say that," said the man suspiciously. "Who is Flora Johns, and what has she to do with me?"

"Her baby lived here."

"Oh, yes. Pretty girl. I saw her a few times when she visited him. You'd better come in."

Lawrence stepped into a dark hallway and was unsurprised to see paint peeling from the walls and a large hole in the wooden floor. But at least his host was not as fearsome as his appearance suggested. He waved Lawrence down the long hallway to a large room at the back of the house with a stove and a pock-marked table. "Take a seat," he said.

Lawrence resisted the temptation to wipe the seat with his handkerchief. Instead, he perched on the edge of the chair with his hands in his lap. He prepared to speak, but the man beat him to it.

"Garrad Bailey," he said, thrusting a meaty hand towards Lawrence. Lawrence returned the handshake and smiled, making a mental note not to judge a man by his looks in future. "Tell me what you want to know. I thought I'd given the policeman everything he needed."

"You spoke to the police about the missing baby?"

Bailey nodded. "They turned up about a week after the young woman stopped calling. Very late to react, but I helped as much as I could. The trouble is that I couldn't tell them very much. She wasn't here long, you see."

"Dorothy Jones?"

"Yes, if that's what her name was."

"What makes you think it wasn't?"

"She called herself Dorothy Jones, but a man came twice while she was here and asked for Miss Hamblin."

"I see." Lawrence reached into his pocket and pulled out a notebook, in which he scribbled the name.

"How long did Mrs Jones reside here?"

Garrad Bailey scratched his cheek as he considered the question. "She paid about twelve weeks rent, give or take," he concluded. "Yes – about three months."

"And did she arrive with the baby?"

"She had a baby with her when she took the room, but not that baby. The first child was older."

"Are you saying that she lived in one room with two children?"

Bailey nodded.

"How many rooms do you rent out?"

"Two," he said. "Both at the back of the house. Mine's at the front."

"Noisy, I would think?" said Lawrence.

"Sometimes," Bailey replied. "The older child was just beginning to move around. I'd hear her toddling around the room from time to time. The baby cried at night, not so much in the day. Mrs Jones kept them reasonably quiet. I've had no complaints from my other lodger."

"Is your other lodger at home?"

"No. John works and doesn't get in until late. I expect that's why he didn't mind the children."

"Did you have any difficulties with Mrs Jones while she was lodging here?"

"No problems at all. She paid her rent on time, wasn't particularly noisy and kept herself to herself. She used the stove and the sink but always cleaned up afterwards. I would have been happy for her to stay longer."

"Why did she leave?"

Bailey sighed. "I don't know. It was most unexpected. She paid a week's rent one Monday but left two days later. That day, she took the children and caught a tram to Clapham, narrowly missing a visitor. A man arrived asking to see her, and I let him in. He waited for several hours, but she didn't return, and he went. I'd gone out by the time she came back, and I never saw her again. She took the babies and all her luggage and left with no notice. It left me quite affronted for a few days, I can tell you. I am a good landlord, and she left so quickly that it felt like a slight."

"Had you seen the man before?"

"No. Never."

"Did he give you name?"

36

Bailey shook his head. "No. He just asked to see her, and I had no reason to question him further."

"And Mrs Jones didn't leave a forwarding address?"

"No. She didn't leave anything at all."

"Is her room occupied?"

"Not yet," said Garrad Bailey. "I have advertised it, but only one person applied, and he was dressed in rags. I'm not stupid – he clearly lacked the means to pay, so I told him that it was too late."

"In that case, may I see it?"

"The room?"

"Yes. It would be helpful."

"There's nothing in it but by all means."

"Thank you."

Garrad Bailey heaved himself off the stool and took a single key from a hook on the wall. "This way," he said as he approached the staircase, and ascended the stairs, gripping the bannister firmly. Lawrence dodged a bowl of water set perilously close to the stairs, relieved that the cat who drank from it was not in position. He would, no doubt, have trodden on it. Glad of the lucky escape, Lawrence followed Bailey upstairs and watched him proceed towards the second door on the left, unlock it, and push the door open. The room was unexpectedly bright, benefiting from a large window to the front and a smaller one to the side. Speckled paper covered the walls, and the floorboards were clean and polished. The furniture was sparse, comprising a bed, a crib, a wardrobe and a chest of drawers, but it was in reasonable condition.

"I made the rooms look nice before I took in lodgers," said Bailey gesturing towards a landscape painting on the far wall. "This house belonged to my mother, and when she passed away, I used the little money she'd left me to tidy the bedrooms. I don't have to work if both rooms are bringing in money."

"It's a nice room," said Lawrence. "May I look inside?" He reached for the wardrobe door.

"If you want. There's nothing there."

Bailey was right. The wardrobe was empty, and so was the chest of drawers. It was as if Dorothy Jones had never existed.

"What's this?" asked Lawrence, pointing to a newspaper lying in the crib.

"Ah. That's where I put it," said Bailey, hitting his forehead.

Lawrence picked up the copy of *The Morning Post*, about to hand it to Garrad Bailey when an article caught his eye. 'Child Murders in London' screamed the headline. He scrutinised the page.

"Bad business," muttered Bailey.

"Shocking," Lawrence agreed.

They returned downstairs, and Lawrence took his leave. "Come back if you need anything else," Bailey offered.

Lawrence walked past the school, deep in thought, wondering whether to visit the Battersea police station to see if they had made any progress. But their arrival at the scene of a missing child more than a week after the event gave him no confidence in their abilities or motivation. He decided instead to seek out the officer named in *The Morning Post* article. From the little he had read, this man seemed to have more about him. And with nothing else to go on, advice on child-related crimes in London was the best for which he could hope.

CHAPTER FOUR

An Interview with Julia Brown

Julia Brown bore no resemblance to the image that Violet had conjured up in her mind's eye. At first glance, Julia looked as healthy as her sister-in-law. Drucilla's hard work had paid dividends and, though thin, Julia was not malnourished. But that's where the comparison ended. Where Drucilla's hair was brown, Julia's was silver grey. And unlike her sister-in-law, her face was etched with worry lines, and her skin an ominous shade of yellow.

Having knocked and waited patiently, and knocked once again, Violet had eventually heard slow shuffling in the hallway. Her first sighting of Julia was not encouraging as she peered timidly around the door frame as if in dread fear of intruders.

"Yes?" she whispered in a faltering voice.

"Drucilla sent me," said Violet, seeking to allay any worries immediately by using a trusted name.

"Oh. What do you want?"

"To help you, Julia. I believe you are seeking answers from the past."

"Oh." Julia clutched the door frame as if about to faint. Her skin blanched, and her hands trembled. "I don't know if I can talk about that today," she said, head bowed and eyes staring at the floor. Violet tried to attract her attention, but she steadfastly avoided eye contact.

"Why not? Has something happened?"

"Not particularly. It's just too hard."

Violet sighed. She hadn't expected a hurdle quite so soon in her investigation.

"You might feel better if you talk about it."

"I won't."

"Then I'm sorry I've wasted your time. I'll call in and let Drucilla know."

"Don't do that," said Julia in a small voice. "I don't want to let her down. She's been so kind."

"She wants to help," said Violet. "She cares for you very much."

Tears welled in Julia's hazel eyes, and she wiped them away with a blackened finger.

"Blackberries," she said, watching Violet's expression. "I picked them for Mr Scott earlier today."

"Mr Scott?"

"It's his cottage," Julia explained. "I keep the house."

Violet nodded. "Is Mr Scott at home?"

"No. He's in Brettenham and won't be home until late."

"Then you're alone?"

Julia nodded.

"These are perfect circumstances under which to talk about your problem," said Violet. "We won't be interrupted, and you can speak freely."

"I don't know…" said Julia, uncertainly.

"And Drucilla will not have to worry about you if she knows we have talked."

"I suppose not," said Julia, opening the door a fraction further. "Who did you say you were?"

"I didn't. My name is Violet Harpham. I mean, Violet Smith. My business partner is Lawrence Harpham." Violet blushed a deep red and spoke rapidly as her clumsy explanation ran away with her. Violet Harpham! Why on earth had she said that? Violet groaned inwardly. Thank the Lord nobody who was acquainted with her had heard. They'd wonder what she intended by it, and she hadn't meant anything. Violet was barely on speaking terms with Lawrence and felt badly let down. The name Harpham was an anathema to her and not an alias she would ever choose to use. She took a deep breath and recovered herself. "Now, is there somewhere comfortable to talk?"

Julia gestured mutely towards the nearest door. It opened into a small but tidy parlour. Two comfortable chairs were set close to the fire with a third underneath the window. "Sit down, if you like," said Julia quietly. Violet took the left-hand seat expecting Julia to sit beside her, but instead, she walked towards the window chair and perched nervously on the edge. "This is my chair," she whispered.

Violet sighed and moved towards the right-hand chair, which she turned ninety degrees until it faced Julia.

"We can't talk to each other halfway across the room," she said.

Julia looked at the floor and did not reply.

"Julia. Look at me." Violet was unusually brusque. The last year had been hard, harder than any other, and there were many places she'd rather be than sat here with this awkward woman child.

Julia looked up startled.

"I can't help you if you don't help yourself," said Violet. "If you don't want my help, say so, and I will leave immediately. Otherwise, please stop making it so difficult."

The minute the words were out, Violet cringed inside. She was never harsh, never unfair and Julia Brown was meek and unable to defend herself. She had no right to get angry.

Julia bit her lip and watched Violet warily, looking as if she might cry.

"I'm sorry," said Violet. "That was unnecessary. Do you want to continue, or shall I come back another time?"

"No. I'll try to be more helpful," said Julia, anxiously worrying her nails.

Violet leaned over and patted her arm empathetically, but Julia winced, and Violet retreated. "You don't mind if I take notes?" she asked, retrieving her jotter and pencil.

Julia shook her head.

"Right. You are seeking justice for your poor boy?"

"Yes, my little Freddy."

"I hear that he died," said Violet.

"Somebody killed him," said Julia. "But not me," she continued, defensively.

"I know," said Violet reassuringly. "That's why I'm here."

Julia relaxed into her chair, appearing more settled.

"Tell me about Freddy."

"He was a dear boy," said Julia, clasping her hands. "Oh, such a dear, polite little man. He had a chubby face and big brown eyes, like mine. He was always smiling, always happy." Violet watched a smile creep across Julia's face. Her eyes lit with pleasure as she recalled happy memories of her child.

"How old was he when he died?" asked Violet.

Julia's smile vanished, replaced by a knitted brow. "A little over three years," she said, staring wistfully ahead.

"And was he healthy?"

"Always. Never so much as a cold."

"Can you tell me what happened the day he died?"

"I'll try," said Julia, hunching over her lap. "I don't know where to start."

"Why don't I ask you some questions," said Violet, "and you can answer as you see fit."

Julia nodded. Her eyes unexpectedly crinkled as she raised a half-smile. Violet thought how much younger she looked when she wasn't frowning.

"Where did Freddy die?"

"At home," said Julia, "that is to say, at my mother's home."

"Who lived there?"

"Mother, Father and my sisters Mary, Hannah and Elizabeth, my brothers William, John and Robert and of course, Freddy."

Violet jotted the names down. "And were you living there at the time?"

Julia looked up as if remembering. "I was visiting, and I stayed the night, but I lived out at the rectory."

"The rectory?"

"Yes. In Brettenham, where Mr Scott has gone today. He's…"

Julia was interrupted by a rap on the door. She started in fright and clutched her chest.

"Who is that? I'm not expecting anyone."

She stared wide-eyed at Violet.

"Would you like me to answer the door?" Violet offered.

The suggestion was calming, and Julia recovered herself. "No, I will go."

Violet patiently waited while Julia opened the door and exchanged a few quiet words with the caller, too soft for Violet to hear.

Presently, Julia returned, looking relieved. "Only Jimmy Gladwell," she said, almost smiling. "He came over from Felsham with a box of groceries for Mr Scott. I had quite forgotten."

"Good," said Violet. "Now, where were we?"

"I was telling you about the rectory," said Julia. "I worked there for the Reverend and Mrs Betham."

"But you stayed at your parents' that night."

Julia nodded. "Yes. I walked home from Brettenham the day before Freddy perished. I will never forget. It was cold to the bone, and had just started to snow when I crossed paths with a woman, who was carrying some cakes."

"They look nice, and I haven't got a present for my boy," I said, and she said, 'you may have some if you like.'. Well, I had just got my wages, so I bought half a dozen and ate one on the way home."

#

Violet listened intently, involuntarily licking her lips at the mention of cakes. It was almost lunchtime, and she was ravenous. She had hoped that Julia might offer her a drink, but no such offer had transpired. Violet began to lose concentration as her mind wandered to the absence of food in her stomach.

"How old were you?" she asked, interrupting Julia's reminiscence.

"When Freddy died?"

"Yes."

Julia pursed her lips and gazed heavenwards. "About nineteen, I suppose."

"Nineteen. And Freddy was three?"

"Yes."

"You were very young when he was born."

"I don't see what that has to do with it," said Julia brusquely.

Violet re-ordered her next sentence to avoid further upset. She was used to speaking plainly, though kindly, but Julia seemed to take offence where none was intended.

"I was only establishing facts," she said. "It must have been a difficult time for you."

"Not really," said Julia. "Ruthie Green, my childhood friend, was chased from her home when her father found out that she was in the family way. She bled to death in an alleyway in Ipswich after she'd tried to get rid of it."

"How awful." Violet shuddered at the thought.

"He said it served her right," said Julia. "Mark Green, that is. But I saw him crying by her graveside one day, so he must have regretted it."

"A guilty conscience," murmured Violet, "and a lack of compassion."

"Exactly," nodded Julia, her face flushed and animated.

"And your parents?"

"They were kindness itself," said Julia. "I did not know how to tell Mother about my condition, but she guessed a few months before Freddy arrived. She told me not to worry and that she would look after him."

"And your father?"

"The same. He did not mention it while I was carrying Freddy, but he loved my boy and treated him well."

"They sound very kind," said Violet.

"The very best." Julia's voice wobbled, and Violet smiled sympathetically.

"So, they looked after Freddy while you worked away."

Julia nodded.

"And you came home with the cakes and saw Freddy?"

"Yes. I arrived home mid-afternoon and Freddy was there with my younger sister Hannah and brother James. They were still young and liked to play with Freddy. I gave them each a cake and had a cup of tea with my mother and my older sisters. After tea, I went out."

"Where?"

"Just out."

Julia stared stubbornly towards the window; her eyes narrowed.

"Where did you go?"

44

"It doesn't matter where I went."

"It might."

Julia's mouth set in a thin line as she hugged her shoulders, rocking gently backwards and forwards.

"Where did you go?"

"I went to meet someone," she whispered.

"Who?"

"Benjamin. Benjamin Dempster."

"Who was he to you?"

Julia was silent again, and Violet decided to change her tactics. She stopped talking and gazed intently at Julia's face. Julia turned away, but Violet continued to stare in silence. Eventually, Julia sighed.

"We had been walking out together," she said.

"He was your young man?"

"For a while."

"But not then?"

"No. Benjamin broke off with me."

"Why?"

"He did not say, except to tell me he had found no particular fault with me."

"Yet you visited him that night?"

Julia nodded. "He sent me a letter asking to see me."

"Did he say why?"

"No. I was curious, so I visited just as he'd asked."

"And he told you what he wanted when you arrived?"

Julia paused, and her face turned a vivid shade of scarlet.

"Well?"

"He wanted comfort. His family were all dead – father, brothers and sisters and his mother lay dying. She was buried soon after, you know. He was feeling lonely and wanted company."

"Did he have other friends?"

"Yes. But he wanted me, and I wanted him, so I went."

"Leaving Freddy with your mother?"

"With my sisters. Mother was ill in bed."

"What time did you return?"

"About half past ten."

Violet raised an eyebrow. If Julia noticed, she ignored it. "I went straight to bed," she continued.

45

"In the same room as Frederick?"

"Yes."

"Just the two of you?"

"No. My brothers shared one bed, and my sister Elizabeth, my youngest brother James, Freddy and I shared the second bed. My other sisters slept downstairs."

"And Freddy was well?"

"Completely well. We all slept soundly. My elder brothers and James woke first and went downstairs. I joined them after half an hour or so leaving Freddy with Elizabeth. I drank a cup of tea, then came back upstairs to say goodbye to my mother."

"Did you see Freddy again?"

"Oh yes. Access to my bedroom was through Mother's room. I chatted to her for ten minutes, then went to kiss Freddy goodbye. He seemed perfectly normal when I took my leave."

"Did you know he was ailing when you left the room?"

"Yes. I had gone downstairs and was preparing to go back to work when Mother shouted to Mary. She said that Freddy was sickening. I followed Mary upstairs, and Freddy had been sick on his shirt. His little face was white. Mary nursed him, and I cried. I could not bear to see the pain on his face."

"Poor little chap." Violet sighed, hating the thought of a child in distress.

"Yes. It was dreadful. Mary gave him warm tea, but he did not rally, and I dressed and prepared to return to the rectory."

"But, you stayed, of course."

"I didn't know what to do, torn as I was between my boy and my duty to the Reverend," said Julia. "Father persuaded me to stay while he sent for the Reverend Anderson and Mr Leech, the surgeon. Mr Leech came after lunch and said that Freddy was a little improved and that I could go back to Brettenham, so I did."

"Oh dear. You weren't there when Freddy died?"

"No, and I will never forgive myself. I should have stayed, but Mr Leech said there was no point in it."

"Were you surprised at the accusation against you?"

"I was shocked." Julia fidgeted with her hands as she recalled the painful memories. "And it was a full week later. I was still grieving for my boy, but I'd returned to work at the rectory. The Reverend came into the kitchen with a policeman one day, and they told me that I would be charged with administering poison to a child. Me – his mother."

"And you had no inkling of it?"

"No. I did not know how Freddy had come to die. I told them I had not done it, but they told me I must leave with them at once."

Julia closed her eyes, trying to block the stream of tears that began to course down her cheeks. "Then, then…" All at once, she couldn't speak for crying. She gulped, trying to find the words. Brushing the tears away with blackberry-stained fingers, she continued. "They searched my room and took away my dress, claiming it was stained with poison."

"What poison?"

"Never mind what poison." Julia raised her voice and pursed her lips. "See what you have done," she cried. "Look at me. I said I could not speak of it. It is too upsetting. You must go."

"But there are things I need to ask you."

"Go." Julia's hot breath flashed across Violet's skin as she snapped the words straight at her.

"I'll let myself out."

Violet slunk towards the door, glad to leave the volatile atmosphere in the house. Julia had turned from passive to defensive to aggressive in no time. If she was capable of that, how could Drucilla be sure that she had not poisoned her child?

#

"At last," said Francis, pushing a grimy tankard across the table. "I was wondering whether to come and find you."

"Sorry," said Violet breathlessly. "It took longer than I expected. I walked as quickly as I could." She sat on the nearest chair and discreetly rubbed her hand across the back of her ankles. It had been an unfortunate day to wear-in new boots, and the tops had chafed the back of her ankles as she walked along the lane. She glanced at her fingertips, now smeared with blood.

"Well, you're here now," said Francis jovially. "Just as well. The beer in here is foul," he continued, lowering his voice.

"I'm surprised you had any," said Violet. "I thought you preferred wine."

"It was that or a long stroll around the village," said Francis. "I can hardly make use of the premises without spending a few coins."

"I suppose not. Shall we go, or are you going to finish your drink?"

Francis grimaced. "I've had quite enough, thank you," he said, making for the door.

"Hey, you!" Francis bolted through the front door as he saw a group of boys beside his car. "Don't touch the brass," he yelled.

"We was only looking," said a young gap-toothed boy as he quickly removed his hand from the steering wheel.

"Well don't," snapped Francis. "Go on, off you go." He gestured vigorously, and the boys slouched away.

"Loathsome creatures," he said, as he opened the passenger door and took Violet's hand.

"They were only curious. They've probably never seen one before," she said.

"Then they should have asked first. No manners at all."

"I expect you were the same at that age," said Violet.

"Not in the least." Francis started the car at the first attempt and smiled broadly. "I was attending preparatory school by that age, and we were disciplined and thus, very well mannered."

"You were fortunate," said Violet. "Those boys are destined for hard labour, no doubt."

Francis grunted, but his features softened as he successfully manoeuvred the car through the village.

"Did you enjoy school?" asked Violet conversationally.

"Not particularly," said Francis, "but it made me the man I am today. I was far happier at my university. It was always interesting, and I forged lifelong friendships."

"Isn't that where you met Lawrence?"

"No. We were at Cambridge together, but Lawrence was a few years below me. We had already met. Our fathers were acquainted, and we all lived in Bury."

"I see. You have known each other for a long time."

"I was best man at his wedding," said Francis.

"You knew Catherine?"

"I introduced them," said Francis, staring into the distance. "It seems like a lifetime ago. I doubt he will need my services this time."

"Services?"

"Best man," said Francis. "He hasn't approached me, and it's dashed difficult to get a firm answer from him, but I understand there is to be a wedding this year. Perhaps it will be a quiet event, though having met Loveday, I find it hard to believe."

"Don't you like her?"

Francis glanced at Violet. "She's perfectly charming," he said. "It's more of a question of how much Lawrence likes her."

"A great deal, I believe," said Violet, quietly.

"May I ask an impertinent question?"

"If you must."

"I won't if it will offend you."

"But I won't know until you ask me."

"Well, I'm not one for beating around the proverbial bush, so I will. Lawrence is a complicated man, moody and capricious. His temper was up and down last year, but when it was up, he was happier than I've seen him in years. And I thought it might be because of your friendship. But it hasn't passed me by that you are hardly speaking. Am I correct in deducing that you do not approve of his choice of wife?"

"It is not for me to say."

"I would have been less surprised if Lawrence had said he was marrying you."

Violet chewed her lip, not trusting herself to speak. During the few weeks they'd spent in Overstrand the previous year, she had thought, hoped, that he might be romantically interested in her. If he ever was, those feelings had disappeared as soon as he encountered Loveday in Liverpool.

"Slow down!" exclaimed Violet as Francis steered sharp right at a junction, carelessly and without the aid of a brake.

"Sorry. I was distracted," said Francis, watching as Violet clutched her arm. "You're not hurt, I hope?"

"No. But I would be happier with less speed," said Violet.

"As you wish. Anyway, you didn't answer my question."

"It was a statement, not a question."

Francis glanced at her pale, set face. She stared dead ahead as if hoping to avoid the subject.

"Well?"

"Lawrence and I are friends. We have never been anything other. I am delighted that he has found someone to settle with."

Francis raised an eyebrow. "I've known Lawrence for years, and I have to tell you that once he's set his mind to something, he follows it through. And if it's Loveday that he wants, then so be it. He's always preferred younger women, and there's every chance that they'll want children, so it makes sense. It's just a shame that your friendship has suffered."

Violet winced. Her skin, already alabaster white, turned a lighter shade of pale. She stared fixedly in the distance, and despite several attempts at small talk, Francis was unable to draw any further conversation from her. Finally, they arrived in Bury. Francis leapt from the car and opened the passenger door for Violet.

"I'm sorry if I spoke out of turn," said Francis.

"You didn't. I'm just a little tired."

"Well, come over for tea tomorrow. Cook's made a batch of plum jam."

"I would, but I must do some research. This poor boy's death must have been reported. I want to check the newspaper accounts against those of Julia Brown."

"Then do it in the morning and join me later."

"Are you sure? You seemed so busy last year."

"Certain. I will enjoy the company, and you can tell me what you find. I promise I won't ask any more intrusive questions."

"In that case, I accept." Violet gave a brief smile, then removed a heavy iron door key from her bag. She waved as Francis pulled away, unlocked the door and made her way to her desk, gazing around the empty room. It was quiet without Lawrence. Still and quiet and empty and lonely. As she sat at her desk, her memories turned to the two years she had worked alone, plodding through case after case without company or advice while Lawrence recovered from his attack. All those wasted years. All that pointless loyalty. And where was she now? A lonely spinster with a broken heart, a barely concealed secret, and a desperate yearning to be somewhere else. Somewhere very specific, with someone vitally important to her. It was time to move on from Lawrence, and she needed to start making plans.

CHAPTER FIVE

The Battersea Baby Farmers

Thursday, September 10, 1896

Sergeant Richard Simms was a dark-haired, prepossessing man in his early forties with twinkling eyes and a ready smile. As Lawrence approached the counter at North Woolwich police station, he felt as if he was in the presence of a well-groomed royal rather than a run of the mill desk sergeant. "How can I help, sir?" asked Simms, flashing a broad smile.

Damn the man. Even his teeth are perfectly straight, thought Lawrence, running his tongue over the sharply jagged edge of his back left molar, the other half of which had sheared away the previous week. "Lawrence Harpham, Suffolk Constabulary," Lawrence lied. It was easier to fall back on his former occupation than reveal that he was a private investigator and therefore less important.

Simms accepted him at his word and held out his hand. "We haven't met, have we?"

"Never," said Lawrence.

"Well, how can I help?"

"I saw your name in a newspaper article," said Lawrence, passing him the battered copy of *The Morning Post* he had taken from Gideon Road.

Simms scanned the page. "Yes. A very distressing case," he said, shaking his head. "Do you have an interest?"

"Not in this crime," said Lawrence. "The one that I'm investigating is in Battersea."

"That's a long way from Suffolk, and a long way from here, for that matter."

"There's a Suffolk connection," said Lawrence vaguely, cursing inwardly for nearly giving the game away.

"I see. Battersea has its own station, you know."

"I know. That's why I'm here."

Simms flashed a knowing smile. "I understand," he said. "But I'm not sure how I can be of help. We hear things, of course, but the distance is too great to share much relevant information."

"Any information will help," said Lawrence. "Can you spare ten minutes?"

"Yes, I can," said Simms, pulling out a pocket watch. "I can give you an hour, and then I have to be somewhere."

"Thank you," said Lawrence, about to remove his coat.

"Not here. There's a little tea shop in Beresford Square. It's only a five-minute walk."

Less than a quarter of an hour later, Lawrence was sipping coffee and eating a large slice of cake in a small, but busy tearoom in the heart of Woolwich. Sergeant Simms was sitting opposite and leaned forward with his elbows on the white linen tablecloth. He raised the teacup to his lips, wiped his mouth and sighed contentedly. "I love it here," he said, crossing his arms and glancing at the pretty waitress. She smiled coquettishly and wiped an imaginary stain from her pristine white apron.

"I can see why," said Lawrence.

Simms grinned. "Tell me what you want before I get too distracted," he said.

"I'm investigating a missing child," said Lawrence.

"Recent?"

"Yes. Three weeks ago. A baby boy. Someone took him from Gideon Road."

"Took? Without permission?"

"Not exactly."

Lawrence explained the situation as concisely as possible. "So, you see, he was there with permission, but should not have been removed."

Simms nodded. "I heard about this."

"Even though it's out of your district?"

"Especially because it's out of my district."

"How so?"

"I've been involved in several child murders, as you know from the contents of this." Simms gestured towards the newspaper. "But what you probably don't know is that I've been following them for several years."

"The same perpetrators?"

"Not necessarily. I've been recording child deaths east of London."

"Why?"

"Because there have been so many."

"You mean they're connected?"

"Not all, but some may be. As a rule, we just don't share enough information, and I've got one or two unsolved child crimes that I can't let go. And the only way they're ever going to be resolved is by collecting facts. So that's what I do. I collect murders. Especially given the recent events in Reading."

"I'm very much hoping that young Bertie is not one of your statistics."

"I hope he is. I've compiled a register of missing children too."

Lawrence smiled. "I'm glad I sought you out. May I take a look."

"Yes, if you need to. But first, let me give you a broad picture of what I've seen recently."

"Carry on."

"At the end of May, a female child was found in the doorway of a shop in Poplar tied up inside a parcel made up of two sheets of brown paper fastened with string. The same thing happened in Cambridge Park in Wanstead; this time a male child born strong and healthy. The results of the autopsy showed that he had struggled for life before being covered in brown paper. Three weeks later another parcel containing the body of a child was found in Snaresbrook, and no less than thirty bodies of children turned up in Epping Forest, all wrapped

54

in parcels. Last week, we found another child in Greenwich. I'm sure you can guess its condition."

"Wrapped in a brown paper parcel?"

"Quite."

"Not Amelia Dyer's doing?"

"Hardly. Mrs Dyer met her end before at least two of the crimes took place."

"But the same perpetrator?"

"I doubt it. That would be an extraordinary volume of deaths for one person."

"Yet the method of disposal was similar."

"Indeed. You were close to the mark with Amelia Dyer. I fear it is the work of baby farmers."

"Good Lord!" Lawrence placed his teacup on the table and spread his hands. "How many of them are out there?"

"More than you think. And there's another thing you should know if you're looking for a missing child."

"Yes?"

"Someone is poisoning children."

"Deliberately?"

"We don't know. But we can't rule it out."

"How many?"

"So far, three children have died, and seven or eight have fallen ill from the effects. And an adult man came perilously close to being fatally poisoned."

"Where have the poisonings occurred?"

"In the Silvertown area – around West Ham and Custom House."

"That's a long way from Battersea, and the boy was only a baby."

"I'm not suggesting that he's succumbed to such a fate, or indeed suffered any crime. But you asked for information, and I'm giving it. Children are dying all over London, by poison, or other nefarious means. I hope your boy is safe, but you must consider the worst."

#

Lawrence stared moodily at the tepid tea in his cup, unnecessarily stirring it for the fourth time. He had formed a picture of young Bertie

Johns in his mind's eye. A happy baby boy, plump and well cared for despite his unfortunate start in life. He imagined Flora counting the hours to her daily visit and Bertie smiling in recognition as his mother reached for him, holding out his hands to touch her face. Dorothy Jones would be smiling benevolently, heart swelling with pride at her decision to mind Flora's child and thinking how unimportant the money was and how being with the child was fulfilment enough.

"As I said, his disappearance may not be sinister at all," said Simms, swiping away the imaginary tableau.

"It's hard to think of a reason why Mrs Jones left without leaving a forwarding address for poor Flora Johns," said Lawrence. "I have racked my brain but cannot think of a circumstance under which this could reasonably have happened."

"Perhaps she was unwell and took the child somewhere safe while she recovered?"

"Both children then," said Lawrence. "There were three of them. Dorothy Jones was caring for a second child."

"Oh dear. That is more worrying," said Simms.

"Why?"

"More money at stake," he continued. "Tell me, were the children well cared for?"

Lawrence nodded. "As far as I can tell," he said. "The landlord said they were quiet children."

"Not too quiet?"

"The baby cried at night, he said."

"Good. Not drugged then."

Lawrence looked up. "Drugged?"

"It has been known," said Simms, pursing his lips. "Now listen. I don't want to alarm you, but I think you should know more about the Battersea case. It may be relevant."

"Battersea case?"

"Yes. It does not have a direct bearing on your missing boy as it pre-dates his abduction, if that's what it was. But the circumstances are pertinent, and the geography is troubling."

"Then tell me about it," said Lawrence.

Simms withdrew a black-bound journal from a smart leather briefcase, opened it and flicked through the pages until he came to an entry with a couple of missing columns. "Here," he said, turning the journal to face Lawrence.

"Caroline Davis and Mary Ann Stevens," said Lawrence, running his finger across the entry. "Fifth of August 1896, Deceased – Marie Grass, Witness – Isabel Smith. Why are the other columns empty?"

"The case was adjourned," said Simms, "pending a second inquest on the other dead child."

Lawrence shuddered, feeling his skin crawl at the thought of two dead children. His thoughts turned briefly to Violet and a sense of relief that she was safely in Suffolk and not having to listen to the awful revelations from London. "What happened to the children?" he asked, swallowing a lump in his throat.

"Childminders must operate in a registered house," said Simms. "In London, at any rate. Regular inspections of the houses take place to make sure that the children are well treated."

"Quite right," said Lawrence, approvingly.

"Quite right, when the rules are followed, but the house concerned in this case was at Amies Street in Battersea, and the registration had lapsed. I'm not sure how it worked because although the children stayed there, the two women who cared for them lived in Isleworth which may have been part of the problem. Anyway, Caroline Davies and Mary Ann Stevens started taking in children, for money. How long this continued for, I can't say, but early in August the mother of a child who had left it in similar circumstances to those you describe went to visit her child."

"Another single woman?"

"Yes," nodded Simms. "A German lady's maid. She gave birth unbeknown to her employer and sought to return to work quickly. She had reservations about leaving her child, but neither of them would have survived without her earnings."

"The same story as Flora," said Lawrence.

"It is the same story all over London, and probably over the entire country," said Richard Simms. "These poor young women are left with no choice in the matter. They take risks with their children's welfare to have the means to provide for them. But what else can they do?"

"Can't the parents help?" asked Lawrence.

"They don't all have parents," said Simms. "And their relatives are often poor. No, there is a flaw in society that we must find a way to manage." He smiled. "I sound just like Isabel," he continued.

"Isabel?"

"Isabel Smith. She is a saint," he said simply. "That probably sounds quite dramatic to you, but she is a shining light, a beacon of hope for those poor children."

"What does she do?"

"She is an infant protection inspector for the London County Council," said Simms. "It is her job to visit registered childminding facilities. She has never married and works tirelessly to keep them safe, working from dusk till dawn and never afraid to intervene on their behalf. She travels all over London with her carriage driver, always rushing from one inspection to the next. I don't know how she finds time to eat and sleep."

"And she was involved in this Battersea tragedy?"

"Very much so," said Simms. "I first met her a year or two ago when she arrived in London. Isabel is from Northumberland originally. Well, she was in Woolwich and had discovered two children in an appalling state. I won't go into detail, but it became a police matter, and our paths crossed for a while and have continued to cross ever since. She has been of great assistance with my register of cases."

"Understandably. And did Isabel inspect the property in Amies Road?"

"She did – and she greatly regrets authorising the registration in the first place. Were she not quite so pragmatic, she could have become seriously distressed at what she feels was bad judgement on her part. But there was no real reason to decline the initial application. The premises were basic but clean, and the women concerned had no known criminal record and seemed genuinely interested in providing a facility for the unfortunate children."

"Yes, something must have gone badly wrong."

"It did. The women were dishonest and inexperienced. The council registration allowed them to keep three children on the premises, but there were more."

"How many?"

"That's a conversation for another day. I must go now, or I'll be late for my appointment."

"But you haven't finished."

"No. But I've had a better idea. "Why don't you go and see Isabel yourself? She can tell you all about it and a lot more besides. There's nobody more informed than Isabel. If she can't help you, nobody can."

CHAPTER SIX

Netherwood

"This story is becoming more and more interesting," said Violet, reclining, legs crossed, in Francis Farrow's grand drawing room. Pages of notes and an old copy of the *Bury Free Press* newspaper were spread across the chaise longue by her side.

"More interesting than tea?" asked Francis, gesturing to the untouched teapot and selection of cakes at the end of the room. "Go on, they're your favourites."

"I'm sorry," said Violet. "I didn't mean to be rude. But it's such a strange affair, and I'm not at all sure that it can be solved."

"Allow me," said Francis, reaching for her hand. He helped her up, and she made her way to the table.

"Lovely," she said, helping herself to a large slice of seed cake. "I'm starving."

"When did you eat last?" asked Francis. "You've lost weight, if you don't mind me saying."

"Yesterday," Violet admitted. "I missed breakfast and was too busy for lunch. But I ate a large supper last night, and you know I have a good appetite. I've been distracted with one thing or another."

Francis nodded sagely, knowing full well that the case was only occupying a fraction of her thoughts. "Have you heard from Lawrence yet?" he asked.

"Hardly. He's only been in London for a few days. He'll write or telegram when he has something to tell me."

"Do you think he'll be in London for long?"

Violet shrugged. "Who knows? He rarely sticks to his plans and does everything on a whim. He could be there for hours or months. It doesn't matter. We are conducting separate investigations."

"Fair enough," said Francis. "Are you going to tell me what you found in the newspaper archives?"

Violet grinned. "Of course. Though how it will help resolve a thirty-two-year-old murder, I don't know. But at least I possess a few more facts, assuming the reporter was accurate, that is. Newspapers are a mine of useful information, but if there's one thing I've realised, it's that they are quick to embellish a situation, especially when murder is involved. Still, the reporter from the *Bury Free Press* seems quite restrained. I ought to be able to check most of the facts fairly easily."

"Show me what you've found then?"

Violet pushed her notebook across the desk. She had written a list of witnesses and a timeline in her little book. "And here's the article," she continued.

Francis took one look at the newspaper and handed it back. "I can't read all that. I've got a headache as it is. Just give me the salient points."

"Well, you know that Julia Brown had a child out of wedlock?"

"Yes, yes. And the boy was poisoned."

"He was a poor little soul. Julia Brown purchased some cakes from a woman as she walked from Brettenham to Felsham and gave them to Frederick and her younger brother and sister when she arrived at her mother's home."

"The cakes couldn't have contained poison, or all three children would have died."

"Exactly. But it didn't stop the police arresting Julia."

"But why?"

"Because there was a great deal of speculation and circumstantial evidence against her."

"Of what nature?"

"A combination of gossip and fact."

"I see." Francis moved from the chair he was sitting on and joined Violet on the chaise longue, craning his neck to see the article from which she was reading. He found himself unexpectedly interested.

"Ah," he said, with a knowing nod. "This is all about a young man."

"Not necessarily," said Violet. "Although that is what they suggested. Julia was walking out with Benjamin Dempster who she met when she worked at a previous position at Gedding Hall. Dempster was not the father of her child."

"And he objected to it?"

"It depends whose account you believe. Julia's sister Elizabeth suggested that Dempster told her that if he took Julia on, he would not like to take the child. But she did not say as much to Julia. And it would not have presented a problem had it been true. Julia's parent's reared Freddy from birth and cared for him as if he were their own. She could have left him and gone off with Dempster, and the situation would have been no different than it ever was."

"So, there was talk of marriage?"

"No. Julia was accused of killing the child because it interfered with Dempster's proposal. But he had not proposed."

"How do you know?"

"Because they put him in the box, and he gave testimony to that effect. He said that he had never promised marriage and never spoke with Julia about the child. He broke off the acquaintance for no particular reason but had no fault to find with her."

"So, no motive then?"

"No. And very little in the way of means."

"Do you think she did it?"

Violet hesitated. "No. There's no reason for her to dredge up these dreadful memories unless she is innocent."

"Yet you said she was reluctant to cooperate?"

"I think it's because it's still upsetting to her, even after all this time."

"I daresay. Anything else?"

"A great deal," said Violet. "Medical evidence of a quite disturbing nature. Forgive the graphic details, but Henry Leech carried out an inquest on Freddy. He was the surgeon on duty that day and attended to the child. Mr Leech could not save him and was suspicious of his condition. According to the newspaper, he found a large quantity of caustic fluid in his intestines and abdomen. Furthermore, there were black, jagged holes near the bowel, of an unnatural appearance. He removed everything and placed it in a bowl to pass to Mr Image, who is another surgeon and something of an expert witness. Between them, they deduced that Freddy had swallowed a corrosive substance. It was later tested in the laboratory and proven to be sulphuric acid."

"Not much room for doubt then?" said Francis. "Who in their right mind would murder a little boy?"

"As you say, they couldn't be in their right mind."

"Is Julia Brown sane?"

"As far as I could tell," said Violet. "But not all mentally afflicted people display their symptoms and could appear perfectly normal."

"You'd get a feel for lunacy, surely?"

"I haven't much experience," Violet admitted. "But Julia struck me as sad and shy. In all other respects, she seemed normal."

"The police must have had some sort of evidence against her."

"They did," said Violet. "And if I'm going to get anywhere with this case, I must investigate it further. Julia worked for the Reverend Betham and his wife. Police Superintendent Durrant arrested her at the home of her employer and searched her sleeping quarters at the rectory. She kept her possessions inside a locked box. A trunk of some kind it would appear. Superintendent Durrant asked her for the key, and she would not give it, so he smashed the box open. Inside was a badly stained dress which was examined by Mr Image. His tests proved that sulphuric acid caused the stains."

Francis whistled. "That's sound evidence against her," he said. "How did she explain it?"

"She didn't."

"Then what makes you so sure of her innocence?"

"The attitude of the judge, more than anything. He was particularly sympathetic to her plight, according to the report. And for all the evidence against her, a motive was singularly lacking. And I don't feel that she is guilty. All my instincts say not."

"You sound like Lawrence," said Francis. "I thought you usually operated from a position of logic?"

"Not always," said Violet. "I learned that when Lawrence was sick. But the facts don't fit her guilt anyway."

"I'm not so sure," said Francis. "And I'll tell you why—"

But the reason remained unspoken as they were interrupted by a knock at the door.

"Come in, Albert," said Francis.

The door remained unopened.

"Albert. Come inside."

There was no sound.

"For goodness' sake." Francis marched towards the door and pulled it open to reveal a young boy of about six years old waiting timidly outside.

"Who are you?" asked Francis bemused.

"Don't you recognise your nephew," exclaimed Michael Farrow striding up the corridor, closely followed by Albert Floss.

"Sidney? Dash it. I'm sorry, young man, but I haven't seen you for two or three years. You're supposed to be in India. What the devil is going on, Michael?"

Michael ruffled the boy's hair. "Go with Mr Floss," he said. "He'll show you to the kitchen, and I'm sure cook will find you something tasty to eat."

He waited until the pair were out of earshot. "Good to see you, Violet. You'd better sit down, Francis, and I'll tell you all about it."

#

"Divorced! No. Impossible. There's never been a divorce in our family." Francis Farrow spat the words through pursed lips. His face was florid, and he was incandescent with rage.

"Calm down," said Michael.

"I will not. Where is Ann? I will speak to her and make her stop."

"It's too late," said Michael. "The divorce has already happened. They are no longer married in law."

Francis sat down on a hard-backed chair and cupped his hands over his mouth. There was a moment of silence.

"Where is she?" asked Francis.

"In Piccadilly."

"What's she doing there?"

"She's visiting a friend," said Michael. "For a few weeks, at least. Then she'll have to find somewhere else to live."

64

"Silly girl. Why on earth would she want to divorce Huntingdon? He has treated her well, hasn't he?"

"You are labouring under a misapprehension, brother. She did not divorce him. Gordon left her."

"What? Just took off, you mean?"

"No. Gordon told her that he wanted a divorce and left with Jocelyn Cookson's wife, Muriel."

"Dear God. As if a divorce wasn't bad enough. Now there's a scandal to boot. And they're already divorced, you say?"

Michael nodded.

"Excuse me," said Violet. "I should go. This is a very personal matter."

"No, don't go on my account," said Francis.

"Or mine." Michael smiled at Violet. "I haven't seen you for months."

"Very well. How is poor Ann, if you don't mind me asking?"

"I'm glad you have," said Michael, looking pointedly towards Francis. "Devastated is the only word to describe it. She had no idea that anything was wrong, and Muriel Cookson was one of her closest friends. It turns out that they were conducting an affair behind their respective spouses' backs and it had been going on for at least a year."

"But you say that Ann is already divorced?"

"Gordon has friends in high places."

"Even so."

"Well, yes. The affair has been going on for a while, but the divorce has only just happened. So far it hasn't been reported in the newspapers, as far as Ann knows."

"That won't last," muttered Francis. "Father would be turning in his grave."

"I think he would want to help his daughter," said Michael.

"Does she need help?"

"She is not without funds," said Michael. "While not unduly generous, neither has Gordon left her destitute."

"Well, that's something I suppose."

"And there is a more pressing problem," said Michael.

Francis raised an eyebrow. "Yes."

"The boy, Sidney."

"What about him?"

"The divorce settlement was agreed on the strength of the boy remaining with his father while Ann took little Mercy."

"Then what the devil is he doing here?"

"Originally, Ann intended to stay in India. It has been her home for over a decade. But the thought of living near her former friend who is now living openly with Gordon was too much to bear. And there was no question in her mind of separating the children, so she waited until Gordon went to Tamil Nadu and hot-footed it to Calcutta. She arrived in England a few days ago."

"How long have you known about this?" The redness had drained from Francis Farrow's face. His eyes narrowed, and his voice was even and cold."

Michael held his hands up. "Since last October," he admitted.

"Almost a year."

"About that."

"And why didn't you tell me?"

"Because of my profession," Michael protested. "She sought my counsel, not just as a brother, but as a priest. I couldn't say no to her even if I wanted to, which I didn't," he added.

Francis softened. "I suppose not. Anyway, you didn't answer my question. What is the boy doing here?"

"Hiding."

"Oh, good God, no. Don't drag me into this. Shouldn't Sidney be in London with his mother?"

"Impossible", said Michael. "Ann is staying with her best friend. It is the first place that Gordon will look."

"She can't seriously expect to get away with it. The boy's place is with his father."

"Why?"

"Because he's a boy. What can she teach him about becoming a man?"

"She'd have no choice if she was a widow."

"Well, she isn't. And I want no part in this."

"But she's your sister."

"And Gordon Huntingdon was a boyhood friend. I cannot choose between them."

"Gordon misbehaved, Francis. Ann did not."

"Well, she's more than made up for that by kidnapping his child."

"You won't allow Sidney to stay?"

"No, I won't. It's out of the question."

Michael shook his head. "I felt sure you would understand," he said. "And I told Ann that you would help her."

"That was your mistake. You shouldn't have."

"I'll take him," said Violet.

The brothers turned to her, both wearing equally bemused expressions. "You?" said Francis. "How can you?"

"I have a spare bedroom," said Violet. "He can live with me."

"The boy needs to go to school," said Francis, firmly.

"Then he can stay with me until your sister finds him a school."

"What about your investigation?"

"He can come with me. It is a historical matter, and not at all dangerous."

"I don't know," said Francis, staring pensively into the distance. "The whole situation is ridiculous."

"Thank you," said Michael. "That will be a great weight off Ann's mind. I'll be in Bury for another day. We can take Sidney out somewhere, and you can get to know him. How does that sound?"

"I must go back to Felsham," said Violet. "It won't be exciting, but if we all go together, I can carry on my investigation and spend time with Sidney too. Then he can stay with me tomorrow night and as long as it takes to secure him a school."

"No, Violet. My family's problems are not yours," said Francis. "This is most unsatisfactory. I don't know what you were thinking of involving us in this, Michael. It's breaking the law, and I'm sure your bishop would have something to say on the subject."

Violet watched the normally mild-mannered Michael glare at his brother. "I have only got one sister," he said. "And I will not turn my back on her. If you knew how unhappy she has been, the depth of her humiliation and betrayal, you would not hesitate to help. There is no reason for the bishop to find out, but if he does, I would like to think that he would understand the bounds of brotherly duty."

Francis sighed and walked towards the drawing room window. The sky had darkened, and a light rain drizzled against the windowpanes. He stood, head bowed, with his hands on the window ledge, staring into space. Michael waited, face still stern with anger as Violet rose, touched his arm and gave a small smile. Finally, Francis turned to face them.

"You will not take the boy, Violet," he said. "This is not your problem. It is mine. Very well, Michael. He can stay with me until Ann has found a suitable school for him. You can tell her that he is perfectly safe with me. I'm sure Albert can keep him occupied."

Michael shook his brother's hand, vigorously. "Ann will be so relieved," he said. "I am going to visit her in a few days, and we can discuss the finer points then, but I'll write to her tonight and let her know what you've agreed."

"Very well," said Francis, thinking of all the plans he had made that looking after a seven-year-old boy would scupper. It would almost be more manageable if Gordon caught up with Sidney first, but he dismissed the thought as soon as it came. "Must do my duty," he muttered.

CHAPTER SEVEN

The Incomparable Isabel Smith

Friday, September 11, 1896

The municipal buildings in Spring Gardens were a fair distance away
from where Lawrence had based himself in a small hotel near
Battersea Park. But despite the uncertain weather, he decided to walk
to his destination rather than use public transport. Though he enjoyed
train travel and his experience of riding the London trams was, on the
whole, good, Lawrence was in no mood for people today. He had
woken up in a decent mood. Yesterday's conversation with Richard
Simms had been enlightening and had given him ideas about where he
could find information on missing children which he was keen to
pursue. But the black dog was upon him, and the buildings of London
loomed gloomily before him, grey and oppressive. It didn't help that
the light was poor, crowded out by rain-filled clouds squatting low in
the sky and threatening a downpour at any moment. And he hadn't
brought an umbrella, nor was his coat waterproof. The weather had
been clement when he'd left Bury, which lulled Lawrence into
thinking that the Indian summer would endure through September. But
there hadn't been much sign of the sun since he'd arrived in the capital
two days ago.

Lawrence's coatless trip was nothing compared to what followed. He'd entered the hotel breakfast room first thing, full of optimism for the day's investigation, to be greeted by a tired-looking waiter who took his breakfast order with a grunt and little in the way of enthusiasm. This lack of care was not unduly concerning to Lawrence, who fully understood the boredom of waiting on guests. He had asked if there was a morning paper and was given a copy of *The Times* which he began to read. The first column of the front page began with births and finished with deaths, but his eye had been drawn inexorably to line after line of marriage announcements. He had read through the declarations from men and women who would soon be living their lives together under the same roof, forming families and creating new households. Lawrence realised, with a jolt, that he would soon be one of them. He would have to give up his rooms in Bury St Edmunds, which were wholly unsuitable for Loveday, and he knew he ought to give some thought to purchasing a house. Lawrence had idly wondered whether the owner of the house he had shared with Catherine would be willing to sell. Seconds later, he had dismissed the thought as visions of flames licking at the burning timbers where Catherine and Lily died flashed through his head like an electric current. No. He was far from ready for that. He couldn't imagine Loveday in an older property anyway. She would, no doubt, want something more modern. Lawrence's musings had been interrupted by the arrival of breakfast which was thrust towards him by the surly waiter with little attempt at grace.

"Tea. Toast," the man muttered in staccato before placing a half-filled toast rack and a leaking teapot on the tablecloth.

Undeterred, Lawrence had buttered a piece of toast and slid it under the fried egg on his breakfast plate. Folding *The Times* small enough to read while eating, he had found himself engaged in an article about the cholera epidemic in Sudan. But after an unsettling feeling of being watched, Lawrence had glanced at the table on his left-hand side. It was occupied by a young woman who examined her nails while picking at a pastry, as she gazed directly at him. Lawrence had turned away, discomfited, and continued to enjoy his bacon and eggs, but he couldn't settle and looked up again. She was still watching him. This time he had raised an eyebrow, and she waved at him and smiled. He froze momentarily. She had behaved as if she knew him, but he couldn't remember ever having met her. Who was she? He didn't have to wonder for long. She had put her napkin on top of the remains of her breakfast, stood, and walked towards him.

"It's Lawrence, isn't it?" she'd said.

"Er, yes. Yes, it is."

"You don't remember me, do you?"

"Sorry."

"Felicity Braithwaite," she'd continued, holding out her hand.

Lawrence took it and nodded, still none the wiser.

"We met at The Pump Rooms, in Cheltenham. I'm Loveday's friend."

"Of course, you are," Lawrence had said, smiling in an attempt to conceal his growing concern that he still could not place her.

"It was kind of you to clear up my mess," she'd continued. "All that smashed glass. You might have injured yourself."

"It was no trouble," said Lawrence, having remembered the incident, though not the young woman who stood before him.

"I hear congratulations are in order," she had continued, with a broad grin. "I bumped into Loveday buying lace for her gown last week. You must be so excited."

"Naturally," murmured Lawrence. "Is she well?"

"Well and happy," the young woman had said. "Will you be in Cheltenham next week?"

"No," said Lawrence. "Why?"

"I thought you'd want to see the houses too."

"What houses?"

"Loveday is looking at properties in Cheltenham for you two to live in when you are married."

The conversation looped in Lawrence's mind as he walked down The Mall towards St James's feeling as if the weight of the world was on his shoulders. He shivered as a growing wind whistled past the buildings while he contemplated his future. It was one thing sleepwalking into a wedding with Loveday. She was a charming girl and had kept his spirits up when Violet had vanished. Loveday had been the only ray of light during the months when he'd felt abandoned and alone. Violet's response had been understandable. He'd behaved badly in Liverpool, indifferent to her feelings and confused at his reaction to Loveday. But Violet had disappeared without any

71

explanation, not caring enough to talk about it or find a way to repair their friendship. It was only natural that he would turn to the young lady who had stepped into the void. But that did not include moving county. Perhaps it was Lawrence's fault for assuming that Loveday would settle in Suffolk, while she had evidently expected that he would be happy to live in Cheltenham. Lawrence loved the Cotswolds, but it would be impossible to make a home there and conduct his business in Bury. And anyway, he didn't want to. It did not feature in his plans at all.

His face set into a scowl as he neared Spring Gardens and Lawrence approached the municipal building oblivious to the structured elegance of Admiralty Arch as he passed through. His mind was buzzing with the difficulties he now faced, and for one moment, he toyed with the idea of bypassing the investigation and going straight to Cheltenham. He needed to resolve the situation before Loveday committed them to a purchase he had no intention of making. But at that moment, a young woman walked past, pushing a perambulator and talking to her young daughter, who gurgled in delight. The little child, dressed in a pink cardigan, was reaching for a row of knitted balls strung across the pram. She wore a wondrous smile across her face and reminded Lawrence of his daughter Lily. No. He would not leave London yet. He had made a promise to Flora Johns and would keep it to the best of his ability. Not until he'd exhausted every possible avenue of investigation would he abandon his duty. But as soon as he had done everything in his power, he would go straight to Loveday and make her understand the necessity of dwelling in Suffolk. Until then, he would try to forget all about it. He straightened his tie, turned into Spring Gardens and entered the municipal building.

#

Getting to see Miss Isabel Smith was nowhere near as straightforward as Lawrence had assumed it would be. It wasn't that she was unavailable. She was present in the building and had no meetings or other interviews that might preclude a visit. Still, the receptionist on the Child Protection counter took her supervisory duties to the extreme. Not since he had attempted to break into Fred Burrage's garden workshop during an investigation had Lawrence encountered such a rabidly diligent gatekeeper. In that case, it had been a particularly aggressive Rottweiler.

The conversation had started amicably enough, with Lawrence wishing the receptionist a good day. But things had gone rapidly downhill when she asked if he had an appointment and he answered in the negative.

"An unplanned visit!" she exclaimed as if it ought to be a capital offence. "Then, no. Most certainly not. Miss Smith has a full diary."

Lawrence sighed. "When is her next appointment?"

"You haven't told me your name."

"Lawrence Harpham, investigator."

"What do you want to see her about?"

"It's a private matter."

The receptionist frowned and eyed him warily.

"I can't help if you won't tell me."

Lawrence gritted his teeth. He was beginning to lose patience. "Tell her that Richard Simms sent me."

"And who, may I ask, is he?"

"Oh, for goodness' sake," Lawrence exploded. "Can't you just ask Miss Smith if she'll see me?"

"There's no need to behave like that." The receptionist pursed her lips and stepped back in pseudo shock, eyes wide. She gave a visible shudder and ran her hand through greying hair. "Move away from the counter or I'll ring the bell."

"What bell?"

"The one we use for difficult visitors."

Lawrence folded his arms. "Good. Please go right ahead."

"You'll be removed from the building."

"Well, at least I'll get to see somebody who might feel like helping me. If that's what it takes to get some assistance, then I'll take my chances."

The receptionist moved her hand away from the bell. "I don't think that will be necessary," she said.

"Then you'll call Miss Smith and tell her that I'm here?"

"No. Leave your calling card, and I'll contact you when I have examined her diary."

Lawrence shook his head, then sat down on a nearby chair with his arms crossed.

"You can go now," said the receptionist.

Lawrence glared and turned away.

He remained like that for twenty minutes while the receptionist glowered at him and pounded on her typewriter keys. For the first few minutes, she ignored him, but the longer he sat there, the heavier her keystrokes became until the speed and ferocity of her typing betrayed her apparent ire. Lawrence glanced sideways and smiled, just as the door behind the counter opened to reveal a tall, willowy, dark-haired woman carrying a folder. She approached the receptionist.

"Has there been any post today, Miss Worthington?" she asked, brightly.

"No, Miss Smith," said the receptionist sullenly.

Lawrence leapt to his feet. "Miss Smith? Miss Isabel Smith?" he asked.

"Yes. Can I help you?"

"I was hoping to see you briefly if you have time?"

Isabel Smith glanced at the wall clock. "I'm sure I can spare you a few moments. Come this way."

She opened the door, and Lawrence followed her out, shooting a triumphant glare towards the receptionist, who pointedly lowered her head and ignored him.

"Has it cleared up yet?" asked Isabel Smith.

"I'm sorry?"

"The weather. It was raining when I arrived this morning. I rather hoped it would improve. I'm expected in Camberwell later, and I was going to walk if it was clement."

"It's still drizzling," said Lawrence. "But you never know."

"Indeed. Here is my office. Do come inside."

They entered a compact room, with a desk beneath the window and a row of neatly arranged wooden filing cabinets. The assiduously placed stack of files was positioned centrally between the top and the left-hand side of the desk. A pen and inkstand lay dead centre and two pencils, an eraser, and a notepad had been arranged with military precision down the right-hand side. A plain, wooden-framed mirror hung above the fireplace, and the only other adornment was a certificate bearing Isabel's name on the opposite wall. Lawrence smiled at the attention to detail. It appealed to his love of symmetry and order.

"Take a seat, Mr...?" said Isabel, pointing to a burgundy upholstered chair opposite the desk.

"Harpham," said Lawrence. "Lawrence Harpham. I am investigating the disappearance of a young child. Richard Simms thought you might be able to help."

"How is he?" asked Isabel, leaning forward and steepling her hands.

"Well, but busy," said Lawrence. "Even so, he spared me an hour yesterday to talk about my case, for which I am very grateful."

"He's a good man," said Isabel, simply.

"The feeling is mutual," said Lawrence. "He spoke highly of you and suggested that you might be able to tell me something of the events that took place in Amies Street."

Isabel Smith's face darkened. "Of course," she said. "Though I do hope that you have no grounds to suspect the same fate might have befallen your missing child."

Lawrence shrugged. "I don't know," he said. "Anything could have happened to the boy. The best that I can do for him now is to find out as much as possible about any crimes involving the disappearance of children."

"I'll tell you everything I know about the Amies Street baby farm, but first, tell me the circumstances of the child's disappearance."

Lawrence recounted every detail of the case from the moment he'd met Flora Johns. When he had finished, Isabel opened the bottom drawer of her desk and removed a large, bound register. "All authorised applications for childminding are in here," she said, opening the cover. "Now, let me see. C, D, E, F, G. No, sorry. There are no entries for Gideon Road. Do you know the woman's name?"

"It could be Dorothy Jones, or it could be Miss Hamblin. She used at least two different names."

"Oh dear. That's not a good sign. I can check another register later. We have arranged this one by location."

"That would be helpful. Can I call in again on Monday to see what you've found?" asked Lawrence.

"Yes, do. Now to the matter of Miss Davis and Mrs Stevens."

"Who are they?"

"The names of the two women who applied to mind children in Amies Street."

"Ah, yes."

"Now. The Battersea matter is most unsettling. I authorised the application and in doing so, was indirectly responsible for the death of two children."

"You weren't to know."

"Of course not. But it doesn't lessen the feeling of responsibility. It is my job to protect children and keep them safe from harm. If I fail in my duty, lives are at risk."

"Do you think you could have done more to protect them?"

"No. I know I couldn't have done any more," said Isabel. "And that is what keeps me from lying awake at night worrying. I signed the application in good faith and made every possible effort following due process to inspect the premises and monitor the children."

"What went wrong?"

"The women lied," said Isabel, simply. "Mary Stevens and Caroline Davis applied to mind three children, but they took in many more and concealed the children whenever I tried to conduct an inspection."

"How did you know?"

"I didn't know to begin with," said Isabel.

"But it became apparent?"

She nodded. "Yes, from the kindly intervention of a neighbour who was roundly abused by Mrs Stevens for his trouble. Most of my journeys take place some distance from the office, and I have the use of a carriage and driver. Well, on this particular day, Valentine Jennings, my cabman, was waiting with the carriage. Exactly how the conversation started, I can't be sure, but the neighbour told him that he'd heard crying one evening and looked through the window to see at least half a dozen children who appeared to be unsupervised. Naturally, Jennings informed me, but not until we had returned to Spring Gardens. My visit rota was full, and it took a few days before I returned to Amies Street. There were indeed six children present, and I issued an immediate warning and reminded them that they should not take in more than three children at any time."

"Were the children fit and healthy?"

"Of course. I would have removed them, if not."

"And you made regular checks?"

"Indeed. More regular than required. I was uneasy about the women and did not trust them. But two further visits passed without incident, with never more than three children present although the lack of cleanliness remained a problem. I visited again towards the end of the twelve-month period when the certificate was due to expire. The rooms at Amies Street were basic, Mr Harpham, and sparsely furnished in a way that did not feel quite right. And two of the three children were sickly and seemed malnourished. I instructed the women to call the doctor, and they agreed, but half-heartedly. I doubted their motives and decided not to renew the licence."

"It sounds like a good decision," said Lawrence. "Innocent children deserve so much better."

Isabel shook her head. "They do, but it wasn't enough. The women carried on taking in children regardless. The neighbour intervened once again, this time in writing and I arrived unannounced at Amies Street and went to see him. The poor man was beside himself. He was adamant that the women were concealing children when we inspected the premises and said he had seen clear evidence of neglect. I left him and went immediately to number forty-eight, but they would not allow me access. It was quite clear that something wasn't right."

"It sounds like the women were running a baby farm," said Lawrence.

"Yes. They were. Not in the manner of Mrs Dyer, and the loss of life was unplanned and came about from neglect. But the result was the same."

"How did you get into the house?"

"I didn't go in that day. I returned to the municipal building and consulted with Mr Newlands. He is one of the other inspectors, and he offered to come with me so that we could watch each of the women to stop them hiding anything. Jennings took us there first thing the next day, and Caroline Davis was so surprised when she opened the door that she failed to close it in time. Mr Newlands barged his way into the hallway, and I inspected the house from top to bottom."

"What did you find?" asked Lawrence, hoping the details wouldn't be too graphic.

"I found a dying child," said Isabel. "The situation was as the neighbour had stated. The women had crammed six children into the front room, two in cribs and the remainder on a dirty mattress on the floor. The children lay in squalor, dirty and unchanged."

"And all this in a short space of time?"

"It was well over six months. Don't forget, we revoked their licence, and they were not supposed to be minding children at all. So, the regular inspections stopped and only began again due to the complaint from the neighbour. I suppose that they threw all caution to the wind, thinking that they could behave as they wished unimpeded by the demands of the council. Thankfully, they were reported."

"But not before their negligence had killed a child."

"Had killed two children," Isabel corrected. "The child who I saw and could not save was a girl, born to a lady's maid who resided near Battersea Park. But several days before she died, a boy child also perished. We did not know either of the children and had not seen them before. They were not the children who were in the house during my previous visits."

"I can see why Simms thought I should speak to you. This case is uncannily similar to that of the young woman I am trying to help. Even down to the circumstances of her child's birth."

"It happens a great deal," said Isabel. "But it does not follow that the child you are seeking met the same fate. By and large, these women do not seek to harm the children they mind. They are simply uneducated and often uncaring. Fatalities occur from lack of attention."

"And I suppose that if the children are sickly when they arrive, there is no motivation to help them."

"That would likely be the case, but the children, or at least little Marie Gras, was strong and healthy when she left her mother's care. She was almost eight pounds and a bonny child. By the time she died, she weighed less than six pounds, was emaciated, and covered in sores from insufficient changes of clothing. I gave evidence at the inquest at Battersea and heard Dr Eginton give his account. Mary Ann Stevens had taken the child to his surgery a few days earlier, suffering from extreme diarrhoea. She said that all the children had contracted the same ailment and began to feed the crying child in his presence. He was horrified at the state of the bottle, which was filthy and smelled disgusting, so he remonstrated with her about it. She left his surgery with enough medicine for all the children, but it was too late to help Marie. She died from exhaustion due to diarrhoea and gastroenteritis, accelerated by the unwholesome surroundings in which she dwelled."

"Does this happen often?" asked Lawrence, sick to the stomach at the thought of the dying children, lying unloved in the stark rooms in Amies Street.

"I see it every day," said Isabel. "It is the nature of my job."

"I don't know how you bear it."

"It takes its toll," she admitted. "At times, I have been tempted to return to Newcastle and find another occupation. But I save more children than I lose," she continued. "It is not an easy job, but it is a necessary one. I try not to dwell on those children that I can't help and thank God for those I can remove from harm."

Lawrence watched her in silent admiration, unable to speak for the lump that had formed in his throat. He bit his lip, realising, to his surprise, that he was close to tears at the thought of the circumstances this woman endured day after day. Her quiet and logical approach to a desperate problem and her humanity in the face of misery and neglect, left him moved. She reminded him of Violet; quiet, understated and rational, and with a gentle heart. Violet. The comparison was with Violet. Not Loveday. Finally, Lawrence felt able to speak without his voice cracking with emotion. "I hope I won't find Bertie Johns in such an establishment," he said quietly.

"You can, at least, be certain that he was not in this one," she assured him. "The inquest was in August."

"Yes, but you say there are others?"

"Many others. But we are dealing with them. It is becoming harder to take children in an unlicensed house. We are building a case to petition parliament to strengthen the Infant Life Protection Act. The day will come when children are far safer."

"It cannot come too soon. Now, do you have any other ideas about what might have happened to Bertie?"

"Several," said Isabel. "But I can't offer any more time today. You're calling in on Monday for news about Dorothy Jones, aren't you? I'll speak to the other inspectors later this afternoon, and by the next time we meet, I'll be able to let you know what kind of cases we're dealing with. I don't know how much it will help you in your endeavours, but perhaps it will provide a starting point."

"You are too kind," said Lawrence gruffly. He left the room and followed the corridor to the front office, too full of emotion to even gloat at the receptionist.

CHAPTER EIGHT

Questioning Rosa

"What's an investigation?" Sidney Huntingdon was sitting on a low stone wall picking at a scab on his leg.

"Don't do that," said Michael, pushing his hand away. "You'll get blood all over your socks. Or at least you would if you pulled them up."

Sidney sighed and swung his leg on top of the wall before yanking his sock as high as possible. "You didn't answer my question," he said dolefully.

"It's what Miss Violet described," said Michael.

"Is that where she is?"

Michael nodded. "Yes, she's visiting a lady to ask her some questions, and we are going to take a nice long walk around this beautiful village and look for some treasure.

"I don't see what's so beautiful about it. It's just a load of houses in a field. It's boring."

"What would you like to do?" asked Michael patiently.

"I want to see my mother," said Sidney, his voice trembling.

"And you will in a few weeks," said Michael.

"I want to see her now."

"She's in London."

"Then, I want to see Violet. She's nice."

Michael removed his pocket watch and passed it to Sidney. "You see that big hand?"

Sidney nodded.

"Well, when it gets there," he continued, pointing to the top of the watch, "and when that little hand gets there, you will see Miss Violet."

"How long will that be?"

"Just over an hour," said Michael. "She said it wouldn't take much longer than that."

"Which house is she in?" asked Sidney.

"That one over there." Michael pointed to a small, cream-coloured cottage on the other side of the green.

"Can we go and see her?"

"No, she's working."

"Please. I promise I'll be good."

Michael sighed. Looking after Sidney was becoming increasingly frustrating the longer he was away from his mother. But the last few weeks had been so turbulent for the boy, that he was reluctant to say no.

"I'll tell you what we'll do. We'll go and sit on the green in front of the house. It's nice and dry, and you can keep a watch out for Violet. I've got a bottle of ginger beer and an apple. We'll have a little picnic. What do you say?"

Sidney nodded vigorously.

"Come on then."

They walked across the grass and towards the little cottage gate.

"There she is," squealed Sidney excitedly, pointing towards the window where Violet was standing with a woman of a similar age. He waved at her and was rewarded with a smile and a wave from Violet.

"Come on now, let's get settled," said Michael. "The sooner Violet can finish her conversation, the quicker she'll be back."

"He's a nice-looking young lad," said Rosa Gladwell as she watched the excited boy waving towards her kitchen window. "Foreign, is he?"

"No. Sidney has just returned from India," said Violet.

"Has he now? The dark skin and fair hair are an unusual combination. I daresay he'll break a few hearts when he's older. He's not yours, then?"

"No, he's not."

"Well, pull up a chair, and tell me what you want."

"Information," said Violet, pulling out the newspaper clipping she'd showed Francis the previous day. "But it's about something that took place a long time ago. I would have asked your mother, had it been possible."

"She died twenty years ago," said Rosa. "And there isn't a day that passes by when I don't think of her. The life and soul of our house, she was. Always laughing, always kindly and always ready to help."

"She's named in this newspaper cutting. Was she a nurse?"

"She didn't train to be a nurse," said Rosa, scanning the newspaper article. "She wasn't qualified, but she was wise and willing and often called upon in times of need."

"According to the newspaper, she tended to little Freddy Brown."

"I can read," said Rosa, slowly digesting the contents of the paper.

Violet paused, waiting for Rosa to finish. Eventually, she looked up and sat back in her chair.

"Well, I knew about Freddy, of course. It was the talk of the village. When was it now?" She glanced at the top of the page. "Eighteen sixty-four. I would have been ten years old at the time. So, yes. I remember the murder, but it's the first I've heard about Mother's part in it."

"That's a pity," said Violet. "I was hoping you'd remember something."

"Like what?"

"I don't know," she admitted. "I can't go into much detail about this. My work is confidential, as I'm sure you understand, but I hoped to find out more about how Freddy died."

"After all this time?" Rosa Gladwell raised her eyebrows and regarded Violet incredulously.

"Exactly. This case is far more difficult than any matter I've ever dealt with. It's an almost impossible task, but if I've any chance of getting to the bottom of it, I'll need to know exactly what was going on in the parish at the time of Freddy's death."

Rosa shook her head. "It's a great pity that you couldn't meet my mother. She would have given you chapter and verse on the doings in the village. She knew everything and everyone. No doubt she would have had her own theories on the matter. I only wish I'd been old enough to remember."

"Were you happy growing up here?"

"Very," said Rosa. "We were a big family and money was scarce. Father worked in the fields, and work was abundant in summer but in short supply over winter. Our fortunes fluctuated with the seasons. My parents were industrious and sober and saved what they could for the winter months. Well, until Mother died, that is. Father didn't fare so well alone."

"He couldn't cope without her?"

"Not so much that, but he became colder. Hard-hearted even. Grandfather John lived with us when Mother was alive. She was very fond of him even though he was only her father by law. But after she died, my father turned him out, and he had no choice but to seek shelter in the workhouse. Shameful and unnecessary."

"Perhaps, money was too scarce for him to manage."

"It was scarce, yes. Of course. Grandfather John left in February during one of the coldest weeks of the year when the ground was iron-hard, and there was no work to be had. I'd left home by then and was married with a child of my own. Only Kate and Oscar remained at home, and Kate kept house for father. I do not doubt that it was hard to feed them all, but my uncles were willing to contribute to Grandfather's keep. Father knew this, but he would not let his father stay. He said that he'd be stuck with him for all eternity otherwise and it was someone else's turn."

"I'm sorry to hear that," said Violet, thinking of her own dear, long-deceased father. She would have starved before sacrificing him to the workhouse, but everyone's circumstances were different. Perhaps even Rosa did not fully understand the nature of her father's financial affairs.

"I shouldn't witter on about it," said Rosa. "As I told you, my childhood was happy. Village life suited me, and I never had any yearnings to leave it. Not much happened in Felsham apart from a bit of poaching and the constant bickering between the shopkeepers. And Freddy's murder, of course."

"Well, it's kind of you to take the time to speak to me," said Violet, rising from the kitchen table.

"I wish I could have helped more," said Rosa. "If only I hadn't been so young. It's a shame that Caroline lives so far away. Mother would have talked to her a lot more."

"Caroline?"

"Yes, my sister, Caroline. She's the eldest and would have been sixteen or seventeen at the time. But she lives in London now."

"That might not be a problem," said Violet. "I was considering travelling to London anyway. Do you think she would speak to me?"

"Yes, I expect so, but I'll write you a note if you wait for a moment. Take it to Caroline whenever you're ready, and I'm sure she will talk with you. Mother would have confided in Caroline. It would be as if she were still here."

CHAPTER NINE

Municipal Buildings

Monday, September 14, 1896

Lawrence walked the route to the municipal buildings in Spring Gardens relieved to have rediscovered the sense of purpose that had eluded him over the weekend. There had been nothing for him to do, at least nothing that he wanted to do. He had nowhere to go, and nobody to go with and had briefly toyed with the idea of returning to Bury St Edmunds for the weekend. It was only the thought of the train journey back to London first thing Monday morning, that stopped him. He'd woken on Saturday, determined to make productive use of the day, but quickly decided that he didn't have anything to investigate until he met with Isabel Smith. And that wasn't until Monday. There was no point in returning to Gideon Road, so he rose late, had a leisurely breakfast, read the paper, then contemplated how to fill the rest of the day as it stretched before him. In the end, he'd plumped for a walk around Hyde Park. He'd crossed the Thames, hopped on a tram and found himself outside Hyde Park Corner a little before midday. The sun was out, albeit faintly, but it had been warm enough to sit outside and watch the world go by. On arriving at Hyde Park Corner, he'd soon realised that a stroll around the park would not be nearly as peaceful as he'd hoped. Most of the inhabitants of London seemed to have had the same idea, and there was a sea of trams and carriages, ladies carrying parasols, and gentlemen dressed in boaters clutching the hands of eager young children.

The clip-clop of hooves, chattering voices and childish squeals had assailed his ears as he passed through the gate searching for a quiet route. Tranquillity eluded him as he headed north, trying to avoid wobbling cyclists, not fully in control of their vehicles and no doubt heading for a fall. As he'd approached Marble Arch, the crowd grew to a heaving, hissing throng and he soon saw the reason for their antipathy in the form of two young women, their shrill voices rising as they tried to impart their message to the unwilling. The women were pleading for political equality, demanding the same voting rights as men. Lawrence had smiled wryly. It was a debate he'd often had in the office with Violet who felt strongly about such things. He would tease her about spending time with her Primrose League friends, many of whom were strictly opposed to the idea of women voting. But Violet was her own person and saw herself as the equal of any man and therefore as able as Lawrence to cast a wise vote. Well, if all women were like Violet, then he would agree. But they weren't, and some were too silly to be trusted at the ballot box. Still, when he came to think about it, so were some of the men with whom he was acquainted. There really ought to be an intelligence test before voting was allowed at all.

By the time Lawrence had reached Marble Arch on Saturday afternoon, he'd had enough. It was too noisy to stay in the park, and he was too irritable to walk. He'd hailed a hansom cab and reclined as they travelled through Belgravia, arriving back at his hotel in a better frame of mind, which did not last. Lawrence had eaten a late lunch, then tried to read a book, but was too frustrated to continue. He'd paced the lounge, poked around the bookcase and found a copy of *The Era* advertising a play at The Adelphi Theatre. The theatre was not particularly high on Lawrence's list of pleasurable things to do in the evening, though he had accompanied Violet a few times in the past. She very much enjoyed that sort of thing, but Lawrence was so bereft of stimulation, that he decided to go anyway, and by the time he was back in bed at eleven thirty that evening, he'd concluded that it had been a sound decision. He had watched a play called *Brothers Together* set in Egypt with a dastardly villain and a persecuted hero. Naturally, they fought over a woman, and it reminded Lawrence of stories he had read in *The Boy's Own Paper*. He had thoroughly enjoyed it, but an enjoyable evening was as good as it got. Lawrence woke on Sunday with the black dog upon him and a full twenty-four hours with nothing to do. The day had been interminably long, and he'd yearned for Monday to arrive.

Now it was here, and he approached the main door to the municipal buildings, worrying that Isabel Smith probably hadn't intended for him to arrive quite so early. He glanced at his pocket watch – only half past eight, and chewed his lip, wondering whether he might have beaten her to it. But as he pushed the door open, he saw her placing an envelope on the receptionist's desk.

"You're early," she said cheerfully. "It's lucky that I forgot to lock the door. We don't normally open to the public until nine."

"Sorry," said Lawrence ruefully. "I didn't think."

"I don't mind at all," she said. "I've got a busy day, and it's quite useful that you're here now. There are one or two things I would like to draw your attention to, unless you're in a hurry, that is?"

"Not at all," said Lawrence. "To be quite honest, I am utterly reliant on any information you can supply. The more I think about this case, the more I wonder whether there's any way to resolve it. That poor young boy could be anywhere."

"Yes," said Isabel. "And I'm not sure how much help I'm going to be. There is no obvious route for you to follow."

"I'll take any hint or clue," said Lawrence, following her down the corridor to her office.

He took the seat in front of her desk, and she poured herself a glass of water and offered him one.

"Not for me," he said, removing his notebook and pen.

Isabel Smith took a small ledger and a handwritten document from a tidy pile on the side of her desk. "Now, first things first. There is no record of anyone called Dorothy Jones on our registers. Not for childcare or anything else we monitor. But there is a childminder in Silvertown who goes by the name of Miss Dora Hamblin. She lives in Albert Road. I'm sure you understand that it would be unethical for me to give you her address. But I'm equally certain that you have the wherewithal to locate her yourself."

Lawrence nodded. "That's a great help," he said. "At least I have a starting point."

"I've also written a few brief notes for you; nothing much, just a short paragraph on each case with which my fellow inspectors are involved.

Lawrence glanced at the page and looked up at her, anxiously. "Almost all of these involve dead children."

"Grim, isn't it?" said Isabel, her forehead furrowed in concern. "We often don't get to hear of problems until it is too late. This little boy here," she said, pointing to the first paragraph, "ran away from home. He was taken in by a man known only as Red Nick who cut his Achilles tendons through and sent him out to beg on the streets. The wounds became infected, and he was abandoned on the pavement where he died. We can't find Red Nick, though we know he operates in Spitalfields, and we have every reason to think that he has other children under his influence."

Lawrence shook his head, too disgusted to say a word.

"Sorry. I know it's shocking," said Isabel sympathetically. "I am not hardened to this, but I see it every day, and I still remember how difficult it was the first time I heard such stories. I've had my fair share of sleepless nights."

"I don't know how you do it," said Lawrence, gruffly.

"Somebody must."

"This boy was six years old, you say?"

"Yes."

"If the sole purpose was to make money by making this boy beg, then Bertie should be safe. He's only a baby and far too young."

"Yes, but if a beggar takes a baby with him, hearts soften more easily. There's nothing that opens the purse strings quite so quickly as a young child in want."

"Sickening. Is there no end to the evil that men do?"

"Here's another report," said Isabel, rotating the page to face Lawrence. "This time, involving babies."

Lawrence read down the page. "Simms mentioned this," he said. "Dead babies wrapped in brown paper parcels. But these children weren't wanted, surely? And it's hard to imagine a more loved child than Bertie."

"You are partly correct. The children weren't wanted by the time they met their fate. The police don't know who they are or how they got there. But you should know this. They all had traces of food in their stomachs. Which means they lived, and someone fed them."

"So not all of the babies were discarded at birth?"

Isabel shook her head. "Worse than that. Feeding indicates some level of nurturing which means they were wanted, at least for a short time. It rather suggests baby farmers."

"Not the two in Battersea?"

"No. All those children died at home. The babies in the brown paper packages appeared throughout London and Essex."

"Are you sure the same person disposed of them?"

"No. Not completely. But according to the police, there were certain similarities in the knots. They were tied in an unusual manner."

"And how did you come to be involved?"

"As I said, the police suspected they came from a baby farm, possibly more than one. There's only a small chance that a place set up for that purpose was registered, but the police sought our opinion anyway."

"So, are you suggesting someone took Bertie for money, then disposed of him?"

"It's possible," said Isabel quietly. "Whoever left the babies in the paper parcels is still at large, as far as we know. It could be anyone."

Lawrence stared quietly at the table, trying to work out what he would say to Flora Johns when they next met. He could offer no words of hope or encouragement, based on the reports he'd heard.

"There's one more," said Isabel, interrupting his thoughts. "It's a little unusual," she continued.

"More dead children?"

"I'm afraid so."

Lawrence sighed. "Go on then. Tell me."

"It's to do with poison," said Isabel, grimacing. "And quite nasty. It's one of Richard's cases. Sergeant Simms, that is. Has he mentioned it?"

"I think he touched on it but didn't elaborate," said Lawrence.

"Hmmm. Well, Richard may not have thought it was relevant. Are you familiar with Silvertown?"

"Not in the least. I'd never heard of it until you mentioned it earlier."

"Yes. It's an uncanny coincidence that it's come up again. Silvertown is in Woolwich, by the docks."

"I know the general area. Is this where the poisoning occurred?"

"Poisonings," said Isabel. "There were more than one."

"More than one child or more than one instance?"

"There were several children," said Isabel, "and at least three separate instances that we are aware of."

Lawrence leaned forwards and steepled his hands. "That sounds intentional."

"Doesn't it? Yet, the police are by no means certain. It could be an unfortunate accident."

"Can you tell me more?"

"Not very much," said Isabel. "We know the bare facts because the police consulted us. A young girl claimed that she was given a poisoned cake, which she shared with her friends. She said that the cake had been given to her by a man, a stranger."

"And the police wanted to know if you'd come across anything like it?"

"No. The girl said she'd seen the man approaching one of the younger children a few weeks before. He'd taken the young boy by the hand and tried to lead him away, but the little boy was frightened and ran off."

"And Sergeant Simms thinks there is a link with the poisonings?"

"Possibly," said Isabel. "But the children are very young and may have been mistaken. It could be two different men, or perhaps they didn't exist at all. After all, the girl was indirectly responsible for poisoning the younger children. She may have made the whole thing up."

"Still," said Lawrence, stroking his lip, "it's worth knowing more about it. I wouldn't bother, but the fact that Dorothy Jones or whatever name she currently goes by, might be living in the same area, is enough to make it worth my while."

"Yes. Well, if you decide it's worth pursuing, then go to Gray Street and ask for Louisa Tullis. A cake of rat poison went missing from her shop on the day of the poisoning. I hope I've been of help to you," said Isabel Smith. "But I really must press on. Jennings is going to deliver this for me," she said, waving an envelope, "and it's rather urgent. I'll…"

But she was interrupted by a knock at the door which opened immediately, leaving her no chance to answer. A grey-haired, handsome man with a weather-beaten face entered. "I'm sorry," he said. "This won't wait. Mrs Newton's had one of her turns. Can you come?"

"Yes, of course," said Isabel, flashing Lawrence a wry smile. "Sorry, I have nursing experience," she explained. "Oh, my letter!"

"I'll take it," said Lawrence.

"Oh, thank you. You'll find Jennings out the front. Black cab and a black horse. He'll be the only one." Isabel rushed from the room, leaving Lawrence on his own. He walked towards the door, then thought better of it and quietly opened the drawer to Isabel's desk where he'd seen the register the previous Friday. He opened it furtively, licked his finger and checked through, but was none the wiser by the time he had finished. Isabel appeared to have shared all the information that had been available to her. Feeling ungrateful and a little guilty he left the room and made his way to the front of the building.

There was no mistaking Valentine Jennings. His horse was black from mane to tail, with dark eyes the colour of its coat. It looked spectral, otherworldly. Valentine, on the other hand, was a stout, middle-aged man with a ready smile. He nodded at Lawrence as he approached, holding out the letter.

"This is from Miss Smith," said Lawrence, by way of explanation.

"Thank you. I'm expecting it," said Jennings. "It's a matter of some urgency, though why I'm not sure. But then, I don't need to know," he continued.

"Where are you going?" asked Lawrence.

"Battersea."

"Ah, my hotel is there."

Valentine patted the seat beside him. "You're welcome to a ride," he said. "You can sit inside if you like."

"That's very kind," said Lawrence, about to decline the offer, but then thought the better of it. "Why not," he said, climbing aboard.

CHAPTER TEN

Return to Battersea

Lawrence enjoyed a long walk as much as the next man, but sometimes enough was enough. He had strolled what felt like the length and breadth of London on Saturday and had taken no less than four short walks on Sunday in his bid to alleviate the boredom. So, a place in Valentine Jennings' cab on what was turning into a pleasant, sunny day, was just the ticket, as far as Lawrence was concerned. He gazed towards Buckingham Palace as the cab traversed The Mall, hoping for a quiet journey, and was rewarded with minimal social interaction from the taciturn cab driver. By the time they passed Westminster Cathedral, Lawrence had decided to make more of an effort. Jennings had offered him a lift, and the least he could do was pass the time of day with the man. A little small talk was in order.

"Have you worked for the council for long?" asked Lawrence.

"A few years, sir," said Jennings. "But I've been a cabman for most of my adult life."

"And you usually drive Miss Smith?"

The cabman smiled and nodded. "I drive all the inspectors, but Miss Smith the most. She's a very nice woman."

"I agree," said Lawrence. "A nice woman with a difficult job."

"The worst," Jennings agreed. "I've seen some terrible things in my time with her."

"I heard," said Lawrence. "You were with her when she uncovered the Battersea baby farm."

Jennings frowned. "Horrible women," he said. "Ignorant and only interested in money. It's a good thing that they were stopped. Who knows how many more would have died.'"?

"Indeed," said Lawrence. "I'd say you'll know how to get around London, with your occupation."

"I should say so. I've spent my life navigating these streets."

"I've got to go to Silvertown later. It's by the docks. Know it?"

"Reasonably well. I have family nearby."

"What's the best way to get there?"

"It's a good ten miles from Battersea," said Jennings. "I'd hop on a train if I were you."

"Hmmm. I didn't realise it was that far," said Lawrence. "Perhaps tomorrow would be better."

The conversation dwindled as they crossed the river and had ceased altogether by the time they reached Lawrence's hotel in Battersea. "Well, thank you," said Lawrence, dismounting the carriage, "much appreciated."

"My pleasure," said the cabman as he took the reins and urged his horse onwards.

Lawrence entered the hotel and made straight for the reception counter, hoping for assistance in arranging his journey to Silvertown. The man behind the counter was familiar with the area and gave detailed directions on how to get there using the Great Eastern Railway. Just as Lawrence was considering whether to bother, the man motioned him back to the counter. "I nearly forgot to tell you. A telegram's arrived."

Lawrence opened it to find a short message from Violet. "Need to go to St Pancras. Arriving in London at 4 pm today. Meet me briefly to discuss cases."

Lawrence frowned. Meet briefly? Why would they meet briefly? If Violet was in London surely they would share details of their cases over a drink, as usual. Had it really come to this?

He screwed up the telegram in annoyance. If they couldn't get along, there was no future for their business. And he didn't want to go back to solo investigations. Violet was a vital asset in their agency, not to mention a valued friend. Lawrence put his head in his hands, wishing he hadn't made such a mess of things. And he couldn't see them improving once he was married to Loveday. God! And that was another problem. He needed to find the time to go and see her and set her right on where they would be living. Somehow, he'd have to go to Cheltenham, and soon. But first things first. He needed to catch Violet at Liverpool Street station, so he didn't lose her in London, leaving her free to set her own agenda for their meeting. He hoped that she'd booked a room in his hotel, knowing he was there, but this version of Violet was very different to last year's. She might do anything or go anywhere. He glanced at the wall clock. It was only a quarter past eleven. He had plenty of time. Lawrence went up to his room, sat on his bed and, using Isabel Smith's records, journaled all his ideas about where Bertie Johns could conceivably be.

#

By three fifty, Lawrence was standing at platform six of Liverpool Street station pacing anxiously. He pulled out his watch and checked it for the third time as the minutes slowly ticked by. Eventually, the small hand dragged itself to the hour, and it was four o'clock, but the train was late, and the platform empty. Finally, at three minutes past four, Lawrence was rewarded by a clattering of wheels on the track, vying with the hiss of steam, as the locomotive drew up by the platform. Lawrence waited for Violet with bated breath, keen to see her, but still annoyed at the sharp tone of her telegram. Passengers spilt from the train, walking briskly towards the exit. They streamed past him, ignoring his concerned glances as Violet failed to appear. He waited until there was nobody else on the platform, then sighed and turned back to the exit. Something must have happened, and she wasn't coming. An unexpected wave of sadness overcame him at the thought of returning to his hotel alone.

Head bowed and resigned to a solo journey, he was startled by a tap on his shoulder and turned around to see Violet, puffing with exertion. Behind her, was a wiry conductor carrying what remained of her suitcase.

94

"The handle broke," said Violet ruefully, nodding towards her luggage.

"Let me help you," said Lawrence. "I'll take it," he continued, relieving the conductor of his burden.

"Thank you so much," said Violet, and reached into her bag for a tip. But Lawrence beat her to it and pressed a coin that he'd taken from his pocket into the conductor's hand.

"Good to see you," said Lawrence, casually. "How have you been?"

"I'm well," said Violet. "The case is coming along, though whether it will amount to anything, remains to be seen."

"Same here," said Lawrence, biting his lip. "Progress is slow, and I'm no further forward. I've only the flimsiest of clues to go on. I wonder whether it's worth it?"

"It is to Flora Johns," said Violet, as they walked towards the row of cabmen outside the station.

Lawrence raised his hand, and the driver of the first cab trotted his horse towards him.

"Battersea," said Lawrence, then turned to Violet. "If that's alright with you?"

She nodded. "I haven't phoned ahead for a hotel. It doesn't matter to me where I stay."

They spent the journey exchanging pleasantries in a way that made Lawrence wonder if things were going back to normal. Violet was her usual cheerful self, not curt and abrupt as she had been since she returned from Cornwall. If Violet's temper remained the same, they might have a pleasant couple of days together, if she stayed that long. Perhaps she would only stay in London overnight. It was a sign of the deterioration in their relationship that he dared not ask her.

They arrived at Lawrence's hotel, and he took Violet's bag to the front desk and waited while she asked whether a room was available. It was, and he dropped her bag outside her bedroom and waited downstairs while she unpacked. Lawrence decided to arrange a table for dinner, and by the time Violet came back downstairs, he was nursing a whisky at the bar. He rose to greet her, and they went straight through to the dining room.

"Well, this is nice," said Violet, looking through the menu. "I'm famished and haven't eaten a thing since breakfast."

The waitress, dressed in a neat pinafore, arrived at the table, smiled, and waited to take their order.

"I'll have the chicken pie, please," said Violet.

"Mutton for me," said Lawrence, passing her the menu.

"Thank you, sir, madam," said the girl. She scribbled their choices and left for the kitchen.

"This is a cut above your usual choice of hotel," said Violet, gazing around the room.

"Yes, I thought I might as well treat myself to something more comfortable."

"Well, you can afford to now," said Violet, without a trace of resentment. "It was kind of your uncle Max to think of you."

"They had no children," said, Lawrence. "Uncle Max always said he'd leave me something. It's not enough to retire on, but more than I expected. It was very good of him."

"Perhaps you can move out of those awful, dark rooms now," smiled Violet. "Although I suppose you will be looking for somewhere for two."

Lawrence grimaced and changed the subject. "Tell me how you've got on so far."

Violet sighed. "Julia Brown is a strange woman," she said. "She's secretive and naive. Almost simple, in some ways. I don't know what to make of her."

"Did she have much to say?"

"She didn't want to talk to me at all, to begin with. But I think she's ashamed of the circumstances that led to her pregnancy."

"What do you mean?"

"The child was born out of wedlock."

"I see, just like poor Flora. Well, it frequently happens. She can't have been the only girl in the village to find herself in the family way."

"No. And her parents were extremely kind and loved the child dearly. It wanted for nothing."

"Then, there's no reason for her reticence."

"Quite," said Violet. "And there is no doubting her attachment to the boy. She loved him and brought him presents. It was one of the gifts that helped to make her a suspect in his death?"

"Really?" Lawrence raised an eyebrow.

"Yes. Julia arrived at her parents' house with cakes for all the children, including young Freddie."

"Did the other children suffer any effects?"

"No. They were perfectly healthy. Only Freddie was taken ill."

"Not from the cakes then?"

"No. Clearly not."

"Any suspects?"

"No. I can't help worrying that this case is unsolvable. There are very few people who could have harmed him. Only family members came into contact with him in the day before he died."

"Which ones?"

"Julia's parents, obviously, and her elder brothers William and John and sisters Mary and Elizabeth. Her other siblings were far too young to be complicit."

"And nobody else visited?"

"Not until Eliza Mayes came."

"Who was she?"

"An unofficial nurse. She tended to the sick if the doctor wasn't available."

"So, it must have been one of the family?"

"Except that it can't have been. I went to the newspaper office and looked at the old accounts of the trial. As you know, Julia was given a not guilty verdict from the jury, but the judge made a point of saying that no other members of the family were under suspicion."

"That doesn't make any sense."

"It does, but only under one circumstance."

"Which is?"

"That the judge thought Julia was guilty. He purposefully removed all doubt against her family."

"So, the judge thought she'd got away with murder?"

"It seems so. What else could it mean?"

"Nothing," said Lawrence. "But why go through this charade?"

"It could be that she's spent so many years trying to deny what she did that she's convinced her sister-in-law and believes the story herself. Ah, dinner has arrived."

The waitress smiled as she placed two steaming plates of food on the table. Lawrence unfurled his napkin and set about the mutton. "That hits the spot," he said, licking his lips.

Violet regarded the large slice of raised chicken pie on her plate, surrounded by vegetables and a rich gravy.

"I do hope I can finish this," she said, spearing a piece of carrot.

They ate in silence for a few moments, and then Violet put her fork down. "The trouble is that I don't think she did it. Logic tells me that she must have, but it doesn't feel right."

A slow smile spread across Lawrence's face. "That sounds like something I would say. And you would tell me to be more rational."

"I know. Julia's an odd character, but I don't think she killed her boy."

"Then who did?"

"That's what I hope to find out from Caroline Bird?"

"Remind me what she's got to do with it?"

"She's Eliza Mayes eldest daughter."

"The nurse?"

Violet thoughtfully nodded as she ate another mouthful of pie.

"I'm not sure how that would help if she arrived after the boy became sick," said Lawrence.

"Nor am I," Violet admitted, "but there is hardly anyone else with whom to talk. Caroline may know what Eliza thought about the matter. She could have expressed an opinion on who harmed the boy, and she would have known the family."

Lawrence dabbed his lips with the napkin. "I agree. It's worth speaking to her. Do you mind if I join you?"

"No. I'd appreciate your thoughts. Mostly I believe in Julia, but the next moment, I doubt her. A second opinion can only help."

"Would you like dessert?" asked Lawrence.

"Rather. I do believe I saw coconut meringues on the menu."

Moments later, the waitress passed by, and Lawrence caught her eye.

"Yes, sir?"

"Coconut meringues for both of us, if you please," he said.

The waitress nodded and bustled away.

Violet removed her napkin from her lap, folded it into four and left it neatly in the centre of the table. Lawrence smiled wryly.

"What?" asked Violet, watching his face.

"You reminded me of someone when you did that."

"Who?"

98

"Nobody you know. Although she is your namesake?"

"Another Violet?"

"As if there could be another Violet," teased Lawrence. "Her name is Smith. Isabel Smith."

"Yes?"

"She is compassionate, intelligent and extremely tidy."

"And of those qualities, tidiness would win the most praise from you," smiled Violet. "She must be neatness personified."

Lawrence leaned back in his chair, letting his arms dangle as if in a state of complete relaxation. He was thoroughly enjoying dinner with Violet. They were chatting good-humouredly, like old times, and he felt a swell of happiness and gratitude.

"She's been helping me with the case," said Lawrence. "Without her suggestions, I would have absolutely nothing to go on."

"How far have you got?"

"About an inch over the starting line," he said, frowning. "It's not encouraging."

"Start from the beginning," said Violet. "Did you visit Bertie's digs."

"Whose?"

"Flora's boy, of course."

"Yes, I did, but there were no clues at all. The only thing of any significance was the suggestion that the childminder went by another name. Flora knew her as Dorothy Jones, but there is reason to think that she also used the name Hamblin."

"Oh dear. Jones is as bad a name as Smith for tracking someone down."

"Not necessarily," said Lawrence. "In fact, a Smith may well have contributed to finding her."

"Isabel?"

"Yes. She is one of the Infant Protection Inspectors at London County Council and keeps a register of authorised establishments for childminding."

"Is Dorothy Jones on it?" asked Violet.

"No. But Dora Hamblin is."

"Well, that sounds promising. Where does Miss Hamblin live?"

"In a place called Silvertown," said Lawrence. "It's by the docks in Woolwich. Miss Smith also gave me a list of cases that they're currently working on – cases that might involve the disappearance of children. And what do you think?"

"I can't imagine."

"One of the cases is also in Silvertown, a poisoning."

"That seems unlikely."

"Yes, that's what I thought. But the alleged poisoner tried to take one of the children."

"Ah. Then it's well worthwhile. I suppose that means you won't be coming to Saint Pancras with me."

"Not at all," said Lawrence. "It will be valuable to work together. We'll see your lady tomorrow and visit Silvertown on Wednesday."

"I intended to return to Bury tomorrow. Annie is still away."

"Just one extra day," said Lawrence. "It will help us both."

"Very well," said Violet. "We'll just have to hope that there's not a sudden stream of visitors to the office in the next few days."

CHAPTER ELEVEN

Stanley Buildings

Tuesday, September 15, 1896

The journey to Pancras Road involved crossing the Thames yet again. The day was set fair, and Lawrence and Violet walked as far as Westminster, retracing their steps as they had in 1891; the year they'd spent considerable time travelling between Westminster and the Embankment. That year had ended badly. Not only were they both victims of cowardly attacks, but Lawrence almost lost his life and was out of action for nearly two years. But before the attack, they had walked the pleasant route to Scotland Yard often, enjoying each other's company as they worked together on their case.

"Penny for your thoughts?" asked Violet as they approached Whitehall Gardens.

"It's nothing. Sorry."

"It must be something. You broke off mid-sentence, and you haven't said a word for five minutes."

"I was thinking about the last time that we were here together."

Violet turned to face him. "You must try to put it from your mind, Lawrence. I know it's difficult, and it doesn't help that your attackers are still at large. But they wouldn't dare try to hurt you again. And anyway, why would they? They've nothing to fear."

"I wasn't thinking about them. Our time here wasn't all bad, and I enjoyed some of it. Life was less complicated back then."

"I don't see how," said Violet, incredulously, looking away. "You hated my friends, you spent most of your time in disguise, and if I remember rightly, you were often covered in fleas from the doss house."

"Hmmm. Now you put it like that, perhaps you're right, and I'm recalling the less unpleasant times."

"I'm surprised to hear that you found any of it pleasing. I seem to recall a lot of complaining." Violet grinned as she teased him.

"Still, times were easier."

"What's wrong, Lawrence? You don't seem very happy for a newly engaged man who has just received a large inheritance."

Lawrence sighed. "I don't know what you mean. Everything's fine."

"Well, what are you getting at when you say that life was less complicated?"

"I don't know. It's just an expression. It doesn't mean anything."

"If you say so. Look, I know we haven't spoken about it, which is hardly surprising since you didn't even have the good manners to tell me yourself, but I'm pleased to hear you're getting married. I'm sure that Loveday will make a wonderful wife and that you will be blissfully happy together."

Lawrence scowled." You didn't seem to like her very much when you lived together in the Fressingfield vicarage."

"What makes you think that?"

"You didn't seem very friendly."

Violet laughed. "She's a different generation. And if you remember, I was the hired help. It was not my place to make small talk with Emily's friends."

"That's low," said Lawrence.

"What do you mean?"

"You know perfectly well."

"No, I don't." Violet frowned. "What are you talking about?"

"The age difference."

"Oh, for goodness sake. I was talking about me. But if the cap fits…"

"And to think I was looking forward to this." The colour rose in Lawrence's cheeks as he hissed the words.

Violet raised an eyebrow and looked down her nose. They walked in silence for a minute or two.

"I'm calling a cab," said Lawrence.

"Fine. I'll go and see Mrs Bird on my own. I was going to anyway."

"A cab for both of us, I meant. I'm coming too. I just can't face a three-mile walk with you in this mood."

"Me?" Violet also flushed an angry red. "I'd rather go alone."

"That's unfortunate because it's not going to happen."

Violet raised her hand as a hansom cab trotted towards them. The driver ignored her and continued his route.

"You won't get very far doing that," said Lawrence.

"I can hail a cab on my own."

"I don't doubt it, but where are you going?"

"Pancras, as you very well know."

"What address?"

"I don't know. You've got my notebook."

"Exactly," Lawrence smirked. "So, let's be sensible and share the carriage."

Violet glared at him but conceded the point and waited with her back turned as he faced the road and waited for another cab. Before long, she heard the clip-clop of hooves and Lawrence hailed the driver, who pulled up beside them.

"Come on then," said Lawrence cheerfully, pleased to have got the upper hand. He held out a hand to help her into the carriage, but she heaved herself up without assistance and sat as close to the edge as possible."

By the time they arrived at Pancras Road, Violet's mood had worsened. She was already furious with Lawrence for many reasons, some trivial and some serious, but this was the final straw. He had no right to control her, and the surge of anger he had provoked left her unfit to be questioning Caroline Bird. She was not in the right frame of mind. Violet wondered how much longer she could realistically work with Lawrence. It was hard to imagine their working relationship would ever be the same, and their friendship was irrevocably damaged.

The cab pulled into a narrow lane off Pancras Road, and they dismounted into a square to see a large, dark-bricked, industrial style block of flats with a depressingly gloomy outlook.

"Is this it?" shouted Violet, over the rumble of a train so loud that it could have been next to her.

"Yes. Awful, isn't it?" said Lawrence. "That's Kings Cross station you can hear," he continued. "I couldn't live with all this noise."

"Neither could I," said Violet, relieved that there was at least something on which they could agree. "What flat are we looking for?"

Lawrence removed her notebook from his jacket pocket and turned a couple of pages. "Number eighty-three," he said.

"I expect that's on the top floor," sighed Violet, looking at the rows of iron-railed balconies.

"It will do us good," said Lawrence, superciliously.

Violet scowled again but walked through the entrance and climbed the stone stairs without complaint.

Number eighty-three was indeed on the top floor, and they located the flat quickly. The door was ajar, and a woman in her forties was singing to herself as she polished the brass door furniture.

"Mrs Bird?" asked Violet, confident that she was addressing the right person. Caroline Bird's singing had not disguised her broad Suffolk accent.

"Yes. Who's asking?"

Violet held her hand out to Lawrence. "My notebook, please."

He handed it over without a word, and Violet turned to the back and extracted a pale envelope.

"This is a note from your sister, Rose. I went to see her the other day to ask some questions. She couldn't help me but thought that you might be able to. She's given me this letter of introduction."

Caroline Bird took the note and eyed it suspiciously. "Silly thing for her to do," she said. "I can barely read. I think she forgets how little education I had," she continued, shrugging her shoulders. "She stayed at school while I went out to work."

She slit the envelope open with polish-stained fingers and removed a small piece of paper with a few lines of writing in the centre. "Yes, that's her hand," she said, screwing the letter into a ball. She looked at it, then up at Violet. "I hope you didn't want that," she said.

"No. There's no need," said Violet.

104

They waited for a few moments, expecting her to invite them in, and when no such invitation was forthcoming, Violet spoke again. "Can I ask you some questions about your mother?"

Caroline frowned. "My mother? What about her? And why have you come all the way from Suffolk just to speak to me?"

#

"I'm looking into the murder of Frederick Brown," said Violet, coming straight to the point.

"Whatever for?" Caroline was staring at Violet as if she'd escaped from an asylum. "And what business is it of yours?"

Violet was taken aback by her hostility. Rosa had been friendly and helpful, but her elder sister was prickly, to say the least.

"We've been asked to investigate his death," said Violet.

Caroline put her hands on her hips. "Who are you anyway, and who's he?" she asked, nodding towards Lawrence.

"My name is Violet Smith and this is Lawrence Harpham. We are private investigators."

"Pleased to meet you," said Lawrence, holding out his hand. Further down the passageway, a door opened, and a young woman carrying a broom emerged from the next-door flat. She looked towards Caroline and started sweeping the area to the front of her door.

"Nosy old cow," said Caroline eying Lawrence's hand suspiciously. She ignored it and crossed her arms.

"Very well," said Lawrence, retracting his hand. "Carry on, Violet."

Violet glanced sideways, narrowing her eyes, then faced Caroline Bird. "Do you know Drucilla Brown?" she asked.

"Yes, I do. I've known Drucilla for years. How is she?"

"In good health," said Violet. "I went to see her a few days ago."

"Why?"

"Because Drucilla asked us to look into Freddie's death, not Julia."

"Oh, I see. Did she say why?"

"She did. Drucilla is fond of Julia Brown and fears her sister-in-law has never come to terms with the death of her child. Drucilla says that Julia is still suffering, and she wants to help."

"She's too kind-hearted by half," muttered Caroline Bird. "I expect Julia's taken advantage of her."

"It was Drucilla's idea. Julia was reluctant."

"I'm sure she was," said Caroline, looking down her nose. She glanced over to the woman who had stopped sweeping and was blatantly listening to their conversation.

"What do you mean?"

"I mean the last thing that Julia Brown wants is all that gossip dredged up again."

"Understandably," said Violet. "It must have been a terrible time for her."

"That's not what I meant."

"Excuse me," said Lawrence, interrupting them.

"Yes?"

"Is it necessary to conduct the rest of this conversation on your doorstep?"

"Lawrence." Violet raised her voice angrily.

He nodded towards the neighbour, who turned away.

Caroline Bird sighed. "I take your point," she said, pushing the door open. "Come inside."

They followed her into a small entrance hall which led to a surprisingly light living room with large sash windows overlooking a railed balcony. Lawrence could still hear the rumbling of trains, but it was nowhere near as audible as it was outside. While he wouldn't have rushed to live in Stanley Buildings, there were worse places to be.

"Sit down," said Caroline Bird, pointing to a dog-eared couch covered by an oversized patchwork cover that had seen better days.

"Mum made that," Caroline continued, pointing to the cover.

"That's nice," said Violet.

"It's alright. Fred doesn't like it much, but it reminds me of her, and he knows not to move it."

"Do you miss Suffolk?"

Caroline looked up as if the thought hadn't occurred to her before now. "I do, I suppose," she said. "Although with Walter living next door, I don't think about it as much as I would, had we come alone."

"Walter?"

"Yes, Walter is my elder brother. He's at number eighty-two," she continued, "the other side of me. Not where she lives." Caroline pointed in the direction of the younger woman who had eavesdropped on their conversation earlier. "He can keep himself to himself," she continued, "unlike some."

"Do you have a family?" asked Violet conversationally, as Lawrence raised his eyes heavenwards wishing she would move things along.

"Yes." Caroline smiled for the first time. "My girls are at school and Fred's working of course."

"What does he do?"

"He's a cabman. Walter is too."

"Hmmm. That could be useful," said Lawrence.

"Fred works for a grocer," said Caroline. "But Walter takes fares."

"Is he at home."

She shook her head. "No, but he should be back within the hour."

"Anyway," said Violet. "We're here to talk about Freddy Brown. Rosa said that your mother tended to him before he died. We were hoping you would remember what happened."

"I remember it well," said Caroline. "Felsham is a small village. Little happens of any note. Freddy's death was scandalous. It was all that anyone spoke about for months."

"I can imagine. And your mother played a part in it."

"A small part, yes."

"Tell me what you remember."

"I remember being there, which was unusual because I was working by then. I must have had a day off or something, but I was at home when John Brown came running in, full pelt, asking for Mother to come and take a look at the child. She left and was back within the hour."

"What did she say?"

"Not a great deal at the time. Freddy was in bed when she arrived. He wasn't agitated or in obvious pain, but he had very little strength. He retched once or twice but wasn't sick, yet it was clear that he was seriously ill, and Mother told John Brown to fetch the doctor."

"Mr Leech from Woolpit," said Violet.

"That's right. How did you know?"

"I've read the newspaper account," said Violet, passing a folded page from her notebook.

Caroline ignored it. "Then why do you need my help?"

107

"Because you were there and the reporter wasn't. There is no chance of solving this mystery without finding out something that wasn't known or thought important at the time."

Caroline exhaled. "I can't tell you much," she said. "And it's all second hand."

"That doesn't matter," smiled Violet. "The most useful thing you can tell me is not what your mother did, but what she thought. Did she have an opinion on who did it?"

"Not to begin with," said Caroline. "She was sympathetic towards Julia to start with, even though she thought it odd that Julia's sisters were nursing the child while he was sick."

"What was Julia doing?"

"She was feeling unwell and stayed downstairs. Julia Brown faints at the drop of a hat. She is known for it. In fact, I can remember Mum saying that Mr Leech found her curled up under a shawl on the floor of the sitting room where she had fallen."

"Poor girl."

Caroline grunted and stared at Lawrence, who was rearranging two photographs on her small side table. The room fell quiet.

"Sorry," he said when he realised that she was studying him. "They weren't quite straight."

Violet closed her eyes, shook her, and continued. "Was that your mother's only visit to Freddy?"

"While he was alive," said Caroline. "But Mr Leech called for her help again when he made the post-mortem examination."

"What – in the Browns' home?" asked Lawrence, surprised.

"Where else?" asked Caroline. "Things are different in a village."

"And your mother saw the whole procedure?"

"Yes. She didn't go into detail, obviously," said Caroline. "But by the time she returned, she had seen enough to know for certain, that Freddy had swallowed a corrosive substance. It had burned through his gullet and bowel and was later identified as sulphuric acid."

"Poor little boy," said Violet. "How dreadful, and how could acid get into his stomach?"

"There's only one way," said Caroline. "Either by eating or drinking it."

"But they didn't find anything?"

"No," said Caroline. "Mum said that they examined one of the cakes that Julia brought for the children."

"Yet no other child was sick?"

"No. They only tested the cake to be on the safe side. All three children who had eaten the cakes the previous day showed no ill signs at all. Mr Leech examined one of the cakes and found it be perfectly safe, so he put the rest in the bin."

Lawrence looked up and stopped fidgeting. "How many cakes did he throw away?" he asked.

"How should I know?" snapped Caroline. "I told you. I wasn't there. All I know is that half a cake was scooped off the floor of Freddie's bedroom and thrown in the bin together with Freddy's soiled nightshirt. Mother nearly cut her finger on some glass fragments when she picked it up."

Violet shook her head and exhaled. "Was that the extent of your mother's involvement?" she asked.

"No," said Caroline. "She attended the inquest, of course, but they didn't ask many questions. The judge was more interested in what the medical men had to say."

"Oh," said Violet, looking disappointed. "Well, it sounds like the newspaper article was accurate. But thank you for your time anyway. It was kind of you to talk to us."

"I haven't finished," said Caroline, sitting tall in her chair." Don't you want to hear about what happened the following year?"

#

"They say that lightning never strikes twice, but it did with Julia Brown," said Caroline, dramatically.

Both Lawrence and Violet gazed towards her in full concentration.

"What do you mean?" asked Violet.

"What's the date on your newspaper article?"

Violet opened the folded paper. "It's the second of April 1864."

"I bet you didn't look any at any more recent reports."

"No. Why would I?"

"Because the same thing happened again."

"Another poisoning?"

"No. Another death – and under the same roof. It must have been early summer – June or July, I think. It was like going back in time."

Violet cocked her head.

"Yes. You may well wonder, and you will barely credit it when I tell you. I was home again, and as I said, it was a rare occurrence. And the same thing happened – another child died, and both Mother and Mr Leech attended the death again."

"Whose child was it?" asked Lawrence curtly.

"Julia Brown's," said Caroline, crossing her arms and wearing a satisfied expression.

"No!" Violet exclaimed.

"As I live and breathe," said Caroline. "And if you don't believe me, then go and get a copy of one of your newspapers and you'll soon see I'm right."

"Oh, I believe you," said Violet, in a conciliatory tone. "It's just such a surprise."

"It was to Mrs Brown, I can tell you."

"The child's death?"

"No, the pregnancy. Charlotte Brown had no idea that her daughter was in the family way again. Julia didn't tell her, you see – kept it secret, as if it's the sort of thing you can keep secret indefinitely."

"It's pointless," said Lawrence. "The truth will come out sooner or later."

"Exactly," said Caroline, "unless, of course, she intended to dispose of the child."

Violet's head jerked up. "Oh, surely not."

"It's not unheard of," said Caroline, scowling. "There were no clothes for the babe, and nobody knew it was coming."

"Tell me from the beginning," said Violet.

"As I said, I was at home," said Caroline. "It was the day before they found the body. I remember it well because it was laundry day and we'd just put the bedding through the mangle and were hanging it on the wall when Mother caught sight of a rainy bug on the bedspread. As she brushed it away, she saw Julia fetching some carrots from the garden, and she tugged at my sleeve. "Look," she whispered, and I gazed at Julia's frock. Well, Julia never wore a dress well. She was an odd shape, thin in some places, plump in others, but not the way you'd expect. Anyway, her dress did not sit right, and it was quite clear that her belly was round. 'Is she with child?' I asked, and Mother nodded and said, 'oh yes, and not much longer to go, if I'm any judge.' Well, she was right. The following morning, Charlotte Brown was banging on our door again asking for Mother to attend to Julia urgently, and off she went."

"Was Julia in labour?"

"No. She'd already given birth, on her own in the night."

"Where was the child?"

"Lying cold and dead beside her."

Violet sat back and chewed her lips, not trusting herself to speak.

"Do you honestly believe that Charlotte Brown didn't know about her daughter's pregnancy?" asked Lawrence.

Caroline thought for a moment. "It could be true," she said. "Mrs Brown was away visiting family for at least three months and only returned the Saturday before Julia's confinement. Mother and I noticed her condition at once, but that's because Mother deals with childbirth every day."

"And there's no reason for Charlotte Brown to lie," said Violet, finding her voice.

"She's not the type," said Caroline, "which is more than can be said for Julia."

"Do you think the child died naturally?" asked Lawrence.

"I don't know," said Caroline. "You see, Julia lies all the time. Not outright lies, but not quite the truth either. I can't remember the exact time that she fetched Mother, but Mother asked what time the child was born, and Julia said that it had only just happened. Well, the child was stone cold, and Mother said it had been dead at least an hour, quite possibly longer."

"Where was the child?"

"Lying in the middle of the bed towards her feet."

"Was there any sign of foul play?" asked Lawrence.

Violet put her hand over her mouth and shut her eyes. Lawrence reached for her arm and patted the back of her hand.

"Not according to Mother," said Caroline. "And I asked her outright. I thought Julia might have smothered it when it was born, but Mother said it was lying clear of any blankets or sheets and there were no marks on it."

"You said they called the doctor?" asked Lawrence, glancing anxiously towards Violet. She was pale and appeared to have lost all interest in seeking further details.

Caroline nodded. "Mr Leech, the surgeon, came again and examined the child in front of Mother. It was a boy child, and the doctor said that it was born full term. Its face and chest were livid red which he said could be from suffocation."

"Did he repeat this at the inquest? I presume there was an inquest?"

"Yes, there was. Mother attended, and so did Mr Leech. He told the coroner that the child's stomach was empty, and it had not suckled. One lung was fully inflated, and the other only partially. He could not say for sure whether the child had a life independent of his mother."

"So, the inquest wasn't conclusive?"

"She got away with it, you mean," said Caroline. "The coroner said that there wasn't enough evidence to show whether the child was born alive, or dead. Mr Leech said it could have been suffocated but could just as likely have died from lack of attention. But I want to know why Julia neglected to get proper treatment for her child. If she had told her mother sooner, it might have lived."

"Who's to say?" murmured Violet. "If it was born dead, then nothing could be done to save it."

"No," said Caroline firmly. "There was a deliberate lack of attention. Mother told me that Charlotte Brown went into Julia's room twice that morning. She took her a cup of tea at about nine o'clock and went back no more than fifteen minutes later to collect the cup. It was then that she noticed bloodstains on the bedding. And had she not seen the marks; she'd be none the wiser. Julia did not attempt to tell her what happened or seek her help."

"Do you think she killed the child?" asked Lawrence directly.

"I wouldn't be surprised," said Caroline, "but Mother thought otherwise. She didn't think Julia had it in her and saw no reason to suppose that Julia had acted against her baby. She told me to forget all about it and said that it must have been a stillbirth."

"But you don't believe that."

"No. I don't. Nothing's ever straightforward with Julia Brown. There's a little truth in everything she says, and therefore at least as much untruthfulness. The child would have been an inconvenience if it had lived. Benjamin Dempster wasn't interested in marriage, at least not to Julia. I think the child was born in the night, probably in some distress and she simply left it lying there. She waited until she was certain that it was dead and only then revealed the blood on the covers. It was a cold, calculated act, in my opinion. She left her baby to die."

CHAPTER TWELVE

Silvertown

Wednesday, September 16, 1896

"What do I do now?" asked Violet miserably as she stirred her morning tea. "What's the point in carrying on? It would be foolish to think that losing two children is just an unhappy coincidence. Julia must have had a hand in it, whether deliberately, or by neglect. I've been awake all night thinking about it."

"I disagree," said Lawrence. "And I could have told you why and saved you a disturbed night's sleep if you'd have turned up to dinner, as we arranged. Where were you?"

"Writing a letter," said Violet.

"All night? What's so important that you would forgo your evening meal, without the courtesy of an explanation?"

Lawrence smiled as if in jest, but his obvious displeasure was not lost on Violet.

"I'm sorry," she said. "It's Aunt Floss."

"The one who lives in Cornwall?"

Violet nodded.

"Couldn't it wait until after you'd eaten?"

"She's been poorly," said Violet. "I haven't heard from her for a few days, and I was worried."

"It doesn't take all night to write a letter."

"I said I was sorry," snapped Violet. "I was tired, so I wrote the letter and fell asleep."

"While I sat in the chophouse alone," said Lawrence. "I'm pleased to report that my dinner was magnificent and the bottle of claret I washed it down with, was quite exceptional."

"You drank a whole bottle of red wine? Well, that explains why you're grumpy."

"Come on, Violet," said Lawrence, quizzically. "This isn't my doing. You didn't turn up for dinner and left me to eat alone. I didn't know what had happened to you and I banged on your door several times when I got back. You must have heard me, yet you didn't answer. So, don't blame this argument on the wine. What is wrong?"

"Nothing," said Violet. "Anyway, why do you disagree with my thoughts about Julia Brown?"

"Because whether she did it or not, is irrelevant to the case," said Lawrence. "We've been asked to find out about Freddy, not the other child. And if it turns out that Julia Brown killed Frederick, then as much as it will displease Drucilla Brown, it resolves the case, and we will have fulfilled our obligation to her."

"She won't believe it," said Violet.

"Then you'll need to prove it."

"How?"

"Come on, Violet. Speak to the doctor. Ask around the village. Caroline Bird can't be the only one who remembers his death. And if you can't get hard proof, then at least present Drucilla with a well-researched case. If she knows that others have good reason to doubt Julia, then she'll have no choice but to listen."

"I didn't want her to be guilty."

"She may not be."

"I wish I had your optimism."

"You usually do, Violet. I'm worried about you."

"There's no need. I'll find the newspaper report when I get back to Bury, and I'll compile a list of people who were there. As you say, there may be others I can ask."

"Good. Now, hurry up and finish your breakfast. I managed to get hold of Caroline Bird's brother last night, and he's collecting us in half an hour."

Violet sighed. "I've decided to catch the train back today, after all."

"Oh, Violet. You promised."

"I know, but I'd rather be at home."

"Why? Your investigation can wait a day or two. Is there some pressing engagement in your diary?"

"Of course not. It's just that my aunt will write to me in Bury."

"I don't understand you, Violet. You barely saw her for ten years, but since you took off last year, you're writing to her every five minutes. I know she was sick, but don't you think you're worrying unnecessarily?"

"You wouldn't understand," said Violet, coldly. "But if it matters so much, then I'll join you."

"Good," said Lawrence, crumpling his napkin onto his plate. "Are you going to eat that last piece of toast?"

Violet shook her head and Lawrence took a bite as he rose and put his jacket on. "I'll meet you in the hotel lobby in a quarter of an hour," he said.

#

The terraces of Silvertown were crushed together in the depressingly familiar way that Lawrence remembered from his time in Whitechapel. If anything, they were even less sanitary, and a wave of nausea engulfed him as the carriage came to a halt beside an open sewer.

"Is this it?" he asked the cabman.

"'Fraid so," said Walter Mayes.

"Can you move it on for a few yards? I can't expect Violet to disembark here."

"Yes, sir," said Walter, tipping his hat. He flicked the reins, and the horse trotted twenty yards up the street and away from worst of the smell. "Will this do?"

"Yes, that's better," said Lawrence, passing him a few coins. "Will you wait?"

The cabman nodded, and Lawrence disembarked, then opened the door for Violet. He reached for her hand and, this time, she accepted.

"Is this it?"

"Yes," sighed Lawrence, pointing towards a street sign. "According to Isabel Smith, Dora Hamblin lives here." He waved his hand in the general direction of the road."

"But it goes on for miles," said Violet.

"I can see that. Miss Smith wouldn't divulge the address, but I assumed it would be easy to find. I certainly wasn't expecting hundreds of properties."

"She must have thought you'd be sufficiently resourceful," said Violet.

"I'm perfectly capable," said Lawrence. "Let's start walking, and I'm sure we'll run into somebody who can help."

Ten minutes later they were still none the wiser. The barber hadn't heard of Dora Hamblin, the old woman who was scrubbing her doorstep couldn't help, and in desperation, they approached a young girl who ran off screaming for her mother before they had even finished asking the question.

"So much for that," said Violet crossing her arms.

"You could help instead of criticising," said Lawrence.

"Perhaps I will."

They walked to the end of the road in silence, following the pavement through ninety degrees, as it continued towards the river.

"How much further does it go on?" complained Lawrence.

"Never mind," said Violet. "Look," she pointed to an area further down the road where the terrace of houses was set further back. In front, a group of women were sitting on blankets on the floor, their arms around a couple of grimy-faced children.

"Stay here," she continued.

Lawrence watched from a distance as Violet approached the women. He couldn't hear the conversation but noticed that one girl was animatedly gesturing as she spoke. He turned away as a second woman pointed in his direction and loitered self-consciously against a nearby lamppost while pretending to ignore them. Lawrence was still facing away when Violet tapped him on the shoulder.

"It's just down here," she said.

"What is?"

"Dora Hamblin's lodgings," said Violet. "But don't be surprised if she isn't there. According to Phoebe Williams, she left in a carriage a few days ago."

"Phoebe Williams?"

"The young lady wearing the blue shawl," said Violet. "Very helpful she was too, though she wasn't particularly complimentary about you?"

"Why? She doesn't know me."

"That's not her fault. You didn't come over. She said you were a jumped-up toff."

"I didn't come over because you asked me to stay," said Lawrence, bristling with indignation. "Honestly, Violet. You seem to go out of your way to paint me in a bad light these days."

"You don't need my help to do that," said Violet. "You manage quite well yourself."

Lawrence sighed. Violet was so prickly these days that anything was likely to set her off. He was beginning to master a level of patience that he hadn't realised he had. "Never mind," he said. "Let's find this house. Perhaps Miss Hamblin is back by now."

"She took a suitcase," said Violet, ominously.

#

"She isn't here," said Violet, leaning on the windowsill with her nose pressed against the front window of the shabby terraced house.

"What can you see?" asked Lawrence. He stepped back from the door after knocking for the third time.

"Nothing, it's empty," said Violet.

"Completely empty?"

"As far as I can tell. There's not a stick of furniture in the parlour."

Lawrence sighed. "We're too late," he said. "We've lost her again."

"Poor Flora," said Violet. "What are we going to tell her?"

"Nothing, yet. I'm not walking away without a proper look."

"It's locked," said Violet, unnecessarily.

Lawrence turned his head and looked towards Phoebe Williams. The group of women were watching intently.

"Damn their nosiness," he said. "I need to get inside."

"Well, you can't."

"Just watch me."

"Don't, Lawrence," said Violet. "Not while they're looking."

"I'll be careful. There must be a back door."

"I'm sure there is, but I expect it's at the end of the terrace, and you'll probably need to walk past all the other houses to get to it. You'll be seen, for sure."

"I've not come all this way to be put off by tiny details," said Lawrence, bullishly. "There's always a way around a problem. First, we must lose our audience. Come along."

He left the property and turned right, briskly walking until they reached the end of the road and were safely out of sight. The last house stood beside a scruffy grassed area with a large factory beyond.

Violet wrinkled her nose. "What's that smell?" she asked.

"Rubber," said Lawrence, "amongst other things. We're deep in the dock area. Many of the men who live here will work at the Royal Docks and the others at the sugar factory.

"I don't think I'd like that," said Violet. "There were times when I felt isolated as a lady's companion and I wished I'd settled on a different occupation, but the thought of labouring in a factory day after day with no glimpse of the countryside makes me grateful for the life I had."

"Not the life you have now?" asked Lawrence.

"Yes, of course. It's just that I could have gone to London when I was younger, and I chose not to. It was the right choice even though I wasn't sure at the time."

"You wouldn't have worked in a factory though?"

"Who knows what my life would have been if Mother hadn't remarried," said Violet. "My father was an artist, and he made a living from it, but he was not a rich man, though talented. Perhaps he would have made money in time, but rheumatic fever carried him off. But for Harold Smith, our lives could have been very different."

"I had no idea that your father was an artist," said Lawrence, surprised. "How interesting, and how strange that you've never mentioned it before."

"You've never shown any particular interest in my family," said Violet. "And I don't talk about him much out of respect to Mr Smith. He's a kindly man who has always treated me like his natural daughter, and I would hate to hurt his feelings."

119

"Well, there's the back entrance," said Lawrence walking around the side of the terrace. "Good. I thought there might be an access path between the house and the garden. I've come across that arrangement a few times during my investigations, but this is easier. It runs between the gardens, and we're less likely to be seen. I was wondering whether to return this evening, but I think it's worth the risk of trying now."

"If you're sure," said Violet, doubtfully.

"I'm never sure," said Lawrence. "Anything can happen, but let's give it a go. Now, first things first. Dora Hamblin's house is quite a long way back. Do you remember what number it was?"

"Yes," said Violet. "I made a particular point of noting it. Number one hundred and seven."

"Good," said Lawrence, approvingly. "We just need to know the number sequencing now."

"It's a mixture of odd and even numbers," said Violet. "And you need to know that because we're going to have to count backwards, so we know when we've reached the rear of the house we want."

Lawrence smiled. "I'm sorry. I didn't mean to appear patronising. There's nothing I can teach you about this profession any longer."

"I'm sure there is," said Violet, accepting the compliment with good grace. "And the one thing I didn't do was check the number of the end house. Wait a moment."

She bustled off and returned quickly. "Number one hundred and twenty-four," she said. "And we'd better go quickly. An old man is coming towards us. He's walking with a stick and won't be swift, but we'd better not delay."

Lawrence ushered Violet forwards, and they trod the narrow strip of grass in between the gardens belonging to the properties in Albert Road, and the boundaries of the properties in the roads beyond. Some of the gardens were little more than yards with tall red brick walls surrounding the garden and obscuring the view of the property. Lawrence counted under his breath as he walked along and eventually arrived outside a brick-walled, gated garden where he stopped. "I think this is it," he said, pressing his thumb on a black painted latch. He pushed, but the door held firm. Lawrence stood on tiptoes and felt along the reverse side of the wooden gate. His fingers closed over a bolt which he worked for a few moments before it finally gave.

"That needs a good oiling," he complained, sucking blood from his knuckle. "Good. The coast's clear. Come through."

Though the row of terraces had looked uniform from the front, the gardens were varying sizes. The end terrace appeared to have considerably more land than those in the centre and number one hundred and seven had little more than a walled yard with enough room for a washing line and a small trough which might have once contained flowers but was now full of dry earth.

Lawrence peered through the glass back door, but his view was obscured by something behind, probably a curtain. He rubbed grime away from the only other window at the rear, to reveal a crack. Inside, the room was empty save for a chairless table. Lawrence tried the back door which was predictably locked. "It doesn't look very promising," said Violet.

"We won't know until we get inside."

Violet sighed, walked to the rear door and knocked several times.

"What are you doing?" asked Lawrence. "The whole street will hear us."

"I'm checking it's the right house before you break in. That's what you intend to do, isn't it?"

"Unless you can think of a better way."

They waited for a few moments, but nobody answered the door. Then, Lawrence reached into his pocket and took out a handkerchief which he wrapped around his knuckles. Violet shook her head and looked the other way as Lawrence rapped sharply on the cracked windowpane, and a large chunk of glass fell into the rear room. Lawrence reached inside and felt for the handle which he tugged open with ease. "Stay here," he said, climbing onto the window ledge. A few moments later, the rear door opened, and Violet went inside.

When Dora Hamblin left the property, she left in a hurry. The kitchen drawers and cupboards were open and still contained a small amount of mismatched cutlery and crockery, and the door to the larder was ajar. A loaf of stale bread lay on the wooden surface with a bread knife and a pat of butter to the side. In one corner, a pair of bottles stood next to a quart of milk.

Violet reached for the bottles and held them towards Lawrence. "Feeding bottles," she said, pointing to the teats." At least they're clean."

"Odd that she left them," said Lawrence, taking a bottle from Violet. "They're in good condition and worth at least a few coins."

"That's not all," said Violet, opening an understairs cupboard. She reached inside and removed a wooden pallet lined with a knitted cream shawl.

"Do you think she used it as a crib?" asked Lawrence.

Violet nodded. "It seems likely. How strange that there is so little furniture, though. She had nothing to eat or sleep on. It can't have been very comfortable."

"What's that?" asked Lawrence, pointing to a piece of paper sticking out from the shawl.

Violet picked it up and looked. "It's just an unaddressed letter," she said, passing it to Lawrence.

Dear Mother, he read before saying, "You're right. There's nothing of interest. Just domestic matters. She couldn't have been here long. Assuming that Dora Hamblin and Dorothy Jones are the same people. At the most a month, if the information given by Flora Johns is correct."

"But a whole month without furniture? It's hard to believe."

"Let's check upstairs," said Lawrence. "Perhaps there's a bed."

He gestured to Violet to go ahead, but as she trod on the first step, he placed his hand on her shoulder.

"Sorry, a force of habit," he said. "This is no time for manners. We can't have you going first in case there's anyone up there."

"There can't be," said Violet. "We've made plenty of noise."

"Even so," said Lawrence. He pushed past and climbed the stairs noiselessly. "Nothing up here," he said when he reached the top. "Up you come."

Violet joined him in the larger of the two bedrooms. "No bed," she said, walking towards the second room. She peered inside. "No bed in here either, but there is a crib."

"So there is," said Lawrence, stroking his chin. "There were babies in the house. But what an odd setup."

"Oh no," said Violet.

"What?"

"Look what was behind the curtain." She passed a brown bottle to Lawrence.

He held it towards the light, squinting as he read the label."
Godfrey's Cordial," he said. "What is it?"

"Horrible stuff," said Violet, shuddering. "It must be old. You can't
buy it anymore. At least not anywhere reputable."

"Yes, but what is it for?"

"To sedate children," said Violet quietly.

"For medical use?"

"No. Well, perhaps, originally. I first came across it in Norfolk
when I saw one of the servant's wives labouring in a field. She'd given
birth to her first child a few weeks before but had no family in the
village. Her husband worked at the rectory, and I asked him who was
looking after the child, and he said Dr Godfrey. What he meant was
that she had sedated the baby and left it in the cot so she could work
without disturbance."

"Is it safe?"

"No. It's not," said Violet. "I've lost count of the number of infant
deaths I've read about in the newspapers. Mothers are often ignorant
of the danger. It's an opiate, you know. Too much can be fatal."

"This bears a close resemblance to what was going on at the
Battersea baby farm," said Lawrence. "And I think it's clear what's
been happening."

"You don't think those poor children were left to fend for
themselves?"

"I'm afraid so," said Lawrence. "They weren't completely
abandoned, but it looks likely that they were fed in the daytime and
left alone at night. As you say, it would be very uncomfortable to live
here without any furniture."

"Poor little mites," said Violet as her eyes filled with tears.

Lawrence patted her hand and walked towards the window, leaning
on the sill as he surveyed the tiny yard. "Hello, what's this?" he said,
placing his scarred left hand on top of a piece of paper. He unfolded it
and passed it to Violet.

"What do you think it is?" she asked. "I mean the drawing. It's
obvious that the clipping is from a newspaper."

"It is something that needs our attention," said Lawrence. "This is
an article about a poisoning in Silvertown. Isabel Smith mentioned the
incident when I saw her the other day. I was in two minds about
whether to follow it up, but as we're here and as this has come to my

notice once again, let's do it now. It's too much of a coincidence to ignore, and you know I don't believe in them."

"You don't think someone poisoned Bertie, do you?"

"Not deliberately, no. Not like the poisonings in the paper. But the existence of the sedative is concerning. Still, there are no signs of any children, sick or healthy, in the house and nowhere to put them outside had there been an unfortunate accident. No. I think she took them with her when she left. The question is, why did she leave?"

"And why so quickly?" asked Violet. "And you haven't answered my question. There's a drawing next to the clipping. The pencil marks are badly smudged, and I'm not sure what they're supposed to represent. It looks like a mouse."

"It's not a mouse," said Lawrence, shaking his head. "Look at the tail. It's a rat."

CHAPTER THIRTEEN

Dante

I knew what it was the moment I saw it. Though tucked away between a glass jar and bottle, the poisoned cake was almost as familiar as the rats that tormented me throughout my childhood. I still live in a small house with a basement, and the horror of the rats has never left me. The thought of seeing one, of being near one, of knowing that one may be close by. No. I would not risk it. At first, I used a propriety brand of rat cake to keep the vermin away, and then any rat poison that I could lay my hands upon. But as I grew into middle age, I became lonely. Fate had not brought me a wife, and though I took an occasional lodger in my spare room, I longed for more in the way of companionship. Noel had married and moved away, and although I met many people during my working hours, the nights were long, and the house filled with the sounds of silence. Creaks and groans heralded the return of the rats. How many times did I lie awake at night wondering whether their filthy, flea-infested bodies would be writhing beneath me in the cellar? How many times, did I rise, heart thumping, and descend the stairs, a trembling hand cupping my nightlight. I have lost count of the number of times I placed my hand on the cellar door and stood, waiting – waiting for the courage to open it and confront my greatest fear. And there I would stay until dawn broke and I could face my enemy in the light of day. And finally, the door would open, and I would descend the stairs to nothing. Nothing but piles of traps and cakes of poison. For the rats prowled at night, stealing from the shadows of silence, cloaked in terror and my imagination. There was only one solution – a cat.

I found Dante one night in April, not long after I had decided that a cat would make the perfect companion. He came to me by chance and reinforced my loathing of children. I had just arrived home after a long and arduous day, travelling around London at the whim of a man who was not my employer. I was not in the best of moods. My small house is gated, and I had unfastened the latch and was walking the few short steps up the path when a scream shattered the still of the evening, and fear raced up my spine. I spun around. The noise was close, only a few yards away. It stopped, then began again, a shrill yowl as if something was fighting for its life. I dropped my bag and hastened towards the sound. It was coming from an alleyway a few doors away. A brisk walk took me to the foot of the passage where I could see three shapes in the dim light. Three children, squatting on their haunches with a dark and screeching mass impaled upon a stick.

As I thundered up the alley, the nearest child jumped to his feet and stood, hands on hips, regarding me with disdain.

"What do you want?" he said, tossing his head contemptuously.

I took one look at him, and another at his two companions as they shuffled in front of the wounded animal and without hesitation, I cracked him around the skull with my fist. He slammed into the wall and dropped to the floor, blood spewing from a wound to his scalp as he hit the bricks. His friends stood, watching aghast as I moved towards them, fired by an out of control rage.

"You've killed him," said one, as I lunged for his jacket, and he squirmed from my grasp and scuttled up the alley. The third boy stood silently, stick still impaled in the cat, which was now panting quietly. I advanced slowly toward him.

"Give it to me," I demanded. "Now."

The boy handed it over without a word and knelt at the side of his injured friend. I raised an eyebrow and regarded him with loathing.

126

And the little coward ran away. Ran off and left his companion lying there, unconscious.

I stroked the cat's head and felt for the entry point. It watched me through slitted eyes, heavy with pain. I could feel the end of the stick embedded in the skin at the top of the leg where it had pierced the flesh. With luck, it had not damaged any of its vital organs. So, I knelt on the floor and scooped the cat towards me as I swiftly pulled the stick from the wound. The cat flinched and groaned but lay there trustingly not attempting to move. Then I took off my jacket and wrapped it around the cat and carried it up the alleyway. The boy moved as I walked past him and rolled onto his back as his eyes flickered open. "Help me," he whispered.

I pulled the cat closer, burying my nose in its silky fur. And then fury overtook me, and I kicked the boy in the head and walked away.

It took several weeks before Dante had recovered enough to move easily around the house. And when he did, it brought a new problem. Rat poison littered the rooms, and it became necessary to remove it. I discarded all the traps and the poison and the rat cake. Everything that had kept the rats at bay for all these years went. Instead, I relied on Dante, and he did not let me down. He didn't catch a rat for there were no rats, but he was a loyal companion and kept the mice away. And at night, when the house relaxed, and the floorboards groaned, it was Dante. It was Dante even when it wasn't. It was quite enough that it could have been. For five good years, I almost forgot about the rats. But nothing good ever lasts. At least not for me.

CHAPTER FOURTEEN

The Girl Who Lived

"Are you sure we're looking in the right place?" asked Violet. "These terraces seem to go on for miles, and I would like to catch the six o'clock train tonight."

"Yes. Louisa Tullis keeps a grocer's shop in Gray Street. She'll be able to tell us more about the poisonings."

"I hope we're not going to wander around aimlessly until we find it," asked Violet.

"No. We're going to find Walter Mayes and ask him."

"Oh yes. I'd forgotten he was waiting."

"We should only need a few moments with Mrs Tullis, and then you can go back to the hotel and pack. I'll ask Mr Mayes to take you straight to the station. You'll be back in Bury in no time."

"Thank you," said Violet. "I do appreciate it."

Lawrence started to speak, then swallowed his words. He was disappointed. Not just because Violet had very little interest in his case, but because she had an equal disregard for his company. He would mind less if she were still angry. But she seemed to have gone past that point and was genuinely eager to return home and leave him behind. He knew that their friendship could not have lasted given his impending marriage. And God knows, he had treated her badly, but not for one moment had he considered losing Violet's goodwill altogether. He felt a momentary flicker of irritation. Why were women so complicated? He didn't see why he had to choose between Loveday and Violet.

"Come on then," said Violet, interrupting his thoughts. "Let's leave before someone sees us."

Ten minutes later they were in the cab and travelling towards Gray Street. They had taken the longest route to avoid Phoebe Williams and her friends. The cabman dropped them outside a shabby looking grocer's store situated next door to a butcher's shop.

"I take it you'll want me to wait again?" asked Walter Mayes and Lawrence nodded.

They entered the grocer's to the clang of a bell like the one in their office in Bury. A short, balding man was standing behind the counter and smiled as they approached him. Lawrence was about to speak when he was stopped in his tracks by a pungent smell, and he sneezed loudly and wiped his eyes.

"Good God, what is that smell?"

"Sorry," said the grocer in a broad Scottish accent. "I dropped a box of mothballs, and my wife stood on them. I've cleaned it up as best as I can. You get used to the smell after a while. But I'm sure that you're not here to discuss our domestic issues. What can I get you, sir?"

"A box of matches, please," said Lawrence wondering what he would do with yet another unrequired purchase. Experience had taught him not to expect information for free and matches were reasonably cheap.

"Anything else?" asked the Scotsman, pushing the matches across the counter.

"Yes," said Lawrence, hesitantly. "Can I speak to Mrs Tullis."

"I dare say. What do you want with her?"

"I'd like to ask a few questions about the poisonings."

"Would you now?" The shopkeeper put his hands on his hips and glared. "And who are you?"

"Lawrence Harpham and this is Violet Smith."

"Yes?"

"That nice police sergeant friend of yours sent us, didn't he Lawrence?" said Violet, jabbing him discreetly in the ribs.

129

"Er, yes. That's right. Sergeant Richard Simms. He spoke with Mrs Tullis."

"She'll remember him alright," said the shopkeeper, curling his lip. "A smarmy devil, I thought, but Louisa liked him well enough. Very well. I'll fetch her through."

"Well remembered," said Lawrence as soon as they were alone. "I only briefly mentioned Simms to you. Glad you were paying attention."

"I wouldn't be much of a detective if I didn't," said Violet.

"No, of course. You just haven't seemed interested in my case up to now."

Violet shook her head and was about to speak when Louisa Tullis entered the room, followed by the shopkeeper. "This is my wife," he said. "I've told her that the slimy copper sent you."

Louisa raised her eyes heavenwards as she puffed a breath loudly. "Don't mind my husband," she said, "Sergeant Simms is a perfectly nice young man."

"I bet he is," growled Tullis.

"Away with you, Alexander," said Mrs Tullis. "Leave me to speak without your interference. Honestly. I don't know where you get your silly ideas from."

"I'll be in the storeroom," said Alexander Tullis, departing without a backward glance.

"The words, dour Scotsman, were invented for my husband," said Louisa. "But his bark is far worse than his bite. Now. I can only think of one reason why Sergeant Simms would send you to me. I suppose it's about this business at Custom House."

"No," said Lawrence. "I don't know anything about that. I was going to ask you about a poisoning here in Silvertown."

"Oh, that one."

"That one?" echoed Lawrence. Have you been involved in others?"

"No, of course not. But I thought it must be connected to the earlier matter?"

"You've lost me," said Lawrence. "Sergeant Simms said it happened in January."

"That was the first poisoning."

As Lawrence opened his mouth to answer, Violet placed her hand on his arm. "Is there somewhere we could sit?" she asked. "It sounds more complicated than we realised."

"Yes, do come through," said Louisa Tullis, then hesitated. "Who did you say you were?"

"We're detectives," said Violet. "Sergeant Simms said that you were an excellent witness and we could learn a lot from your account."

Louisa's cheeks coloured as she ran a meaty hand through her hair. "Such a nice young man," she said, as she opened the door. "Come through and don't mind the muddles."

Louisa guided them towards four hard-backed chairs curiously arranged in a line across the room. A large, rusty bicycle rested against a table, containing a brass cycle horn and a bottle marked 'Club Black enamel, hand drying'.

"Alexander's repairing his bicycle," she said unnecessarily. "And I wish he'd get on with it. I want my table back."

"Stop yer moaning, woman," a Glaswegian voice bellowed from an open doorway off the kitchen.

"Sit down," said Louisa as she strode towards the door and shut it firmly.

"Now," she continued, sitting next to Violet. "As you say, I think there's been some confusion. You want to talk about poor little Joseph Yeo."

"Yes," said Lawrence, still far from certain."

"I feel very responsible," said Louisa Tullis. "You'll know that from speaking to Sergeant Simms. I didn't sleep for a week after it happened, wondering why I didn't think to lock it away. But why would I?"

"Lock what away?"

"The rat cake, of course. Isn't that what you're after?"

"Yes," said Lawrence eagerly, turning to face her, feeling that he was making progress at last.

"Do you think I should have put it higher?"

"Why don't you start at the beginning," suggested Violet.

"Yes, dear," said Louisa. "I suppose it started back in January when we found mice in the storeroom. I asked my husband what we should do about it, and he said he would lay some traps, but they didn't work. The mice were crafty so Alexander said I should try some poisoned

131

cake. I said no, of course. I mean it's a storeroom and the mice were getting into the flour, but Alex said I was silly – the mice were under the floorboards. It would be perfectly safe to put the rat cake there and take up one of the boards when they had died. So, I bought some."

"Did it work?" asked Lawrence.

Louisa Tullis jerked her head back in surprise. "Are you being funny?"

"No."

"I didn't put it down, did I? The rat cake went missing."

"Ah," said Lawrence, enlightened.

"Where was it?" asked Violet.

"On the end of the counter in between two bottles," said Louisa. "Alexander was standing on the wooden steps trying to reach a jar," she continued. "And he asked me to take it from him. So, I put the rat cake down."

"Did the child take it?" asked Violet.

"He couldn't have done," said Louisa. "It was at the back of the counter. It's a stretch for me to reach it from the front. Only an adult could have taken it."

"When did you notice that it was missing?"

"At about three thirty, four o'clock the same day. I'd only been home for a few hours."

"But you don't know how the child came by it?"

"I don't even know if the child died from my rat cake. But it went missing the same day that the children were struck down."

"Did you report it immediately?"

"As soon as I heard about the Yeo children."

"Children?"

"Oh yes. The little boy died, but they were all ill. Three of them. The two girls lived, but they were older, you see."

"Who came into the shop that afternoon?" asked Violet.

"Sergeant Simms asked the same question," said Louisa. "He used those very words, and I'll tell you what I told him. Lots of people came in. People were in and out all afternoon starting with Nance."

"Nance?" asked Lawrence.

"Nancy, that is. Well, her name isn't Nancy, but we call her that as she doesn't like her real name. Says it's silly. But you don't care about that, do you? Anyway, Nancy is my good friend, and she came in at about one o'clock, and we had a natter while I was serving customers. There were at least five or six while she was there. Then her brother came in out of the blue with a message. I'd never seen him before, and he thundered in giving me quite a turn and Nancy left. Then what happened? Oh yes. A woman arrived with a child in a perambulator. A sickly-looking thing it was. I can't remember what she purchased. Then Bert Baxter came in. He's the lodger at number twenty-seven, and a few more who I can't remember. By then it was late afternoon, and somebody told me about the Yeo children, so I went straight to the police station."

"Remarkable," said Lawrence.

"What is?"

"Your memory. This incident happened nine months ago, and you can recall almost every detail."

"That's because they've asked me about it so many times. Up at the police station, then they sent Sergeant Simms to the shop, then I had to stand up at the inquest. It's hardly surprising that the details are set in my mind."

"It's our good fortune that they are. Well, you've certainly given us food for thought. I wonder how the children got the rat cake."

"One thing's for certain. They didn't take it from here," said Louisa. "The only child I remember being in my shop that afternoon was a baby. I would ask Mary Parker if I was you."

"Who's Mary Parker?"

"The girl who gave the other children the poisoned cake."

#

"I can't believe our luck," said Lawrence. "She only lives a few doors away."

"Who?"

"Mary Parker, of course."

"What time is it?" asked Violet.

"It's a quarter to four," said Lawrence. "There's plenty of time."

"Plenty of time for what? I've got a train to catch."

"Yes, I know," said Lawrence abruptly. "But Mary Ann Parker lives at number thirty-four. That house there," he said, jabbing his finger towards a terraced house identical to the others.

133

"No, Lawrence," said Violet. "It won't do. I've done as I promised, but I am not missing this train."

"It will only take ten minutes," said Lawrence. "There's no point coming all this way tomorrow for the sake of a quick chat today."

"But what's it got to do with Bertie Johns?"

"The newspaper clipping as you well know."

"I think it's fanciful," said Violet. "I thought you were stretching your imagination yesterday, but I went along with it because there's very little else for you to go on. The paper scrap is unlikely to have any relevance and could have been intended for anything if you think about it. Dora might have wanted to jot down a note, or wrap something, or simply been interested in the poisoning. Some people are fascinated by such things, as you well know. And that's if Dora Hamblin and Dorothy Jones are the same women. We don't know that either. Now, if you want to spend your time following up unlikely clues, then go ahead by all means. But I have a train to catch, and you promised I wouldn't miss it."

Lawrence stared at Violet in disbelief. She had never raised her voice to him before. Even yesterday, when they were squabbling, Violet had kept her temper. But she was standing beside him, red-faced and agitated, looking as if she were about to cry. "I'm sorry," he said. "I understand. If it's that important, then go back with Walter. He's expecting to take you anyway. You feel safe with him, don't you?"

"Perfectly safe," she said. "Are you staying here?"

"Do you mind?"

"Not in the least," said Violet. "As long as I can go, then you can do as you please."

"It would be a wasted opportunity, not to mention a wasted journey if I did not."

"As you wish."

They walked the short distance to the waiting cab in silence. Lawrence opened the door and offered a hand to Violet. She climbed inside and turned her face away. "Please take Miss Smith to the hotel and wait for her to pack a bag. Her train leaves at six o'clock. Can you get her there on time?"

Walter Mayes withdrew a battered watch from his top pocket and squinted at the chipped face. "As long as she's quick packing," he said, "I'll get her there."

"Thank you," said Lawrence, pressing money into the cabman's hands. "I'll make my own way back."

"Very generous, sir," said Mayes, tipping his cap as he pocketed the fare. Walter Mayes cracked the reins, and the horse trotted off. Lawrence waited by the side of the road and waved towards Violet, but she did not look back. He stood for some time watching until the cab was a distant pinprick wondering what had really upset Violet. Her story about waiting for her aunt's letter didn't ring true and certainly didn't explain the urgency of her need to return to Bury. There was something she wasn't telling him. Small wonder, he supposed, when their friendship had suffered so badly. He was determined to make more of an effort when he got back home, wherever that was destined to be.

"Watch where you're going." A woman's voice cut through his reverie as he gazed at a young boy running down the opposite side of the road, arms out as if he was a bird. "You nearly knocked my basket off my arm, Daniel Parker. I'll tell your father."

Daniel Parker. Perhaps he's a relative of Mary Ann Parker? thought Lawrence as he walked towards 34 Gray Street. Lawrence felt flat and subdued and hoped the conversation with the Parker girl would be worth it, assuming she was available to talk. He knocked on the door and waited. Eventually, the door opened, and a young man answered. "What do you want?" he asked bluntly.

"Does Mary Parker live here?" asked Lawrence.

The young man nodded.

"Is she in?"

"No. Mary is at school. In fact, she's likely on her way back by now." He stepped out of the house and looked up the street. "That's her over there," he said, pointing to a trio of children at the top of the road. "She's the tall girl in the middle. What do you want with her?"

"Sergeant Simms sent me," said Lawrence, trotting out the same fabricated story that had worked so well earlier.

"Righty-ho," said the boy and closed the door.

Lawrence walked up the road and approached the group of schoolgirls. The girl in the middle was only a fraction taller than her friends. "Mary Parker?" he asked, uncertainly.

The schoolgirl nodded. "Yes," she said. "Who wants to know?"

"I'm Lawrence Harpham," said Lawrence. "A friend of Sergeant Simms."

"Oh, not that again," said Mary, planting her hands on her hips. "What do you want."

"A few words, if you don't mind."

"I do mind," said Mary. "I don't want to talk to you. I'm sick of it all."

"That's not very helpful," said Lawrence.

"I don't care. Go away," she said, linking arms with the red-haired girl to her side. "Let's go and play, Hannah."

"You're very rude," said Hannah, removing her arm. "Why won't you help him?"

"Why should I?" Mary stuck her bottom lip out.

"Because Joe died, and nobody knows why."

"I know," said Mary. "And I've tried to tell them, but nobody believes me."

"I promise I will listen," said Lawrence. "And I will take anything you say very seriously indeed."

"They all promised that," said Mary. "But Sergeant bloody Simms was the worst. He called me a liar."

"Mary!" Hannah stared at her aghast.

"Well, he did," said Mary, crossing her arms.

"You shouldn't use bad words. My mother says I won't be able to walk to school with you if she hears you do it again."

"My mother says your mother is hoity-toity and full of herself."

"That's not nice," said Hannah, looking close to tears.

"Let's go," whispered the third girl who had been standing quietly in the background. "I don't like her when she gets like this."

"Oh bloody, go bloody off without me then," said Mary. "Bloody, bloody, bloody horrible girls. This is your fault," she said, glaring at Lawrence.

"Why did Sergeant Simms call you a liar?" asked Lawrence.

"Because he's stupid," said Mary.

"That's a reason, but not the reason," said Lawrence. "What didn't he believe?"

"That I'd been given a cake," said Mary. "But that's because he remembered the wrong answer."

"It sounds complicated."

"Not really. A decent policeman ought to know the difference between a normal cake and a poisoned cake."

"He should," said Lawrence. "I can see why you're angry. It must be very frustrating to take the time to explain things, only to be misunderstood."

"Exactly," said Mary. "And to be called a liar at the inquest, just because he hadn't been listening properly.

"Why don't you tell me all about it?" said Lawrence. "I promise to listen very carefully and not to leave until you are satisfied that I understand."

"I suppose I could. I've got to get home for tea, though."

"I won't keep you long. Shall we go and sit on that old log over there," Lawrence continued, pointing to a small grassed area.

"Come on then," sighed Mary, leading the way.

#

Lawrence perched awkwardly on the log, rested his elbows on his knees and steepled his hands. Mary sat beside him and flung her satchel on the ground. Books spilt from the flap, half-open due to a missing buckle.

"Bugger," she said.

Lawrence raised an eyebrow.

"Oh, don't you start. My brother swears, and nobody minds."

"How old is your brother?" asked Lawrence.

"Fourteen."

"And how old are you?"

"Eleven. What's that got to do with it?"

"You're not a child anymore, but a young lady and that means people will judge your behaviour differently."

"I don't see why. If my brother can do it, then I should be able to."

"It doesn't work like that," said Lawrence, stroking his scar.

"How did you do that?" asked Mary, nodding towards his hand.

"I burned it in a fire," said Lawrence, placing his hand in his jacket pocket.

"Can I see it?"

"No. Why would you want to?"

"Because the man had one like it on his arm. I wanted to see if it was the same."

"Which man?"

Mary stamped her feet in frustration. "You weren't listening. You said you would listen carefully and you're just as bad as the other one."

"I know what we'll do," said Lawrence removing his notebook from his top pocket. "Why don't I interview you properly and I'll make some notes which you can read after. If there's anything you don't like, we'll change it. How does that sound?"

Mary chewed her knuckle and regarded him sullenly. "I suppose so," she said.

"Good," said Lawrence. "Let's start at the beginning. What was the name of the little boy who died?"

"Joseph Yeo," said Mary.

"And how did you know him?"

"We went to the same school. Joseph was a lot younger, of course."

"He wasn't in your class then?"

Mary tutted and raised her eyes. "Don't be silly."

"Then why was he with you that day?"

"Because of Florence."

"Florence?"

"His sister. She's in my class, and she's the eldest, so she has to walk with Mary Ann and Joseph."

"Oh, I see," said Lawrence. "Were they all with you on that day?"

Mary nodded.

"Florence, Mary and Joseph Yeo – you see, I'm writing it down exactly as you say."

Mary craned her neck, examined the notebook and nodded approvingly.

"Were you coming from school or going to school?"

"Going to school, but it was after lunch."

"You had lunch at home?"

"Yes."

"I know it was a long time ago, but can you remember what you ate?"

"Of course I can. I had a slice of bread and dripping as usual and a piece of seedy cake which wasn't at all usual. It was a lovely surprise, and that's why I remembered it, and that's what stupid Sergeant Simms got wrong."

"And then you returned to school?"

"Yes. I met Florence, who you saw earlier. The quiet girl, not haughty Hannah. She was with Mary and Joseph, and we walked together for a few moments, but as we passed the corner of the road, we saw a man standing there, and he winked at me. The others didn't see him, but I thought it was strange, so I looked again, and he put his finger to his lips and beckoned me over. I told Florence to wait, but she said she'd be late, and they went off without me."

"What did he want?" asked Lawrence.

"I was coming to that," glowered Mary. "He said I looked like a nice girl and he wanted to share some cake with me. I said I'd just eaten a big slice of seedy cake, and I didn't want any, and he said that I should take it anyway and have it for my supper. But be sure to share it with my friends."

"And you took it?"

"Actually," said Mary, rising from the log, "I said no. I didn't want his cake, and if I wasn't going to have it, then I wasn't going to share it. He told me not to be silly and to take the bloody cake."

"Did he use those words?"

"As I live and breathe," said Mary, crossing her chest.

"What did you do?"

"I walked away, and do you know what he did?"

"No."

"He grabbed me around the waist and tried to drag me into the alley. Have a guess what I did next?"

"I can't imagine."

"I bit his bloody arm. And that's how I know about his scar. I bit him and grabbed his horrid cake, and then I ran up the road as fast as I could."

"What did this man look like?" asked Lawrence.

"Oh, I don't know. Ordinary, I suppose."

"How was he dressed?"

"Trousers, jacket, black coat and hat."

"Was there anything notable about him?"

"No."

"And did you tell anyone when you got to school?"

"No, why would I?"

"Weren't you frightened?"

"Not really. I didn't think much more about it until the next day."

"Tell me what you did with the cake?"

"I put it in my satchel, went to my lessons and forgot all about it until the bell went. I saw it when I put my book away, and I was hungry again by then, so I nibbled a bit when I left the classroom. But it tasted foul. Then I saw Florence and gave her a piece while we waited for her brother and sister. Florence didn't like the cake much either, and there was quite a bit left, and she gave it back to me. I didn't want the bloody thing and gave a small piece to Mary and a big piece to Joseph because I liked him better. Then I went home."

"Did you see the man again?"

"No. I have never seen him to this day," she said.

"When did you find out that the other children were poorly?"

"Next day at school," said Mary. "Well, I sort of knew before school actually. Florence always waits on the corner, and she wasn't there. I nearly called on her, but I was cross that she was late, so I went without her. But she wasn't in our class by registration, and then somebody said that none of the Yeo children were at school. When I got home, Mother told me that they had all been taken poorly and were at home in bed."

"Were you ill at all, Mary?"

"I had a bad tummy," she said. "I felt sick all night, but I wasn't sick."

"And you only had a little piece of cake."

"Hardly any. Only a few crumbs."

"When did you realise that the cake might have been poisoned?"

"Not for ages," she said, "which is odd because I'm quite smart. But Florence is always missing school. She's weak. None of them is as strong as me. But a day or two later, Mother went to the general store and said Mrs Tullis had been going on about a missing cake of poison. She'd heard that the Yeo children were sick and was having the vapours about it. She's always like that. A worrywart. And that was all, until the next day."

"And then what?"

"I woke up looking forward to the weekend when I didn't have to go to school so it must have been a Friday, and I was just dressing when Mother shouted for me to come down at once. Well, she'd seen Bill Bailey walking past the house, you know, the butcher – and he said that Joseph Yeo had died at home that morning. The two girls were still very ill, and the doctor thought they had eaten something poisonous. Mother asked if I had been unwell and I told her that I'd felt sick and then I told her about the cake."

"And what did she say?"

"Nothing. Mother boxed my ears until they were ringing and made me sit in the corner until school time without any breakfast. And instead of letting me go to school, she marched me off to the police station to tell Sergeant Simms what had happened. Then he shouted at me as well and said I was silly for taking food from strangers. How was I supposed to know the food was bad?"

"You said that he didn't believe you?"

"He didn't. I tried to tell him about the poisoned cake, but he confused it with the seedy cake. Then he outright accused me of lying."

"About the cake?"

"No. Sergeant Simms wouldn't listen about the cake. He said I was lying about the man."

"He didn't believe you?"

"No. He's a hippo something."

"Hypocrite?"

"Yes. A hypocrite. He told me off for taking food from a stranger, and in the next breath, he told me he didn't believe the man existed at all."

"I wonder why he thought that?"

"Because he's stupid. And the stupid judge believed him too."

"Did it go to trial?"

"I don't know what you mean."

"Were you asked questions in a court?"

"No. I was asked questions at the Railway Hotel."

"Ah. An inquest then."

"If you say so. And that's where Sergeant horrible Simms called me a liar for the second time."

"Tell me about it," said Lawrence.

"Well," said Mary scraping grooves in the earth with her feet. "Mother and I were told to go to the hotel a few days after Joseph died and the judge man..."

"Coroner?"

"Yes, that's right. That's what they called him. The coroner made us sit and wait while Dr Hill talked. It was very boring until he got to the bit where he said that Joseph was poisoned by arsenic. It's a very bad poison, you know?"

Lawrence nodded. "I know. You were fortunate not to have been more severely affected."

"Anyway, after Dr Hill, it was my turn, and the coroner asked me lots of questions. And I told him that a man had given me the cake and that I'd given it to the other children. He asked if I had eaten any myself and I said that I had and that it had made me feel sick in the night."

"Was he satisfied with your account?"

"He was until Sergeant Simms poked his nose in."

"Simms was called to the stand immediately after you?"

"Yes. Horrid man."

"What did he have to say?"

"Lots of lies about me, starting with the cake."

"What about it?"

"He said that the story I told the coroner was completely different from the story that I told him and that the cake was given to me by my mother. Then he said that I told him I hadn't given it to the other children."

"He was wrong then?"

"Mostly." Mary stopped digging in the dirt with her shoe and rubbed the end of her nose. "He was wrong about the cake, but I might have made a mistake about giving the cake to the children."

"Either you did, or you didn't."

"I did, but I told him that I didn't."

"At the police station?"

Mary nodded.

"Why?"

"Because my mother boxed my ears and I didn't want her to do it again. So, I told Sergeant Simms that I ate the cake but didn't give it to the others."

"Did he believe you?"

"No. And then Florence told her father that I'd given them the cake and he told Sergeant Simms, and then I had no choice but to admit it. And now he thinks I lie about everything. But I didn't. There was a man, and he did give me a cake."

"Thank you, Mary," said Lawrence, turning to face her. "Here you are." He handed her his notebook.

Mary bit her lip in concentration as she scrutinised the page. "You're writing is difficult to read," she said.

"I'm sorry."

"This will do," she continued, snapping the notebook shut after reading the first page. "I think you understand."

"I do," said Lawrence. "And I will use the information wisely. Are you going to find your friends now?"

"No. They're cross with me, and I don't want to see them."

"You could apologise."

"Why should I?"

"Because you're a young lady and it's a good life skill to be able to apologise, even if you don't mean it. It's called diplomacy."

"Hmmm. I'll think about it."

"Good luck then," said Lawrence, offering his hand.

She took it and shook it surprisingly firmly, then walked away.

Lawrence pulled out his pocket watch. It was late afternoon, and he still had to negotiate his way back to Battersea. He sighed and set off for the station.

CHAPTER FIFTEEN

Vermin

Children are vermin. Utter vermin. Filthy creatures with neither conscience nor kindness. I disliked them enough when I was one of them, but over the years I have come to despise them. They make my skin crawl, and I shudder at the thought of being near one. I loathe children as much as rats, and I would be hard-pressed to choose which I would least like to encounter in my cellar. Rats would be worse, but only because I fear them.

The children from whom I had rescued Dante must have known who I was. I had recognised one of them, and he at least must have lived nearby. But they must have been afraid of me, for they never bothered me again, nor sent angry parents my way. Dante and I lived our lives peacefully and crossed into middle age around the same time. His sleek black fur glowed with silver edges, and my hair did likewise. I left the house every day to fulfil my employment while Dante remained at home, coming and going through a latched window at the rear of my house. During those years, we took in several lodgers, one of long-standing. They were all kind to Dante, and the last one became unexpectedly dear to both of us, only leaving when her employer insisted that she must live-in. I dwelled alone for a long while after that, but it was tolerable, as long as I had Dante.

Then one day, he left me. He wasn't there when I got home. The house was, by now, untenanted and there was nobody to ask where he was. The scraps of food that I had left him were gone. He must have remained in the house long enough to finish them, which was something, at least. I anxiously waited for him to return, sitting in the parlour until an ungodly hour, but there was no soft pad as he landed on the floorboards, no purr as he crawled beside me on the bed. The house was silent, and I waited with bated breath. The night dragged by and I rose early the following morning and set off to look for my friend. I trod the streets until the last moment before I had to leave for work, arriving just before my appointed hour. I watched the clock all through the day, eager to return and resume my search. When I finally arrived home, I unlatched the door, hoping against hope that Dante would come padding towards me, rubbing his head against my ankles. I knew from the moment I inserted the key that it was not to be. A cat fills every part of a home, from the outside in, and its absence is palpable. My house felt bereft, long before I registered that Dante was still missing.

I left the house knowing that the only way to find out what had happened to Dante was to ask around, which meant conversing with the neighbours. I kept myself to myself by choice, and it was not natural for me to seek out conversation. I had to steel myself for the ordeal, but it was worth it to find Dante. I knocked at the doors of the houses either side of me. Both occupants seemed surprised to find me on their doorsteps, and neither had any information to offer, although Mrs Barnett said she had seen him recently. I walked up the road, speaking to everyone I encountered, to no avail, and finally called in at the corner shop where Alf Meredith flogged his seedy wares. I asked him about Dante, and he replied almost immediately.

"Speak to Ivy Bellamy," he said. "She was in here yesterday complaining about a bunch of children throwing stones at an old cat."

He directed me to the Bellamy house, and I ran up the street, sick with worry and exertion. I hammered on her door and she answered immediately.

'Yes, she had seen children throwing stones at a cat. No, it was not in a good way. The poor thing had run off into the path of a cart as it tried to escape them and had crawled off to die. Where? The cartman had left it lying a short distance away, and she'd got her son Norman to put it in a ditch, out of the way by Lower Field. Yes, of course, it was dead. He wouldn't have left a suffering animal. No, she didn't know who the children were, but they were girls.'

I felt sick, and my heart hurt. Perhaps it wasn't Dante. I raced, puffing and panting to Lower Field, took a stick and dragged it along the ditch removing leaves and debris for a better view. And I found him halfway along, mouth hanging open, eyes closed, black fur matted with dried blood. I removed my jacket and held him in my arms, ignoring his stiff limbs and the smell of death, and I buried my nose in his fur as I had all those years ago. When I arrived home, I laid him beneath the window in his favourite spot in the sun while I dug a hole in the flower bed, dislodging plants in my hurry. Then I put him in the hole and stood over him until the sun went down, vacillating between sadness and unquenchable anger. That night, through broken sleep, the rats returned.

CHAPTER SIXTEEN

Back to Netherwood

Thursday, September 17, 1896

"Did you get your letter?" asked Francis Farrow, reclining in his favourite high-backed chair.

"Yes," said Violet, biting her lip.

"Not good news?"

"My aunt is still unwell," said Violet. "She says it is nothing, but she rarely ails."

"Can't you go and see her?" asked Francis.

"It's complicated," said Violet. "And she lives so far away."

"But at least she writes to you often."

"She does, and I'm grateful. Her letters mean a lot."

"If it's a question of travelling costs, you know I can help."

"Francis, you are kind, but that's not it. Thank you anyway."

Francis smiled benevolently, uncrossed his legs and walked towards the window. "How's that old reprobate, Lawrence?" he asked.

"It's hard to tell," said Violet. "He doesn't seem very happy."

"Oh. Why is that?"

"He hasn't said much, but I get the feeling that he isn't particularly keen to get married."

"What makes you think that?"

"He says his life was less complicated before."

"It is when you're unattached. It doesn't mean anything."

"Do you think he loves her?"

"Loveday?"

"Who else?"

"Yes, I do. Lawrence has had designs on Loveday on several previous occasions. She's like catnip to him."

"He seems to be lacking in enthusiasm."

"That's just the way Lawrence behaves. He's never been one to wear his emotions boldly."

"Is she like Catherine?"

"Loveday? Good Lord, no. Catherine was one of a kind – poised, elegant, and a more handsome woman, it's hard to imagine. She could light up a room. Her ability to mingle, to make everyone feel special, it was a gift. She had it all, Violet. Looks, charm, a well-regarded family. Everything." Francis stared into the distance, lost in thought.

"He was lucky to have her," said Violet.

"God, yes. He married well," said Francis.

"And she loved him?"

"Yes, she did. It's no wonder he wants to remarry. Not that it will ever be the same."

"You don't think Loveday measures up to Catherine?"

"No woman ever could," said Francis.

Violet sighed and picked at a jagged piece of nail.

"You shouldn't bite them," said Francis.

Violet moved her hands from sight. "I don't," she said. "They're just not very strong. Do you think Lawrence will be happy with Loveday?"

Francis approached her and looked down. "He will be happy, Violet," he said. "And you must allow him his happiness. I know it's difficult to let go of your friendship, but you must. He cannot make a good marriage if he is reliant upon the affections of another woman."

"But will we be able to work together?" asked Violet, her brown eyes soft and sad.

"That's a matter for your conscience," said Francis.

"But…"

The door opened, and Alfred appeared.

"Ah, I wondered where you were." Francis collected an envelope from the table and handed it to his butler. "Post this, will you, there's a good chap."

"Certainly," said Alfred. "May I ask Miss Violet if there is any news from London?"

"Very little," admitted Violet. "Lawrence is still searching for Bertie. He is doing everything he can but is making slow progress."

"Oh dear." Alfred seemed to shrink a little as he listened. "Flora has written again. She is desperate for news."

"Poor thing. I'll ask Lawrence to call on her. Perhaps that will help."

"Oh no. That won't do at all," said Alfred. "Her employers will let her go."

"Of course," said Violet. "But I promise to let you know whenever I hear anything."

"Thank you," said Alfred, turning to leave.

"What did you want anyway?" asked Francis.

"Oh, Master Sidney needs a new pair of trousers," said Alfred. "I'm afraid he ripped them climbing a tree."

Francis sighed and reached for his wallet. "Take this. Get him whatever he needs."

"How is Sidney," asked Violet as the door closed.

"Still here," sighed Francis. "And to be honest, he's in the way. I should have let you have him."

Violet opened her mouth to answer.

"I didn't mean it," he continued. "But the sooner he's at school, the better. Now, what are you doing for the next few days?"

"I'm glad you asked," said Violet, retrieving a list from her pocket. There are a few people that I need to speak to, and I might need your help."

149

CHAPTER SEVENTEEN

Journey to Hitcham

"So, you don't know where we're going?" asked Francis, trying to conceal his impatience. When he'd asked Violet to join him for a coffee earlier, he hadn't expected her travel needs to occupy the whole of his day. It was now early afternoon, and far from having gone home, she had roped him into another trip to Felsham.

"Not exactly, but everyone knows everyone around here. It shouldn't take much effort to track them down."

"Them?"

"My list of people."

"How big is this list?"

"Only half a dozen names and I may not need to speak to all of them. Some of them may have moved on anyway as Caroline Bird did."

"Where are you going to begin?"

"There," said Violet, pointing to a man pushing a load up the road in a small barrow. "Pull over, please. I'll start with him."

She hopped from the vehicle and strode towards the man before Francis had even applied the handbrake.

"Excuse me," said Violet, holding her hat on her head. A blustery wind had chased them for most of the car journey and showed no signs of relenting now they had arrived.

"How can I help you, miss?" asked the man, gruffly.

"I'm looking for somebody," said Violet. "Several somebodies, actually. Do you live here?"

The man sighed. "Yes. I live here. Have done for years. Who are you looking for?"

Violet produced her list and started reading from it, but the man interrupted her. "It will be easier if you give it to me," he said. "Don't worry. I can read."

Violet's cheeks flushed as she offered the paper. He had uttered almost exactly what she had been thinking.

"Yes, yes and yes," he muttered as he read the list. "Rosa Gladwell. What's she doing on there?"

"Do you know her?"

"We are distant kin," he said.

"Oh. Are you Jimmy Gladwell?"

He nodded. "That's me."

"You were delivering groceries to Julia Brown while I was visiting her," said Violet.

"If you say so. Now, back to your list. Hmmm. It must be old. Anna Nobbs is married now with a couple of girls. You'll find her living in Hitcham. There's a big apple tree outside her house with a swing on the bough. You can't miss it. And Charlotte Betham is at the rectory in Brettenham. You're out of luck with Benjamin Dempster. He moved a long way north years ago. Oh, him." Gladwell's face darkened and his brow furrowed as he stared at Violet. "Alf Chipperfield. That's an unwelcome name from the past." He turned the list over and re-read it. "What is this? Why are you looking for these people after all this time?"

"Does it matter?" asked Violet, trying to maintain confidentiality.

"Not really, but why you want that miserable old bugger, I don't know."

"You didn't like him?" asked Violet unnecessarily.

"It went much deeper than that," said Jimmy Gladwell. "We hated each other. Healthy competition is one thing, but he damn nearly drove me to bankruptcy with his underhand ways."

"You were a grocer?"

"We both were. Chipperfield sold his shop a few years after me and made a handsome profit. I let mine go for next to nothing. Fed up with it, I was..." Gladwell shook his head and stared into the distance.

"Mr Gladwell?"

"Sorry, yes. It was a difficult time. That sort of mistrust drives a man to make bad decisions."

"I'm sure luck plays its part," said Violet.

"Hmmm?"

"The right buyer being there at the right time."

"Yes, I suppose so." He scrutinised Violet's list again. "Is there anything else I can help you with?" he said, returning the paper.

Violet took it and re-read it. "I'm sure there were more names than that," she said, eyeing the list with suspicion. "Oh, no. It's the wrong list. This one is for reminders. Oh dear. That explains why Chipperfield was on there. I wonder who I've forgotten?"

"Sorry, I can't help you there," said Jimmy Gladwell, retaking the weight of the barrow.

"Not to worry," said Violet. "And thank you. You've been very helpful."

She returned to the vehicle to find Francis quaffing from a hip flask.

"Get what you wanted?" he asked, screwing the top down.

"Mostly," said Violet. "It was lucky that I brought the wrong list."

"Where are we going, then?"

"Hitcham," said Violet.

"I know it – not too far. Hold onto your hat."

Twenty minutes later, they had arrived outside Hannah Fisher's cottage. Jimmy Gladwell was right. There was no mistaking her property. The bough of an ancient apple tree was just the right height and shape to accommodate a swing which had been carved long ago in the form of a shallow bowl. For a fleeting moment, Violet felt compelled to try it.

"You won't want to come inside?"

"No."

"Then, I'll see you shortly. Thank you, Francis."

Violet smiled as she knocked on the cottage door, which opened at her touch. "Hello," she called, as she peered into the hallway.

"Up here?" A voice croaked hoarsely, and Violet stood where she was, feeling awkward.

"I said, up here."

Fighting her reluctance to bother someone who was clearly unwell, Violet tiptoed upstairs and into a small, dimly lit landing.

"Hello," she whispered.

"In here."

Violet turned into a room on the right-hand side. The drawn curtains excluded most of the light, and she could barely see the shape in the bed reclining under the bedspread.

"Who are you?" croaked the voice.

"My name is Violet. I'm sorry to disturb you. I came to ask you some questions, but I wouldn't have bothered you if I'd realised you were ill."

"I thought you were Edith," said the woman. "My youngest. It's her half-day."

"Are you well enough to speak to me?"

"I'm bored enough," said the woman.

"And you are Anna Fisher?"

"Yes, I am. What do you want with me?"

"Can I talk to you about Julia Brown?"

Anna sighed and patted the bed. "Take the weight off your feet," she said.

#

"I suppose this is about the murder?" asked Anna.

Violet nodded.

"Why, after all this time?"

"Because nobody ever answered for it," said Violet.

Anna seemed satisfied. "Poor little fellow," she said. "Carry on."

"I've read the newspaper reports," said Violet. "And I know that you worked as a servant to Reverend Betham at the same time as Julia."

"I did," said Anna.

"And I've read that the little boy was poisoned, probably from ingesting sulphuric acid."

"So they say."

"But the accounts are very complicated," said Violet. "The scientific report is beyond my comprehension. From my limited layman's knowledge, the doctors seemed to think that Julia had sulphuric acid on her clothes."

"She may well have done. She certainly changed her dress on the day she returned to the rectory."

"How do you know it was that day?"

"I was called upon to give evidence not long after. I remember Sergeant Durrant apprehending Julia. Rumours were afoot, but nobody really believed it until he turned up at the rectory and arrested her. I was in the hallway when he charged her with poisoning the little boy. She said she hadn't done it, but she was emotionless and matter of fact. I had seen her more agitated after being told off for not polishing the brass properly than when they accused her of murder."

"You didn't find her convincing?"

"Not at all," said Anna, placing her hand over her mouth. She coughed a little and caught her breath, then another cough came and another until she was gasping for breath.

"Can I get you some water?" asked Violet, and Anna nodded, panting as she strove to recover.

Violet returned a few moments later with a glass and handed it to Anna.

"That's better," she said.

"Are you up to this?" asked Violet.

"As much as I will ever be," said Anna. "My health is failing."

"I'm sorry."

"They made me go to her room, while they broke open her box," said Anna.

"Box?"

"Yes. Julia's trunk. You know, for storage."

"Why?"

"Because they wanted to know if she had anything that she could have used to poison her child."

"But they didn't find anything?"

"Only the stained dress."

"Now," said Violet, removing her notebook from her bag. She withdrew the newspaper clipping and flattened it with her hand. "The account says that a bottle of vitriol went missing. When they asked Julia about it, she said you told her that it was useful for cleaning, but denied it in the courtroom."

"Did I? It's such a long time I ago, I simply can't remember."

"I'm not sure what relevance it has," said Violet.

"Only that it implies that I took the bottle for cleaning when I didn't," said Anna.

"I see. Now, what tasks did Julia perform in her duties?"

"She was the cook," said Anna. "And thought herself a cut above me, just because she kept the kitchen and I cleaned the house. And sometimes when she wasn't busy, she played with the Betham children."

"Were they fond of her?"

"The children liked her well enough, I suppose, though I think her attention to them was all for show. Mrs Betham thought she was kind and gave her extra things. She had a set of handkerchiefs on her birthday, while my birthday was forgotten. But then, I didn't make a big fuss about it, and Julia made sure she told the children who told their parents. She was like that. People thought she was slightly simple, but she wasn't." Anna Fisher sighed. "But then again, it was a very long time ago."

"I'm sorry," said Violet. "It's a bit much to expect you to remember conversations that happened in the past."

Anna said nothing but turned her head and gazed towards the wall.

"Did you like her?" asked Violet, breaking the silence that had descended on the room.

"We weren't close," said Anna, "but I didn't dislike her."

"Why do you think she changed her dress as soon as she returned from her visit?"

"I expect it was soiled. Why else would she do it?"

"I'm sure you're right," said Violet closing her notebook.

"Have you finished?"

"Yes, thank you," said Violet.

"Good. I'm feeling tired now."

"Well, hopefully, you can rest and recover from your illness."

Anna laughed hollowly. "It's not the kind of illness that gets better," she said. "My days are numbered."

Violet squeezed her hand. "I'm sorry," she whispered. "I'll let myself out."

CHAPTER EIGHTEEN

High Tea at Fortnum's

Lawrence strode briskly into the dining room, watching anxiously for signs of the waiter clearing breakfast away. His journey from Silvertown had been unendurably long after he had boarded the wrong train. Lawrence hadn't noticed; he was halfway out of Essex and heading north to Suffolk before realising his mistake. He had leapt out at the next stop but needed to change trains several times before arriving back in Battersea. The hotel kitchens were closed by the time he got as far as the dining room, and he was too tired to find a restaurant. He had lain on his bed having every intention of reading through his notes but had fallen asleep fully clothed, not waking until it was almost half past nine.

Having woken both tired and stiff, Lawrence was also famished. As he entered the dining room, his eyes darted towards his usual table. It was free and still set with cutlery and a napkin. Lawrence grabbed a rolled-up newspaper and settled nonchalantly on the chair, trying to ignore his crumpled clothes and the fact that he hadn't washed.

After a few moments, a waiter arrived, took his order and set off for the kitchen without glancing at his watch. Lawrence exhaled with relief, unfurled the newspaper and spent two minutes reviewing the weights and handicaps of the racehorses running at Kempton Park that day. Making a mental note to place a bet on Cockroach, just because he liked the name, his eye was drawn to the headline immediately below. 'Singular Poisoning Case' the text screamed. 'The coroner for West Ham opened an enquiry today into the death of Edith Eliza Beard last Thursday. It will be remembered that eleven children were poisoned by eating rat cake, which they found in the street.' Eleven children! Lawrence examined the newspaper again. Surely it couldn't be a coincidence. Perhaps that was what Louisa Tullis had meant when she'd asked if he was investigating what happened earlier. Lawrence continued reading. While the connection to the Silvertown affair was unproven, there was wild speculation about a possible link which was now the subject of a police investigation. And clearly, there had been other incidents in between the Yeo poisoning and this latest. He needed to find out more.

Lawrence was on the verge of walking away from breakfast when he heard a voice coming from the lobby.

"Through there, miss, I think you'll find," said a young man as he entered the restaurant, followed by the familiar form of Loveday.

"What on earth are you doing here?" asked Lawrence, jumping to his feet. "How did you find me?"

"Nice to see you too," said Loveday, kissing him on the cheek.

"Well, of course, it's good to see you," spluttered Lawrence. "Just unexpected. I'm investigating a case."

"I know," said Loveday. "Felicity told me."

"Felicity?"

"Felicity Braithwaite. Keep up. You only saw her a few days ago."

"Ah, yes. I remember."

"Well, she came straight back to Cheltenham, and I happened to meet her in The Strand. And when she told me where you were, I thought I would pop up and surprise you."

"You've certainly done that," said Lawrence, looking discreetly at his watch.

"Your breakfast, sir." The waiter appeared with a plate of toast and marmalade, which was not what Lawrence had ordered. Lawrence

158

gazed disappointedly at the mound of toasted bread. He wouldn't have lingered had he known that this scant offering was all he would get for his tardiness. "Would you like some?" he asked, offering the plate to Loveday.

"No, thank you. I've already eaten. Anyway, I thought you could take me to Fortnum's when I've dropped my bags off."

"Where are you staying?"

"In Chelsea, with Sally Goodall. You know, Jonty Goodall's sister."

Lawrence shook his head, quite sure he'd never heard of either of them.

"You must know the Goodalls? They made their money in Tanzania. Never mind. I'll drop my bags, and you can pick me up from Cadogan Gardens at midday."

"I can't, I'm afraid."

"Why not?"

"As I told you, I'm in the middle of an investigation."

"Lawrence, I've come all this way to see you, and we can't meet tomorrow as I have a fitting in Bond Street. No, it must be today. Anyway, we need to talk about the wedding."

Lawrence moodily buttered a piece of toast and cut it into four equal portions, before individually coating each piece with marmalade, working with unwarranted precision.

"Why do you do that?"

"Hmmm?"

"Butter your toast that way. It must take hours."

"Never mind that. There's been another poisoning. I need to see Sergeant Simms and find out what's going on."

"See him tomorrow."

"You could come too?"

"Me?" Loveday started at him incredulously. "Where?"

"Woolwich."

"I haven't travelled all this distance to visit a policeman in Woolwich," she said. "I would like you to take me to Fortnum's."

Lawrence folded the newspaper and stashed it in his jacket pocket, then pushed the toast away, uneaten."

"Very well," he said.

#

"That's Charles Fortnum," whispered Loveday, nodding towards a distinguished-looking man who was standing at the entrance to the restaurant.

Lawrence glanced at the tall, white-whiskered man. "Who?" he asked.

"He's a historian, something to do with the British Museum," she said.

"Does he own it?"

"No, I don't think so. But he is one of the Fortnum family."

Whatever point Loveday was trying to make, was lost on Lawrence. The delicate cucumber sandwiches that had just arrived in front of him were no substitute for having missed three meals. He had tried and failed to persuade Loveday to order a cooked lunch. Instead, she had opted for afternoon tea and had insisted that he did likewise. Lawrence wasn't enjoying the perfumed tea that Loveday had selected and was hoping that the promised selection of cakes would make up for the lack of meat in his meal.

"Isn't this wonderful?" said Loveday, beaming at Lawrence as she sat back in her chair.

"It's a fine building," he agreed. In truth, Lawrence liked Fortnum and Mason. It was a fascinating and elegant store and if he weren't so damned hungry, he would, no doubt, be enjoying the meal.

"Have you chosen your best man yet?" asked Loveday, pouring another cup of tea.

"Not yet," said Lawrence. "I'm still thinking about it."

"Well, you haven't got long. The wedding's only three months away."

"I know. I can't make my mind up about who to ask."

"Who were you thinking of asking?"

"Either Michael or Francis," said Lawrence. "But Francis was best man at my wedding to Catherine."

"He won't do," said Loveday. "And whoever heard of asking a parish priest to be their best man. Why haven't you asked Colonel Melcham?"

"Tom? It never occurred to me. And he travels a lot. I don't know if he's in England at the moment."

"He is," said Loveday. "I met him at the assembly room ball last weekend. He seemed quite amenable to the idea."

"What idea?"

"Of being your best man, naturally."

"Loveday. Please tell me that you didn't ask Melcham?"

"Of course not. I just told him that you probably would."

"I wasn't going to do anything of the kind."

"Who else if not him? You've already ruled out the Farrows."

"I haven't ruled out Michael. He is by far my first choice, if he agrees."

"Why wouldn't he?"

Lawrence opened his mouth to speak but then shut it again. Michael's objection, if any, was likely to be due to his perception of how he had treated Violet, and that was not a topic he could discuss with Loveday.

"That's settled then. You'll ask Tom Melcham when you visit Cheltenham next Saturday."

"Nothing is settled," said Lawrence.

"Stop shouting," hissed Loveday as a waitress walked towards them, pushing a laden cake stand on a trolley.

"Here are your cakes, sir, madam," she said breezily. "Didn't you like your sandwiches? I can fetch you something else."

"They were perfectly acceptable," said Lawrence. "I wasn't in the mood. Please take them away."

"Enjoy your cakes," said the waitress as she bustled off.

"I wasn't shouting." Lawrence removed an almond cake from the stand and chewed it with gusto before resuming the conversation. "And I will select my best man, Loveday. No, don't argue." He put his finger to his lips as she began to speak. "You've decided on everything else, and I have gone along with your wishes. But a man should choose his own groomsman, and it is not up for discussion."

"Have it your way," said Loveday. "But Tom Melcham would have been far more suitable. You'll have to tell him that he isn't needed when you see him on Saturday."

"I'm not going to see him on Saturday," said Lawrence. "I'll probably still be here and if not in London, then certainly in Suffolk."

"You can't. We're looking at houses."

161

"No, we're not," Lawrence spoke quietly and reached for Loveday's hand. "I don't want to talk about it in here," he said. "It's neither the time nor the place."

"But I won't see you until next week. I suppose I could squeeze you in on Monday before I return. Yes, you can take me to the station, and we can talk then."

"Why do you want to marry me?"

"What an odd question. Why does anyone marry?"

"Usually for love."

"You are very quaint, Lawrence. And a little provincial in your outlook. But we get along splendidly, you and me. We will make an excellent partnership."

Lawrence smiled and stroked her hand. "Do you think so?"

"Of course." Loveday smiled and looked into his eyes, flashing a glimpse of perfect white teeth. "You'll love the houses that I've selected. Now, eat up and then we can browse the household department."

CHAPTER NINETEEN

Woolwich Police Station

Friday, September 18, 1896

Lawrence had spent an unsettled night mithering over the quandary in which he was now firmly mired. Loveday, quite clearly, had every intention of remaining in Cheltenham and he couldn't see a way forward without disappointing her. Nor could Lawrence see any compromise in the situation. He had considered the problem from every angle, and there did not seem to be a resolution. It had disturbed his sleep to the extent that he was now considering forgoing his intended visit to Woolwich police station, and it was only his commitment to Flora Johns, that kept him on track. Dressing with no enthusiasm for the task at hand, he took coffee in his room and left without eating breakfast again. Lawrence wandered moodily towards the station with his hands in his pockets and his head bowed against a gusty breeze. Before long, the heavens opened, and his strides grew longer as he sought to avoid what was threatening to turn into a torrential downpour. His mind was in such a state of concentration that

Lawrence didn't see the carriage pull up beside him or hear the friendly voice that shouted his name. The first moment he became aware of Isabel Smith was when he heard a deep voice bellowing beside him, and he started at the sound.

"Sorry, sir," said Valentine Jennings, as he lunged towards the carriage door and pulled it open.

"Mr Harpham, I thought it was you. Can I offer you a space in my carriage?" asked Isabel.

Lawrence tipped his hat. "Thank you. You've very kind, but I'm going to Woolwich," he said.

"Don't worry," said Isabel. "If you can tolerate my company as far as Trafalgar, Jennings can take you to Woolwich."

"In that case, it would be my pleasure," said Lawrence, entering the carriage.

"How are you getting on with your search?" asked Isabel, smiling pleasantly.

"I'm making a little progress," said Lawrence. "I found Dora Hamblin's house in Silvertown, and there's something not quite right about it. There was a newspaper clipping about the Silvertown poisoning."

"I won't ask how you came to enter the premises," said Isabel, "but it sounds like you are on the right track."

"I'm on *a* track," said Lawrence, "whether it's the right one, remains to be seen. I found evidence that Dora Hamblin was drugging children."

"Oh dear. That's disturbing. Presumably, she wasn't there?"

"No, but we only just missed her. She'd left in a hurry the previous day."

"I wonder why?"

"I assume it's because she was worried about being caught with the children, but perhaps there was another reason."

"Mr Harpham. The abuse of children is of the greatest concern to my department. Please don't hesitate to ask if there is anything that I can help you with, be it information, transportation or any other matters arising in your investigation. If you keep me informed of your progress, I promise I will not question your methods. We must find these children and soon."

"Thank you," said Lawrence. "That will be a great help."

The carriage came to a stop outside the municipal buildings. The cabman alighted and opened the door, and Isabel instructed him to take Lawrence wherever he needed to go. She took her leave and waved as she entered the building.

"Where to, sir?" asked the cabman.

"Woolwich police station," said Lawrence, sinking back into the carriage as he mulled over the case.

#

Richard Simms was scribbling on a chalkboard as Lawrence entered the back room of the Woolwich police station.

"Have you got a moment?" asked Lawrence, walking past two young constables inconveniently loitering in his path.

"I should think so," said Simms good-naturedly. "Hopkins, Barrow, go and find something useful to do." One of the constables raised his eyes to the other, but they left the room without complaint.

"How can I help you?"

"It's this poisoning business," said Lawrence, sitting on the edge of the table. "Ah. It appears that you are working on the same thing." He pointed towards the blackboard where Edith Eliza Beard's name appeared in full view.

"What do you know about it?" asked Simms.

"Only what I read in yesterday's paper. My investigation is leading me the same way."

"What do you mean?"

"The missing baby that I mentioned yesterday. I spoke to Miss Smith, as you suggested, and she pointed me in the direction of a house in Silvertown. We missed the occupant by about a day, but we found a clipping about the poisoning. I've subsequently spoken to Louisa Tullis."

"And, no doubt, the charming Mr Tullis," said Simms.

"He was there," said Lawrence, ignoring the sarcasm.

"But what has it to do with your case?"

"To be honest, I don't know. But all the clues, such as they are, point to it being relevant."

Simms sighed. "My superiors don't encourage our cooperation outside of the police force. I've already told you more than I should have."

"And I appreciate it. But if I must rely on the Battersea police to follow this through, the poor child will never be found."

"Hmm. I forgot about their involvement," said Simms. "I wouldn't want that on my conscience. What do you need from me?"

"Details, please," said Lawrence. "I've read an account that suggests there were eleven children involved."

"Don't believe everything you read in the press," said Richard Simms. "That number isn't strictly accurate. There were four children involved in the first case – Mary Ann Parker and the three Yeo children. A further eight also suffered poisoning symptoms, but this may have been a different incident. The Parker girl denied any involvement with them, but then she is known to be economical with the truth. Then, in May, two little girls living in a road near Custom House were both poisoned with rat cake. That case is likely to be connected to the first as is the third case, which involved a seaman. Interestingly, the coroner came up with a theory that rat cake used at a nearby shipyard was carried insecurely in unfastened bags and routinely fell on the ground when the rat-catchers did their rounds. The seaman concerned didn't die immediately. He staggered into the Seamen's Hospital in East London, gravely ill but conscious. He said that he'd eaten some cake that he found in the street, after which he became exceedingly unwell. When asked why he would eat food from the ground, he said he found it in the street, not on the street, and the poor chap expired soon after."

"Isn't that the same thing?" asked Lawrence.

"Yes, as far as the coroner was concerned," said Simms. "But I don't like to take things at face value. The seaman, even in his weakened condition, was offended at the suggestion that he'd picked the cake from the road, which suggests to me that he may have found it in a more sanitary position. On a wall, or some other surface. Something less unpleasant than lying in the dirt. It wasn't wrapped, you see. That much, he did say. Anyway, the poor man is no longer with us, so it is all conjecture. The coroner ruled it as death by misadventure, and that is the end of that."

"And Eliza Beard?"

"Well, I can't be sure," said Richard Simms. "The child went to school perfectly well and arrived home with sickness and diarrhoea. She died the next day. I wouldn't necessarily have connected the two things were it not for the fact that young Edith lived in Cleaver Road, which is very close to Martindale Road where the Cochlin girls died. Both in Custom House, you see. It warrants an investigation."

"Could they have been poisoned deliberately?" asked Lawrence. "Mary Ann Parker was adamant that someone gave her the cake."

Simms rose, walked to the chalkboard and pointed to the last name in a column on the left-hand side. It read 'Mary Ann Parker' and below it was a single phrase – 'unreliable witness'. "She's a storyteller," he said. "There's possibly a little truth in some of the things she says, but it's damn near impossible to weed out fact from fiction. Don't postulate a theory from anything she says."

"And there was nothing similar in any of the other accounts."

"Not really. Edith Beard was put to bed, having said very little. You know everything the seaman said and the two Cochlin girls were too young to impart anything reliable. There was another girl with the Cochlins, eight-year-old Alice Shaw, who was offered some of the cake but didn't eat it. She saw the red colourant, and it was enough to put her off. Just as well that one of them was sensible."

"I wonder if I should see them," mused Lawrence.

"I'm not sure you'll get much from the family," said Simms, "but nobody has questioned them recently, as far as I know, and I've no objection. Wait a moment." Simms strode from the office, leaving Lawrence alone with the chalkboard.

He advanced towards it and took a closer look, realising at once that there was very little information displayed of which he wasn't already aware. He resumed his position perched on the edge of the table and was studiously examining his notebook when Simms returned to the room.

"There," he said, passing a scrap of paper to Lawrence. "That's Mr Cochlin's address. Let me know if he tells you anything of importance. I think you're wasting your time, though."

"Probably. But there isn't much else to go on, so I'll take my chances. Thank you for your help."

Lawrence rose and offered his hand to Simms before leaving the room and the police station. He walked absent-mindedly towards the front of the building, forgetting for a moment, that the cabman had gone. As realisation dawned, Lawrence set off towards the station at a brisk pace, which fell to a trudge as his mood changed from optimism to concern. The lure of a useful clue always kept Lawrence's spirits high, but he was down to his last lead, and it was a poor one. And the matter of the location of his future home weighed heavily on his mind. Try as he might, he could not imagine a life in Cheltenham. Yet it shouldn't matter where he lived. He could be a private investigator anywhere, and it would not be difficult to start again in Cheltenham where he already had many useful contacts, not least Tom Melcham. But the flaw in the plan was Violet. He would be starting again, alone. It was a stark choice between being with Loveday in Cheltenham or with Violet in Bury St Edmunds. The decision should be easy, yet it wasn't. By the time Lawrence reached the railway station, he was in turmoil. He needed to speak to someone, a friend. Someone who knew him and would listen. Francis or Michael, perhaps. He looked at his watch for inspiration, but nothing came. He wasn't due to see Loveday next until Monday. Almost without conscious effort, Lawrence found himself boarding a northbound train. Several hours and a few changes later, he arrived in Bury.

CHAPTER TWENTY

Brettenham Rectory

"What a lovely old building," said Violet, looking towards Brettenham rectory. Francis smoothed a newspaper over the car steering wheel as he reclined in the seat, ready for another bout of waiting. "Thank you so much for driving me again. I hope it isn't becoming too much of a burden."

"Not at all," said Francis. "Any excuse to take the old girl out. I meant her, not you," he continued, patting the bonnet, as Violet arched an eyebrow.

"I'm truly grateful," she smiled, unable to keep up the pretence of being offended. "I don't know what I'd have done without you."

"Will you be long?" asked Francis.

"I doubt it. I told Mrs Betham that I'd only be ten minutes."

"You're never that quick."

"I know, but I thought she might object if I said it would take longer. And perhaps it won't, especially if she refuses to talk to me."

"Nobody ever refuses you, Violet," said Francis.

Violet's smile was replaced with a frown as she turned towards the rectory. Francis had been a godsend, but she was beginning to worry that she was taking advantage of his good nature. And not only that, she was concerned that he might want something more than friendship. He was more solicitous than their platonic relationship warranted and, as much as Violet liked him, her feelings could never be more. Perhaps her imagination was running riot, but she decided to spend a few days away from Francis, after today, just to be on the safe side.

Violet rang the doorbell and was greeted by a formally dressed housemaid in stiffly starched apron and pinafore dress. "Yes, ma'am," she asked, bobbing a curtsy.

"May I see Mrs Betham," asked Violet. "I have an appointment."

"Come this way. The girl led Violet up a hallway and into a brightly lit morning room overlooking the garden where Charlotte Betham was sitting at the table, counting a pile of coins.

"Ah, Miss Smith, I presume," said Mrs Betham offering a hand, which she drew back before Violet could take it. "Sorry. Filthy stuff, money, isn't it? I'll wash my hands first." She disappeared through a door leaving Violet standing over the pile of money and feeling extremely uncomfortable. She made her way to the farthest end of the room and stared at the bookcase while she was waiting.

Presently, Charlotte Betham bustled back in. "Come, sit," she said, indicating the seat opposite the coins. "Let's try again." She offered her hand, and this time Violet shook it. "Good, now that's out the way, you won't mind if I write this in my cash book while we are talking."

"Not at all," said Violet.

"One pound, three and six in case you're wondering," said Charlotte. "And I know I won't be missing a penny. I'm a good judge of character, and I wouldn't have left you if I'd thought for a moment you'd pilfer."

"I don't know what to say."

"You looked very uncomfortable standing by the bookcase, and it's quite evident that you couldn't get far enough away from this money which indicates that you are either a consummate thief or thoroughly honest. I don't doubt that it is the latter."

"Perhaps you would be better suited to my occupation," said Violet.

"You haven't told me what it is yet."

"I am a private investigator."

"And what is it that requires investigating?"

"Do you remember Julia Brown? She worked for you as a servant back in sixty-four."

"Julia Brown. Yes, I remember her very well. I only had her for a few weeks, but so much disruption followed behind her, that she is one of my most memorable servants."

"Did you like her?"

"Very much. Why are you asking about Julia Brown after all this time?"

"We have, that is my business partner and I, have been asked to investigate Freddy Brown's death. Nobody was ever held accountable, and Julia's family still feel that she is judged harshly and considered a murderess even after all these years."

"They're correct in their assumptions," said Charlotte. "I have heard it said on many occasions and I have rebuked everyone who has uttered it in my presence. The court found Julia not guilty, and that is the end of it."

"I suppose you were not able to form much of an impression about her in the short time you knew her."

"On the contrary. My children formed an immediate attachment to her. She was kind and solicitous to each of them. They liked her, and I liked her, and more to the point, I trusted her."

"You don't think she harmed her child."

"No. The idea is preposterous."

"Yet the evidence you gave to the Crown Court, hardly helped her case."

"They asked for facts, and I gave them. I talk plainly, Miss Smith. I find that it makes life easier."

"That is very true. Would you be prepared to tell me what you told the inquest?"

"If you think it would help Julia. In all honesty, it is hard to see a gain after all this time, but equally, I suppose that it cannot do any harm."

"Thank you. From what I've read, much of the case against Julia came from a bottle of oil of vitriol with similar properties to that which caused Freddy Brown's injuries."

"Correct. It was an important part of the prosecutor's case."

"Why was that?"

"Well, Julia joined us early in the year, February I think it was, and at that time I had a bottle of oil of vitriol in my storeroom."

"What for?"

Charlotte Betham raised her eyes and bit her lip as she tried to remember. "If I recall correctly, I bought it to remove some marking ink stains from a piece of furniture. But when I used it, the vitriol was so strong that it burned the table. It was no use at all, so I put it in the storeroom and forgot all about it."

"When was that?"

"Probably at the end of January. I am quite sure that it was before Julia came to work at the rectory."

"And from what I understand, the bottle of vitriol went missing?"

"Yes, it did – probably while I was visiting family. I was away for a month, you know. I never saw it again after that."

"Who lived in the house while you were away?"

"My husband, obviously, my son Charles, the younger children and the two servant girls."

"And where was the key kept?"

"Usually in a locked drawer. I held the key but gave it to the Reverend while I was away. As I told the court, the key is sometimes left in the lock, and my husband will not have thought to check for its safe return. I cannot guarantee that it was routinely put away on that occasion."

"Could anyone else get hold of it other than the occupants of the household?"

Charlotte Betham cupped her chin and gazed across the table. "Almost anyone who visited," she admitted. The door to the storeroom is off the passageway. It is the tradesmen's entrance, and all deliveries arrive there. The grocer and gardener come weekly, the coal merchant and sweep monthly, not to mention occasional visits from the rag and bone man. And the baker calls daily, except at the weekend."

"Then why did suspicion fall on Julia?"

"It didn't until the little boy died."

"Really? Bear with me a moment." Violet delved into her bag and retrieved the newspaper cutting, which she placed on the table. "It's getting very dog-eared," said Violet, nodding towards the paper. "Now, let's see. Ah, yes. According to Julia, Anna Nobbs told her that vitriol was good for cleaning utensils, but Anna denies this."

"She would," said Charlotte Betham.

"You don't believe her?"

"I would give more credence to her story had she told it before the police arrived. It was a little too convenient after the fact."

"When did they come?"

"A few days after the child died. They arrested Julia and asked to see her storage box."

"You mean a trunk of some kind?"

"Exactly that. Julia kept her soiled linen in it, amongst other things."

"I understand that there were acid stains on the dress which she wore on the day Freddy died."

"And no doubt you have also read that she would not give the police the key to her box."

"That's right. The article reports that she lost it."

"Julia did not lose it. She was too frightened to give it up after her arrest, knowing what they would find there. I knew where she kept the key and was quite prepared to keep that knowledge to myself, but Anna Nobbs intervened and told them where it was. But it was too late by then. They'd already broken the box."

"But you are married to a man of God. Why would you conceal such a thing?"

"Think about it, Miss Smith. Julia's son died from ingesting acid. She held the boy, tended to him and at one point, she fell on the floor in a faint. Of course, there was acid on her clothes. It would have been more suspicious had there not been."

Violet nodded. "You are right, of course. In their haste to arrest Julia, the police assumed that having acid on her clothes was evidence of guilt. But the reverse was true. May I presume from your comments that Julia and Anna didn't get on?"

"You may. And I will be explicit on the matter. Anna was jealous of Julia. Though the quieter of the two, Julia was naturally drawn to children. She played with them and indulged them and was kind and loving. As a mother, this pleased me, and I gave Julia one or two small items in appreciation. It appears that this did not sit well with Anna, who had been with me longer and felt that she deserved them better. Silly really, as most of the things that I gave Julia were intended for Frederick and would have been of no use to Anna."

"How do you know that Anna misled the police?"

"As I said, I am a good judge of character. Anna said she didn't mention using vitriol for cleaning, but she did. I heard her. She said it the day before the police arrived and must have known by then that they suspected poison. Julia repeated this, not in the context of having taken the bottle, but just to be helpful about why it might be missing. Do you see?"

"I do," said Violet. "Do you suspect Anna?"

"No. Anna couldn't have harmed Freddie, so what would be the point? In my opinion, she saw an opportunity to discredit Julia in front of me and took it."

"I've seen her, Mrs Betham. She has not admitted half of what you say nor has she much sympathy for Julia."

"Envy is a hard master to break from," said Charlotte Betham. "Anna Fisher, as she is now, is very sick. She is not long for this world, and it may be that if you approach her in the right way, she will be more forthcoming. If I were you, I would try it."

CHAPTER TWENTY-ONE

Back to Bury

Saturday, September 19, 1896

The short walk from Violet's cottage to 33 The Butter Market was usually a quick and pleasant stroll, but not today. Instead, Violet struggled against a blustery wind while trying to shield her face from the rain with a poorly functioning umbrella. From the moment she had woken in the early hours of the morning, the elements had worked against her. The wind had caught her latched bedroom window and flung it against the brick wall, waking her and necessitating an urgent check of the other windows, so they didn't suffer the same fate. Once awake, sleep was impossible. The wind whistled against the cottage walls, and her neighbour's garden gate incessantly banged as it slammed into the low garden wall. Violet gritted her teeth, wondering why they didn't go and close it and almost took action herself. Only the thought that the latch might have broken stopped her from putting on her coat and going downstairs. She'd risen at daybreak, knowing that any further rest was unlikely, and had decided to go to the office to marshal her thoughts. Lawrence had constructed a noticeboard while working on the Ripper case and it had been beneficial to them ever since. The solution to Freddy Brown's death seemed impossible to resolve with the information she had acquired, none of which seemed any different to that available at the time. But perhaps if she took the facts and rearranged them on the board, she might be able to see the case differently. It was a method that worked well for Lawrence, so why not try?

Violet left the house with an umbrella in one hand and her notebook in the other until she reached the corner of her road. Then, a sudden squall whipped the umbrella almost out of her hand, and she dropped her notebook, which landed in a puddle. Violet stopped, retrieved the soggy mess and battled her way until she reached The Butter Market, then lowered her umbrella and reached into her pocket for the door key.

As she approached the door, a movement through the window stopped her in her tracks, and she wondered whether Annie Hutchinson had come in early to clean. Violet wiped the rain from one of the small panes and peered inside. Her heart lurched as she saw Lawrence hunched over the desk with his head in his hands. His eyes were downcast, and the slump of his shoulders suggested abject misery. She stood staring for a moment, heart heavy with regret at what might have been. For all the unintentional anguish Lawrence had caused her, she still cared about him and wondered what had happened to cause this change in his demeanour.

Violet unlocked the door and walked in, greeted by the familiar jingle of the bell. Lawrence started. "What are you doing here?" he exclaimed.

"What am I doing here?" she countered. "I work here. You're supposed to be in London. When did you return?"

"Last night."

"Why?"

"I needed a desk and some peace to work on the case," said Lawrence, scratching his nose. "It's too difficult to concentrate with all the noise in the hotel."

Violet hung her coat on the stand and sat at her desk. "Nonsense," she said.

"Fine. Then you tell me why I'm here if you don't believe me."

Violet turned her chair to face him. He looked away, not meeting her gaze.

"What's wrong?"

"Nothing."

"Something is."

"Why does anything have to be wrong?"

"Because you're here."

"So?"

"Nothing stops you sleuthing in the middle of a case, Lawrence. Yet you've turned up in Bury out of the blue, walking away from your commitment to Flora. There must be a reason unless you've found a clue that leads you here."

"I haven't."

"No. I didn't think so. What is it? Have you come here to speak to Francis?"

"I haven't thought that far ahead. I wanted to get away from London, that is all."

"I see. Did you get anywhere with the Parker girl?"

"She was helpful enough. I'm not sure it has moved the investigation forward."

"Anything else?"

"I saw Richard Simms again yesterday. He told me about some other poisonings and suggested that I speak to the children's father."

"You're making progress then?"

"Some, I suppose." Lawrence picked up a pencil and chewed the end reflectively.

"Don't do that."

"It's mine."

"I use it though," said Violet.

Lawrence placed the pencil on the table, watching as it rolled slowly to the floor.

Violet sighed and leaned over to pick it up, but Lawrence was quicker. Their fingers connected as they both reached for the pencil at the same time, and a frisson of electricity passed between them.

"Oh, Violet, I don't know what to do." Lawrence grasped her hand and pulled her towards him.

She recoiled. "No, Lawrence. Don't."

He shook his head. "Sorry," he said. "How things have changed. Do I repulse you now?"

"No, but you're engaged to be married," said Violet.

"I know. I'm sorry."

"You should be. Anyway, as you're here, the quarter rent is due at Michaelmas, and there's not enough in the account. I don't know why."

"I borrowed some money," said Lawrence. "Don't worry. I'll put it back. It was easier to use our business account. But I don't know whether we should pay it at all."

"We must. Rent comes before any of our other obligations."

"It's not that. I don't know whether I'll still be here."

Lawrence chewed his lip, waiting for an outburst that never came.

Violet sat silently watching the scene outside.

"Say something."

"There's nothing to say. I wondered if you would move to Cheltenham, but as you never mentioned it, I assumed Loveday would come here."

"So did I."

"But she has other plans?"

Lawrence nodded.

"And that's why you're here. When was this decided?"

"She told me yesterday."

"Told you! She can't tell you where to live. It's a choice you make jointly. How could she have told you, anyway?"

"She's in London."

"Loveday is in London, and you are here?"

Lawrence nodded.

Violet stood up, walked to the fireplace and rolled a spill which she lit with a match.

"It's not cold enough for a fire."

"I need to dry my notebook," she said, peeling back the soggy pages. She ripped them out and placed them around the hearth together with the newspaper clipping.

"You won't be able to read them."

"They are perfectly legible," said Violet. "Just wet."

Pausing only to take a letter from the mantlepiece, Violet returned to her desk. She opened her drawer, removed a box of pins, and tore a large piece of paper into twelve equal pieces using the edge of a rule.

"How is your aunt?" asked Lawrence, searching for something to say.

"Still unwell, but she's rallied a little, thank goodness." Violet's eyes momentarily filled with tears.

"Good. I'm pleased," said Lawrence, expecting Violet to continue the conversation. Instead, she took a pen and began writing words and phrases on the slips of paper."

"I thought you'd have more to say," said Lawrence.

"About what?"

"Cheltenham."

"What about it?"

"For goodness' sake, Violet. This move affects you too. Do you care so little about the business?"

"I'm not the one who's leaving."

"Do you think I want to go?" Lawrence slammed his hand on the desk as he shouted at Violet. "I hate the idea of it. I don't want to leave Bury. It's my home."

"Then why are you telling me and not Loveday?" asked Violet.

"This is such a bloody mess." Lawrence stood and paced the room. "And I don't know what to do about it."

Violet watched him, trying to fight the urge to put her arms around him and tell him everything would work out. But he'd hurt her too much, and his infatuation with Loveday was too intense.

"You'll have to tell her," said Violet. "You can't start your marriage with a lie."

"She doesn't like Bury," said Lawrence. "She thinks it's too provincial."

"It's the same size as Cheltenham," said Violet.

"She won't come."

"What will you do?"

"I'll have to go there."

"And take the business?"

"We could both run it from separate locations."

"I don't want to. I spent too much time investigating alone while you were ill. Most of the appeal is in being able to share information. I will find another position."

"You've been so good to me," said Lawrence. "This isn't fair."

"Life isn't fair."

"I won't do it," exclaimed Lawrence. "There must be another way."
He picked up his jacket from the stand. "I need to get away from here
and do something. Have you finished your case yet?"

"No," said Violet. "I have one more person to see. I was going to
leave it until Monday, but we can go together now if you want. It might
be the last time."

#

Violet's second approach to Anna Fisher failed as soon as they arrived
at the cottage. It was bad enough that they'd travelled by cart after she'd
become accustomed to being driven. But her resulting stiff back was
nothing compared to the reception she'd received when the door
opened to reveal a rough-looking man, who Violet assumed was
Anna's husband.

"She's sick. Go away," he said, glowering at her through deep-set
eyes heavy with lack of sleep. He looked exhausted.

"Please. It will only take ten minutes?"

"No. I don't know who you are. Go away."

"I'm Violet Smith, and I only spoke to her a few days ago."

"I don't care who you are. You're not speaking to my wife. And
neither is he." George Fisher nodded angrily towards Lawrence before
slamming the door in their faces.

Violet sighed. "That's that then. We've come all this way for
nothing."

"We should wait," said Lawrence. "A man like that won't stay
inside all day."

"It's still wet," said Violet.

"Trust me," said Lawrence. "The chances are he will be working,
and if not, he'll leave at some point."

They walked a circuit of the village with Violet prepared for a long
wait, but as they drew closer to Anna's house, they saw George Fisher
walking towards them. He gazed at them with undisguised antipathy
but carried on walking in the direction of the village centre.

"You were right," said Violet.

Lawrence resisted the temptation to agree, choosing instead to
appreciate his time with Violet and enjoy the walk without
controversy. Presently, they arrived back at the cottage, and Violet

knocked at the door and waited. There was no reply, and she popped
her head through the door and called upstairs.

"Who is it?" asked Anna, and Violet announced herself, asking if
she would mind if Lawrence joined them.

Anna was in bed as she had been previously and was paler and
seemed thinner than before.

"Thank you for seeing me," said Violet.

"I heard you arrive," said Anna. "But George is in a bad temper
today, and there is no point in arguing with him."

"Does he treat you kindly?" asked Violet, concerned.

"Oh, very much so. You mustn't judge George by his short temper.
He is angry because I am ill, and he cannot make me better. If
anything, he cares for me too well."

"I'm glad," said Violet.

"Why are you here? And who is your friend?"

"Sorry. Where are my manners? This gentleman is Lawrence
Harpham. We work together. And I am here because I saw Mrs
Betham yesterday."

Anna's face fell. "Oh. You didn't say you were going there."

"I thought it would help to understand what happened."

"And do you understand?"

"No. You see, Mrs Betham tells the story differently."

"She would. She always preferred Julia."

"Yet Julia was only with her for a few weeks."

"I know. I'd been there for so much longer."

"How did that make you feel?"

Anna Fisher licked her lips and reached a feeble hand towards the
glass by her bedside. Lawrence noticed her struggle and filled it from
a nearby stone jug before passing it back over. Anna took a sip of water
and composed herself.

"I didn't feel good enough," she said simply. "Mrs Betham never
warmed towards me as she did towards Julia. I tried to work harder,
but she didn't notice."

"That must have made you resentful," said Violet.

"Not really." Anna was suddenly terse and defensive.

"Do you believe in God?" asked Lawrence.

"Of course."

"Then I'm sure you would want to put things right, while you still can."

"What things?"

"Why did you deny telling Julia that oil of vitriol was useful for cleaning kitchen utensils?"

Anna sighed. "It doesn't matter now and it didn't then."

"Of course it did," said Violet. "Frederick Brown was poisoned by sulphuric acid, and Julia was working in a household with access to a substance containing sulphuric acid. Now she may not have known what it was or why it was there. But if someone told her that it would be useful for cleaning, then she might have taken it for that purpose. Did you lie because you were trying to harm her, or were you actually trying to protect her?"

"Neither," said Anna. "I did lie. But it was because I was angry with her and I wanted to contradict her. It wouldn't have mattered what she said. I would have gone against her either way."

"Why were you angry with her?"

"I was still upset about the handkerchief and all the other presents."

"Most of them were for Freddy," said Violet.

"How do you know?"

"Charlotte Betham told me."

"Oh." Anna looked down at the counterpane and picked at the fabric. "I didn't know that."

"How was Julia in the days following the death of her child."

"Sorrowful," said Anna. "She cried all the time."

"Do you think she loved her son?"

"Yes, she did. She kept going over the day's events. On and on. At first, I thought it was from guilt, but her distress was so great that I knew it was genuine. She wasn't there at the moment Freddy died, and she regretted it. And she wished she hadn't given him the cakes in case they had made him poorly. But of course, they hadn't. The cakes were tested and found free of poison."

"What cakes?" asked Lawrence.

"Didn't I tell you?" asked Violet. "Julia met a woman on the road from Brettenham and purchased some cakes which she gave to the children when she arrived at her parents' house. It's a pity we don't know who sold them."

"I do," said Anna. "She mentioned it often enough. Julia bought the cakes from Deborah Lister. She still lives in Felsham, but it won't help. As I said, Mr Image tested the cakes, and there was nothing wrong with them."

"Still, I'd like to speak to her," said Violet. "If nothing else, it would be useful to know how Julia's mood was that day."

"I'm sorry I lied," said Anna. "I wasn't unkind to Julia when we lived together. I kissed her and wished her well after the inquest, and I told her that everything would get better. I was just a little jealous. I still feel it, even after all these years. Sometimes people make you feel inadequate. They don't mean to be hurtful, but even an unintentional slight can linger."

"I hope you feel better for telling us," said Violet. "It wasn't a big lie, and in the end, it didn't matter. But it's good to unburden yourself. Please don't feel bad." She reached over and took Anna's hand.

"Be off with you," said Anna, smiling. "George will be home soon, and he won't take kindly to you being here."

"Of course," said Violet, walking towards the bedroom door.

"Miss Smith?"

"Yes?"

"Tell Julia I have remembered her and hope she is well."

Lawrence and Violet left the house and located a carriage to return them to Bury. While they were in the cottage, the rain had stopped and their journey was pleasant. They chatted about the case while watching the sun climb high in the sky and shine over a verdant landscape.

"Can I take you to dinner?" asked Lawrence as they pulled up by The Butter Market.

Violet considered it for a moment, then agreed and they were discussing where to eat as they walked towards the office. They had almost arrived when they heard the parp of a horn and Francis pulled up beside them.

"You're back," he said, waving to Lawrence. "Are you here for long?"

"No. I'm going back tomorrow."

"Pity," said Francis. "We've found a school for Sidney. He starts on Monday."

"I need to be back in London by then."

"I'll take him, if it's not too far away," said Violet.

"Capital idea. It's in Clerkenwell. I'll drive if you like?"

"There's no need," said Violet. "I'll go down and back in a day."

"Well, come and eat with me tonight as a thank you."

"We were going out to dinner," said Lawrence.

"Don't do that. You can join me at Netherwood. Come on. Hop into the car. I'll drive you."

Lawrence looked at Violet. It would only take a single sign from her, and he would risk offending Francis and say no. But she looked relieved. "We'd both love to join you, Francis," she said.

CHAPTER TWENTY-TWO

London Calling

Sunday, September 20, 1896

Lawrence idly looked through the window as he relaxed into the seat. The clatter of the steam train and the familiar sound of a whistle had a soporific effect and he felt almost drugged as he watched the bucolic scenery slip by. It was early evening, and despite his disappointment at not spending time alone with Violet, Lawrence had enjoyed the previous evening at Netherwood. Francis was a marvellous host, full of bonhomie and generous to a fault with his wine cellar. His cook had rustled up a delicious three-course meal at little notice. After dinner, they went for a walk before returning for a hand of cards and a half-hearted attempt at charades. There were times in the evening when Lawrence almost felt the outsider, so close was the friendship between Violet and Francis. It seemed to have grown stronger the more they had been thrown together. Lawrence briefly wondered whether it could become something more, but Francis was always attentive to women. He had been the same with Catherine. Why he had never married was a mystery as Francis evidently enjoyed female company, yet still led the life of a confirmed bachelor.

Lawrence watched the sunset through bleary eyes, regretting his decision to return to the capital early. He wasn't looking forward to another lonely night in his hotel room, yet he did not dare risk travelling back on Monday in case there was a problem, and he didn't arrive on time. If that happened, Loveday would find out about his journey to Bury over the weekend, and she was unlikely to approve. Though she had a full diary, she would, no doubt, expect him to be available to her. Lawrence was confident that she would not have called on him but equally sure that being late on Monday would lead to trouble. And he was settled for the first time in a week. Lawrence was surprised at how much he had enjoyed his weekend in Bury – perhaps the thought of moving away had given him a greater appreciation for the town in which he lived.

As these thoughts flitted gently through his mind, he relaxed further into the seat and shoved his hands into his jacket pocket. They connected with a piece of paper which he pulled out and opened. It was the unaddressed letter he had found in Dora Hamblin's rented property when they had visited Silvertown, which he had dismissed at the time for its dull domestic news. Lawrence was almost alone in the carriage, except for one other man sitting a few seats away. Risking the wrath of the guard, he stretched his legs until they rested on the opposite seat and, having nothing better to do, he read the letter.

Dearest Mother

I hope this note finds you well. I am sorry it has taken so long to write, but I have been trying to decide what to do with myself since leaving the asylum. But I expect you don't know that I've gone. How could you? You'll still be in Edinburgh, no doubt. Were you going for five months or six? I bitterly regret losing my address book. I have no way of contacting you until you return to Dorking. If only father were still alive, or Maudie hadn't gone to Virginia. But I cannot think of anyone who will know Great Aunt Clara's address. You will think I do not care and to a certain extent, you will be right. I have been careless in my assumption that you will always be at home and available to me. I am tempted to go to Dorking and knock upon the neighbour's door.

But Mrs Harmon is elderly, and the chances are that she will not remember where you have gone, even if you told her. I wonder if you left a key with her? Perhaps I shall visit after all.

I have written my new address on the back of the envelope in which I intend to post this letter. I have taken lodgings in a house on the south side of the Thames. Do not scold me, but the only other occupant of the house is a man. There is nothing improper, I assure you. He is kindness itself. Actually, there is another occupant of the property – a great black cat with a ragged ear and a sweet temperament. I am happier here than in the nurse's accommodation at the asylum, but my meagre savings will not last many months, and I must find another way to keep myself.

It is a good four weeks since I began this missive, Mother. And in that time, I have become more intimately acquainted with my landlord. He prepares meals for me sometimes, and we walk together. He has suggested a way in which I could earn a good living without resorting to working in another asylum or waiting on tables, an occupation which I would have considered if there was no other. He says that he will help me in this regard and has been most solicitous and helpful. By the time you read this, I expect to be gainfully employed in this new venture.

Oh, Mother. Nothing is ever as it appears. Here I am another month on, and my plans are unravelling at the seams. I have received payment in advance for the services I perform and can meet my financial obligations. But something is wrong. Insidious comments and fleeting suggestions, so subtle that I am not sure whether they are real or imagined. And now this request to prove my devotion without revealing how. Living here seemed such a good idea, such a ready solution. But when I ask myself why I followed this route, I wonder about the motivation of the one who guides me which seems healthy in every way yet is perhaps too good to be true. What would you have to say on the subject? How I wish you were here to ask.

It has been four months and three days since our last conversation, Mother. Surely you must be nearing the end of your visit. I am in a real quandary, and I don't know which way to turn. I have left the room at the lodging house for another. The new place is not comfortably furnished, but the relocation is a wise move. Yesterday, I wrote to Mrs Harmon in desperation, giving the address of the corner shop for her reply. Today, I will finish this letter and post it to you at home in the hope that you will return within the next few weeks. I cannot leave London for reasons which will become clear when we finally meet. But you could come here, couldn't you, dear? I wish you would. I have lost the envelope intended for this letter and must go and find another. I will close now and post it on my return...

Lawrence turned to the back of the second sheet expecting the letter to continue, but it did not and had been left unfinished. The writer probably died of boredom he thought as he folded the letter and returned it to his pocket; a dull letter detailing an ill-advised romance. The young lady's mother would, no doubt, have something to say about it when they finally met, her words probably loaded with disapproval. As the train slowed and they approached a platform on the north side of London, Lawrence considered the letter again and wondered whether it had been penned by Dora Hamblin or Dorothy Jones, assuming they were the same person. He had somehow imagined her to be older, colder and less hysterical. The letter did not fit the character of a woman who had cruelly stolen a child from his mother. No. A previous occupant of the house must have written it. After all, it was a rented property. Any number of tenants could have lived there. Lawrence withdrew the letter, scrunched it into a ball and tossed it under the seat. But something gave him pause – a small voice niggling at the back of his mind. Lawrence sighed, stooped to retrieve it and returned it to his pocket. He was still mulling over the character of the child stealer when his train arrived at Liverpool Street station.

CHAPTER TWENTY-THREE

A Tricky Conversation

Monday, September 21, 1896

Lawrence paced the hallway of the Goodhalls' townhouse in Cadogan Gardens waiting for Loveday with trepidation. On the one hand, he was looking forward to seeing her but on the other, he dreaded the conversation that must take place on the journey to the railway station. He checked his watch for the third time and fumbled as he returned it to his pocket. The timepiece clattered as it struck the tiled floor. The Goodhalls' butler raised a greying eyebrow as he regarded Lawrence from emotionless eyes.

"Does sir need assistance?" he asked, superciliously.

"No, sir does not," said Lawrence stooping to retrieve the object, a red flush covering his face and neck. The watch had fallen open, and the silver cover had splayed against the hinge. Lawrence tried to snap it tight, but it was misaligned.

"Damn it," he said aloud.

The faintest tic appeared around the butler's mouth, just noticeable enough to present as a sneer.

In total, Loveday had kept him waiting for twenty-four minutes, each one of which was more excruciatingly painful than the last. He wanted, no needed, to get this conversation out of the way before his inaction decided the matter for him. Finally, he heard a noise at the top of the stairs and Loveday glided down wearing a lavender day dress. As usual, she looked faultless. She flashed him a smile as she tossed back her blonde curls, and he remembered how lucky he was that such a beautiful and accomplished young woman was interested in him.

"Ah, Lawrence, you're here," she said, blowing him a kiss. "Excellent. The Goodhalls sent my bags to the station this morning. I would like to call into a little shop in Knightsbridge for my mother. I'll have the carriage stop there."

"Why don't we walk?" asked Lawrence.

"Whatever for?"

"It will give us more time to talk."

"What about Mother's errand?"

"We can do both, can't we?"

"I suppose so. Stay here a moment. Sally's in the garden, and I must say goodbye." Loveday swished through the rear hallway and disappeared.

Lawrence couldn't face another moment in the presence of the butler. "I'll wait outside," he said gruffly. "Please tell Loveday where I am."

"As you wish, sir." The butler walked towards the front door, but Lawrence arrived first and let himself out, heaving a sigh of relief as he loitered on the pavement. The air was fresh and crisp, and the day set fair, though low black clouds held the threat of showers. Even so, he would rather be outside than in.

Despite his occupation, Lawrence's family background was like Loveday's, their status equal. Yet she flitted in and out of a much higher social set with ease and was obviously comfortable within it. It was also becoming increasingly clear that she aspired to it. Though Lawrence's newfound wealth allowed him some nods to luxury, not previously available, the idea of joining these social circles horrified him. All butlers should be like Albert Floss, he thought, unpretentious and useful without airs of their own.

190

"I'm back," said Loveday, as she breezed through the door and linked arms with Lawrence. "They are so sad to see me go and said I should return next month. You can come too," she continued as they left the property.

"I don't know what I'll be doing yet," said Lawrence, appalled at the idea.

"You can spare a few days."

"Not if I'm working on a case."

"Well, you won't be, will you? You don't need to work now."

"We need to talk about that."

"Ah, there it is." Loveday pointed to a smartly dressed shop, with a large window in which pedestals containing small items of decorative houseware had been positioned for maximum exposure. "Come and help me choose."

Lawrence joined Loveday, but after ten minutes of viewing overpriced and artless gilded statuettes, he gave up and went outside. By the time Loveday reappeared carrying several packages, his impatience was boiling into anger.

"Have you finished?" he asked curtly.

"It depends. Let's walk along here," said Loveday, pointing to another row of shops. "Symonds is nearby."

"No," said Lawrence firmly. "We are going to talk now and without the distraction of the shops. Follow me."

He took her hand and guided her across the road and through the gates of Hyde Park.

"Must we?" asked Loveday, wrinkling her nose at a steaming pile of horse manure. "I'd rather not."

"Well, you're going to. Come and sit down."

"Not near the horses."

"Over here then." Lawrence pointed to a gazebo in the distance.

Loveday sighed but didn't argue and followed him to the covered seats.

"What is it?" she asked.

"I'm not moving to Cheltenham," he said, with a finality that surprised him. "It's not happening, Loveday. If you want to be my wife, you will move to Suffolk."

She stared at him, aghast.

"No," she said. "Why would I do that? All my friends are in Cheltenham."

"And my friends are in Bury."

"You have friends in Gloucestershire."

"I know. But my business and my home are elsewhere."

"You don't need to work."

"But I want to. I like it."

"I don't understand. You can't prefer Suffolk to Gloucestershire. Nobody could."

"Well, I do, and you will learn to love it as much as I do."

Loveday snorted. "I won't because I'm not going."

"Now, that's silly. Just think about it. We will buy a nice house anywhere you like. You can have a servant, and you can attend the local balls and make lots of new friends."

"Friends? In Bury? Like that ageing former companion, you employ? I don't need friends like her."

"I hope you're not talking about Violet."

"Who else?"

"That's a horrible thing to say, and quite beneath you."

"She's an old witch, Lawrence, and she's wrapped you around her finger, though why I can't imagine. Violet is plain and boring, and you should release her from your employ so she can go off and live in obscurity somewhere like the silly old spinster she is."

"Violet is not in my employ," said Lawrence quietly. "We are partners. I gifted her half of the business, and she earned every penny of it."

"How? By scratching around doing a few menial tasks for you while you take on the lion's share of the work?"

Lawrence shook his head as he watched Loveday. Her beautiful, delicate features were twisted into a hostile glare, her naked dislike of Violet etched across her face.

"You really don't know me," said Lawrence regarding her with sadness. "You weren't around when I was injured and unable to work for two years."

"That old story again," said Loveday. "I know. You were in the hospital and she did some investigating alone. It's not as if she had anything better to do. Like get a husband or make some friends."

192

"She didn't just keep my business alive. She kept me alive, Loveday. She buoyed up my spirits when the world was too dark to bear. I owe her everything."

"Then perhaps you should marry her," said Loveday, laughing at the suggestion.

"It hurts me when you talk about her like that," said Lawrence. "It's not nice to see the woman you..." His voice trailed away as he tried and failed to say the word, love.

"Don't let's argue," said Loveday, "not about her. We have a future to plan, and I want to suggest a compromise."

"Yes?"

"You do not want to live in Gloucestershire."

"Correct."

"And I am not willing to come to Suffolk, so there is only one sensible solution."

"I'm all ears," said Lawrence, waiting for the worst. When Loveday's proposition came, her suggestion was even grimmer than he'd expected.

"We should move to London," she said excitedly. "We can live in Chelsea, or Knightsbridge, perhaps. Somewhere central, anyway. And you can carry on with your occupation if you must. See? How clever am I?"

CHAPTER TWENTY-FOUR

The Cocklins

Lawrence was still reeling from the shock of Loveday's suggestion when he made his way back to Silvertown to seek the parents of the poisoned girls, mentioned by Richard Simms. He'd left Paddington station and walked without thinking to Isabel Smith's offices at the municipal buildings. Isabel had been available, and although he suspected that she must be getting fed up with his visits, she had greeted him amiably and offered him a glass of water.

"What can I do for you this time?" she asked, with a twinkle in her eye.

"The usual," said Lawrence, "if that's still appropriate?"

"Where are you going?"

"Back to Silvertown. A different address this time." Lawrence consulted his notebook. "Martindale Road," he continued, "number sixty-two."

"And why are you going there?"

"To speak to the parents of Norah and Lavinia Cocklin."

"I see." Isabel steepled her fingers and frowned. "Henry Cocklin, their father, took the deaths of his girls very badly. The poor man was devasted and blamed himself for their loss."

"Many fathers do," said Lawrence, bitterly.

"There was nothing he could have done. He was as blameless as any other man who loses a child through no fault of their own," said Isabel, looking straight at Lawrence.

"Nevertheless, he will always feel responsible," he said.

"Then be gentle with him and don't be surprised if he is reluctant to talk."

"I will," said Lawrence. "Does my visit qualify for a driver?"

Isabel nodded. "Of course, but please continue to share any concerns you may have, and don't do anything to upset Sergeant Simms."

"I'm seeing the Cocklins with his blessing," said Lawrence. "Henry Cocklin was never interviewed. The police didn't deem it necessary."

"Really? I doubt he can tell you much, but best not to leave any stone unturned."

"Exactly," said Lawrence. "I don't expect much from it, but there's very little else for me to investigate."

"Good day, Mr Harpham." Isabel offered her hand, and Lawrence shook it gratefully. Her willingness to assist him with his transport needs had made what could have been a series of laborious trips, much more manageable. And he liked her. She was pleasant company. He left the office whistling and went outside to the coachman's hut where he found Jennings reading a book.

"Sorry to disturb you," said Lawrence catching the coachman by surprise. He slammed his book shut and stood to his feet.

"I didn't hear you, sir," said Jennings. "You'll be wanting a ride, I suppose?"

The journey to Silvertown was becoming depressingly familiar, and the sounds and smells of the East End began to jar. Lawrence tried to imagine what it must be like to live near the clamour of the docks with the constant smell of India rubber mingled with sugar and chemicals from the nearby factories. The smell and the noise, the hustle and bustle, a visible daily grind of people living in boxes and working for pennies made him bone-weary and heartsick. Lawrence was thankful for his privileged background, and the opportunities life had given him. For all his faults, he was grateful that he had never endured the deprivations of poverty, though his gratitude wavered when under the pall of the black dog.

His spirits fell further still when he pulled up outside Martindale Road, a decrepit terrace of poorly built, unimaginably small, red brick houses set close to the roadside. The windows were tiny, and as Lawrence approached the entrance to number sixty-two, he noticed that the bricks were crumbling around the arch above the door. He rapped the door knocker, feeling an overwhelming depression at the squalid conditions and the malodourous fug that enveloped the homes and was surprised when the door opened to reveal a young woman with a pleasant smile. "What can I do for you, sir," she asked in a lilting Irish accent.

Lawrence tipped his hat. "I'd like to speak to Mr Cocklin if he's about."

"You're in luck," she said. "He's out the back. There was no work for him at the dock today."

Lawrence sighed as the girl retreated, knowing that a man sent away from his workplace was unlikely to be in a good mood.

Sure enough, when Henry Cocklin appeared, he wore the weary expression of a man who was wondering how to feed his family with no money to buy food.

"What do you want?" His Irish accent was thicker than the girl's, but with enough of the East End to suggest that he had lived in London for a long time.

Lawrence offered a hand. For a moment he thought the man would refuse him, but he grasped it with a half-hearted, insipid shake. "My name is Lawrence Harpham. Sergeant Simms gave me your address."

"Did he now?" said Henry Cocklin. "You'll want to talk about my girls then?"

Lawrence nodded. "If it's not too painful."

"Of course it's bloody painful." Cocklin slid a stone away from the doorstep with a patched boot. It ricocheted against a pail and clattered across the street.

"I know how you feel." The minute he said the words aloud, Lawrence regretted it.

"I doubt it." The Irish man's reaction was more measured than the careless words warranted.

"I mean it. I lost my daughter in a fire."

"How old was she?"

"Three."

196

"Lavinia was three. Norah was eight. Bonny girls the pair of them. Wasted."

Cocklin shook his head, bitterly.

"I'd like to tell you it gets easier, but it never does."

"What do you want to know?"

"I'm looking into the poisonings," said Lawrence.

"I thought that was Simms' job?"

"It is. I'm a private detective. I'm looking for a missing child."

"And you think it's got something to do with this?"

Lawrence shook his head. "I don't know," he said, honestly. "There are certain parallels, and one or two clues, nothing definite, but enough that I need to check and be sure. There's very little for me to go on, and I'm almost at the end of the road."

"And you'll give up?"

"I'll have no choice."

"I'll help if I can. Come through."

He led Lawrence down a narrow passage and through the rear door. The house was so small that no sooner was Lawrence in it than he was outside again. At the back of the house was a walled yard, with a scrubby patch of garden. Two packing crates had been placed side by side in the centre.

"Sit down," said Henry Cochlin, offering Lawrence a pouch of tobacco.

"No, thank you."

"Mind if I do?" asked Cochlin, more as a matter of fact than a question.

"Feel free."

"What do you need?"

"Your girls…"

"Lavinia and Norah."

"Quite. Did they tell you anything about what happened that day, or were they too sick by the time they got home?"

"They told me enough to send me running for the doctor. He prescribed emetics, but it was already too late. They died the same night."

"I'm sorry."

"I dare say. It won't bring my girls back."

"I know. What did they tell you?"

"It was that girl, Alice," said Henry Cocklin. "Alice Shaw. She saw a piece of cake on the road and pointed it out to my Norah who picked it up and offered her some. Alice saw bits of red stuff in the cake and refused."

"Did Norah tell you this?"

Cocklin nodded. "Anyway, Norah ate some and gave a piece to Lavinia. They finished it between them. Silly girls. How many times has their mother told them not to pick things off the road? I shouldn't have lost my temper. Not when she was so poorly. It was probably the last thing she heard me say."

"Said what? To whom?"

"Norah, of course."

"What did you say?"

"I told her off, told her how reckless she had been giving cake picked from the road to her little sister."

"It's a natural thing to say."

"She didn't think so. It hurt her feelings. She said that it would be fine to eat the cake because the man had told Alice where to find it."

"Which man?"

"I don't know. Norah died before she could tell me, so I spoke to Alice, and she wouldn't say much at first. Thought I was blaming her for my girls' deaths, but it wasn't her fault. She was only eight herself and the only one with enough sense not to eat the stuff."

"What did she say?"

"She backed up Norah's story. A man she had never met before told her that he knew where she could find some cake and she should share it with her friends."

"What did he look like?"

"Ordinary," said Cocklin. "She said his clothes were black, and he wore a black hat, that's all."

"That's not all," said Lawrence. "It's not much of a description, but it's exactly the same one as that of the man who poisoned Joseph Yeo."

CHAPTER TWENTY-FIVE

The Bird Has Flown

Tuesday, September 22, 1896

Lawrence woke to the sound of someone knocking at his door. It took a few moments for him to remember that he'd asked for an alarm call and a further few seconds to remember why.

"Are you awake, sir," called a voice from the corridor.

"Yes, thank you," said Lawrence rubbing his eyes as he remembered the telegram that had been waiting for him when he'd returned from the Cocklin house. Lawrence had come to dread the sight of telegrams, which all too often contained bad news. He'd opened it with trepidation, but the information inside was pleasing. Sidney Huntingdon was to start school on the morrow and Violet would be bringing him. Perhaps they could enjoy that quiet dinner together, after all.

Lawrence whistled as he dressed, looking forward to the day ahead. He slid on his freshly pressed trousers and collected his shoes from the hallway where he'd placed them the night before to find they had been shined to mirror-like perfection.

He arrived in the hotel restaurant, pleased that for once he was the only guest present. He checked his watch and realised to his satisfaction, that far from being late, he was so early that breakfast was only just available. Service was swift, the waiter pleasant, and the food was piping hot. Lawrence made a mental note to adjust his timekeeping for the rest of his stay.

After a delightful repast of kedgeree followed by toast and jam, Lawrence sauntered across the Thames to Goswell Street and waited for Violet outside the Merchant Taylors' School. He had purchased a newspaper en route and stood happily reading at the front of the school, quite oblivious to the passers-by until Sidney pulled down the top of the paper and announced his presence with a 'boo'.

Lawrence jumped theatrically, leaving the boy in peals of laughter as he looked ahead for Violet. He saw her in the distance and to his immense disappointment, realised that she was walking with Michael. She waved and smiled, and Michael nodded as they made their way towards him.

"Sorry we're late," said Violet breathlessly. "We called in to see Ann. She'll be along shortly. You might meet her if you stay long enough."

"How long are you here for?" asked Lawrence.

"Just today," said Michael.

"Can't you stay longer?" Lawrence addressed the question to Violet, but Michael answered.

"No. I must be back in the parish tonight, and Violet will travel with me."

"That's a shame. I'd hoped we could dine together."

"Sorry," said Michael coldly.

"Can we go in?" asked Sidney.

Michael checked his watch. "I don't see why not," he said, ruffling the boy's hair. "Our appointment is in fifteen minutes. Hopefully, your mother will be here by then."

"Let's go," said Sidney tugging his hand, before turning to Lawrence. "Are you coming too?"

"Three's a crowd, young man," said Lawrence.

"Four," said Sidney. "Mummy's joining us."

"I'll wait outside," said Violet.

"No need," said Michael. "I'll take Sidney. Why don't you two go off and talk about your case? I've got a meeting with Canon Blessop, anyway. I'll collect you from the hotel later, Violet."

"Thank you," said Violet. "I'll say goodbye, Sidney. This is for you." She handed him a square package wrapped in brown paper.

"Ooh." The boy's eyes widened. "What is it?"

"It's a surprise," said Violet. "Open it later."

"Thank you." Sidney smiled and held out his hand.

"I'll miss you," said Violet.

"I'll write."

"Make sure you do." She smiled and waited while Lawrence offered his hand and said goodbye.

"He's a well-mannered little chap," said Lawrence when they were out of earshot. "A strange choice of school, though."

"Why?"

"Well, with all that money, I thought Huntingdon would have sent him to Eton."

"Merchant Taylors' is a day school," said Violet. "It's ideal. Ann has decided she'll stay in London. Besides, Eton would be the first place her husband would look for the boy. He won't easily find him here."

"But will he get a good education?"

"Of course. It's an excellent school. Sidney will learn mathematics and the classics, of course, not to mention all the sporting activities available. He will be happy here, and by the time Gordon finds him, if he bothers to look, Sidney will be established, and the headmaster might be able to influence him to make the right decision for his son."

"Good. Well, I'm glad his future is settled. Sidney is a nice young man."

"I agree. How are you getting on with the case?"

"I'm making slow progress. Would you like something to eat? We can talk about it inside."

"I'm not hungry. A coffee, perhaps?"

"We could go somewhere nice. I'll take you to Harrods or Fortnum's?"

"Don't be silly. A nice tea shop will do perfectly well."

They walked towards Clerkenwell, searching for a suitable venue when a waft of something baking caught their attention.

"How about there?" Lawrence nodded towards a busy cafe, and they peered through the window. Only one of the gingham covered tables was available.

"It looks popular," said Violet.

"Good."

They entered, and a friendly waitress showed them to a table in the corner. "What's that wonderful smell?" Violet asked.

"Chicken pie," said the waitress. "Proper good it is too, miss."

Violet and Lawrence exchanged glances.

"I thought you said you weren't hungry," said Lawrence.

"I know, but shall we?"

"Two pies and two coffees," said Lawrence.

"Right you are, sir. Be with you in two shakes of a lamb's tail."

"This is very naughty. It's only just after ten o'clock."

"Who will ever know?" smiled Lawrence. "Now, back to the case."

He told Violet about the visit to the Cocklins and the man in black.

When he'd finished, she looked up with a concerned expression on her face. "That was an important visit," she said.

"I know. These poisonings are quite deliberate. But I still don't know if it has anything to do with Bertie's disappearance."

"Neither do I, but you must tell Sergeant Simms."

"I will," said Lawrence. "But I'm going to tell Isabel first."

"Isabel?"

"Your namesake, Isabel Smith. She's been very accommodating, and I promised to keep her informed. Without her, I wouldn't have got this far. But you're right. I will have to tell Simms. There are no more clues, and I have nowhere else to turn."

"Here you are," said the waitress, balancing a large tray on her arm. "Pies and coffees." She beamed as she placed the steaming plates in front of them.

"My goodness. Look at the size of it. I was expecting a slice, not a whole pie," said Violet.

"Don't waste it."

"I won't." Violet picked up her cutlery and cut into her pie with relish. "It's delicious," she said, licking her lips.

They ate quietly for a few moments, then Lawrence put his fork down. "How about your investigation?" he asked.

"I haven't done anything since we visited Anna Fisher, though I really must track down Deborah Lister," said Violet. "I've been helping to get Sidney ready for school and not hearing from my aunt this week has been an unwelcome distraction. I didn't want to make a half-hearted visit to Deborah."

"It can't be more than a week since your aunt's last letter."

"It feels like longer. I do worry so."

"I'm sure she's well," said Lawrence. "Try not to think of it."

Violet bit her lip. "I know. But there are so many bad people around. Your poisoner, that dreadful Dyer woman. Wicked people."

"The baby farmer? She's dead, Violet. And she wouldn't have harmed your aunt anyway."

"I know that. I don't want to talk about it." Violet put her cutlery down and pushed her plate away.

"Don't leave it," said Lawrence. "You were enjoying that."

"You can't just abandon Bertie," said Violet, changing the subject.

"I don't want to, but I've run out of ideas."

"You've checked everything?"

"Yes."

"I suppose we'll have to break the bad news then. Poor Flora. She'll be heartbroken."

"I'll tell her tomorrow after I've seen Isabel and Richard Simms."

"Flora's not in Battersea."

"Where is she?"

"Staying with friends in Poplar. I'll write down the address."

Violet reached inside her bag. "Oh dear. I've left my notebook in Suffolk. Have you got a piece of paper? I can just about remember the address."

"I haven't got mine either," said Lawrence ruefully, patting his inner pocket. He slid his hands inside his coat. "Use this," he said, thrusting a folded sheet of paper towards her.

Violet opened it, and turned it over to write on the reverse, then looked again. "What's this?" she asked.

"Only that letter we found in Albert Road."

"How interesting." Violet placed the letter on the table, picked up her fork and absent-mindedly resumed her attack on the pie as she read.

"It's not in the least bit interesting," said Lawrence, "just another failed love affair."

"Yes, but if Dora Hamblin wrote the letter, then it's relevant."

"I doubt she did. Any tenant could have written it."

"But suppose for one moment that it was her."

"Yes?"

"She mentions a corner shop."

"So?"

"The nearest corner shop to Albert Road belongs to Louisa Tullis."

"I know."

"She could have had an account there."

"I see what you're getting at."

"Exactly. There might be a forwarding address."

"We should go there now," said Lawrence, finishing the last mouthful of pie.

"Have we got the time?"

"If I prevail on Isabel's kindness again."

"Then I'll join you. Anything to keep Flora's hopes alive."

#

Valentine Jennings was taking a rare day off, but thanks to the continued generosity of Isabel Smith, they were offered the services of another driver who returned them to Silvertown and dropped them with a cheerful wave and a promise to wait.

"Isabel is very taken with you," said Violet.

"I'm not surprised. It's my charming personality, no doubt."

"Most amusing. I mean she's very dedicated and clearly wants you to succeed in finding Bertie. But it's more than that. She genuinely thinks you have a real chance of tracking him down."

"I wish I had her confidence," said Lawrence. "It seems an impossible task."

"We need some luck," said Violet. "Let's see what Louisa Tullis says." She gestured towards the door of the corner shop, which was standing ajar. As they walked towards it, they heard peals of laughter from inside.

They entered to find Louisa Tullis and another woman sitting on a stool behind the counter. The two women nursed cups of tea and were whiling away the time between customers by catching up on the week's events. Louisa stood as she saw them. "Don't I know you?" she asked.

"We called by a few days ago," said Lawrence, "to ask about the poisoned rat cake."

Louisa's smile slid away. "Oh, yes. I remember. He's the chap I told you about, Nance," she said, turning towards her companion.

"Those poor children," said Nance. "What a thing to happen. And now Edith Beard has died. I know her mother, did I tell you? When I say I know her, I mean I met her at Norma Carter's house a couple of times."

"Well, I never."

"It's true."

"And Norma's the woman whose husband set the smithy alight."

"Harold Carter? Spiteful."

"Very spiteful. All that mess and a man nearly died, just because Mr Allen was a better blacksmith and took all Carter's customers away.

Lawrence coughed. "Were you here the day the rat cake went missing?" he asked.

"You've got a good memory," said Louisa. "Yes, she was here."

"But you didn't see anyone take it?" said Lawrence turning pointedly to Nance.

"No. I was in and out dealing with my brother. Perhaps he saw something while I went to fetch the key."

"And you don't know who else was in the shop."

Nance pursed her lips. "Yes. Sheba Collins was poking around with one of her sisters."

"Sheba? That's an unusual name," said Lawrence.

Nance scowled. "People should be more careful choosing names for their children. They're stuck with it for a lifetime. And don't laugh at it," she continued wagging her finger at Lawrence who was smiling broadly.

Louisa shook her head and put her finger to her lips, indicating to Nance to stop talking, but it was too late. Nance continued angrily. "It's not a laughing matter – parents giving girls boys names and boys girls names and stupid flower names. I've heard it all. Why would anybody want to call their child after a place or a season or a dog? It shouldn't be allowed."

Louisa patted Nance on the hand. "Why don't you go and make another tea, dear," she said.

Nance grabbed the cups in one hand, carelessly clattering the china together as she left.

"She's a bit touchy about names," said Louisa, by way of explanation.

"Hers must be awful given that reaction," said Lawrence, tactlessly.

"It's really not that bad. I don't know why she gets so worked up about it. But then my aunt Gladys couldn't abide the colour green and we couldn't go near her if we were wearing it. There's no accounting for folk. Anyway, that's not why you're here. What do you want from me?"

"We're looking for someone," said Violet. "She might go by the name of Dorothy Jones or Dora Hamblin."

Louisa shook her head. "I don't know that name."

"She lived at a hundred and seven Albert Road."

"That sounds familiar. Let me check." Louisa returned to the rear of the counter and withdrew a tattered ledger from a cupboard below. "You've got the name wrong. It's Jane Venables," said Louisa. "I remember now. Nice, quiet young woman."

"Just as I thought," said Lawrence, turning to Violet. "It was one of the other tenants. I'm not surprised."

"What did she look like?" asked Violet.

"Youngish – in her late twenties or early thirties," said Louisa. "Dark hair, a thin face, and she always looked as if she carried the weight of the world on her shoulders."

"Did she come here regularly?"

"A few times a week. She bought odds and ends of food, bits for the children, you know."

"Children?" Lawrence's interest was immediately reignited.

"Yes."

"Two?"

"There were two the first few times I saw her. Then only the baby."

"Boy or girl?"

"I don't know. I didn't pay that much attention. It was in a perambulator."

"And the older child?"

"I'm sorry. I really don't know."

"Did she have a tab?" asked Violet.

"No. She always paid by cash. I only give credit to locals," said Louisa. "I didn't know her that well."

"Then why is her name in your ledger?"

"Because she said she was leaving and asked me to give her forwarding address if a woman asked for it. But on no account must I give it to a man."

Lawrence and Violet exchanged glances.

"And did you?" asked Lawrence.

"Yes. I gave it to her mother."

#

"Don't get too excited," said Lawrence, striding towards the cab. "It could be another red herring. We don't know if Jane Venables is another alias or a different person altogether."

"It's her," said Violet.

"You seem very certain?"

"It feels right."

"You would have scolded me for saying that a few years ago."

"I've learned from you as you have from me. It's called a partnership."

"Can we go back through Poplar?" Lawrence wrenched open the door of the carriage and offered his hand to Violet.

"I've no objection. It's on the way, sir," said the cab driver.

"Number forty-seven High Street," said Lawrence.

"Very good, sir."

"You're quiet," said Violet five minutes into the journey. It had started to rain, and Lawrence was staring from the window and picking a splinter of wood from the door frame.

"I'm trying to remember what Garrad Bailey told me about the children."

"Who?"

"You were in Suffolk when I went to see him. He's the landlord at Gideon Road. A nice chap. That's where Bertie went missing. He said there was an older child, but I don't think he said whether it was a boy or a girl."

"I hope we find him, Lawrence." Violet's eyes suddenly filled with tears. "Poor little chap. I can't bear to think of him alone out there."

Lawrence took her hand. For a moment she let it linger, then pulled it away.

"I'm not going to Cheltenham," said Lawrence, suddenly.

"Oh good."

"It's not good. Loveday wants to live in London."

Violet sighed. "You must do what you think is right."

"What do you think?"

"It doesn't matter what I think."

"The right word from you..." Lawrence left the sentence unfinished.

"You must decide, Lawrence. You and you alone."

"I've made a commitment, given my word. You may think badly of me, but how could I go back on my promise? What sort of man would that make me?"

"Do you love her?"

"I admire her."

"Do you love her?"

Lawrence opened his mouth to speak, then closed it.

"Did you love Catherine."

"With my heart and soul."

"Then you've answered your question."

Neither uttered another word until the carriage drew up near a multi-paned window on Poplar High Street. Further down the road, small pockets of people were going about their business, but the terrace of red brick properties to the side was strangely deserted.

"Look," said Lawrence pointing to a card inside one of the lower panes of what appeared to be a haberdashery.

"If that's forty-five, the house we want must be here," said Violet walking towards the next-door property. Like the rest of the terrace, the house was three floors high and with large sash windows overlooking the street.

"We won't be long," said Lawrence, waving at the cab driver as he knocked on the door.

#

The large, red-faced woman who opened the door to Lawrence and Violet was nowhere near as jolly as her appearance suggested.

"Yes?" she barked curtly.

"We're looking for Jane Venables," said Lawrence, reading from the note he'd scribbled earlier.

"Well, you've come to the right place, but she isn't in. She's gone, and I don't know if she's coming back. Thoughtless baggage."

"When did she leave?"

"Yesterday afternoon. She said she was going for a walk and I haven't seen her since."

"Perhaps she met a friend."

"Well, if she did, she shouldn't have promised to watch Billy for me. It's just plain inconsiderate."

"Billy?"

"My baby. I would have left him for a few hours if he'd been asleep, but he was wide awake and screaming, and that's an evening's earnings wasted because of her. I'm glad she's gone. I could have let the rooms to someone else if she hadn't left her bags behind. They'll be going in the furnace tomorrow."

"She's left her bags?" echoed Lawrence.

"That's what I said."

"Can we see them?"

"No. You can mind your own business. Who are you anyway?"

"We're looking for a room," said Violet.

"Not here," said the woman, closing the door. "There'll be no funny business in my house."

"Not both of us," said Violet, putting her foot in the door. "Just me. Mr Harpham is helping."

"Can you pay?"

"Yes," said Violet. "I'm willing to pay eight weeks in advance for the right place. I work in Poplar, and a room in the High Street is ideal."

The woman smiled, and her eyes lit up. "Come in, my dear," she said. "And you," she continued, nodding at Lawrence. "Up there, on the left. It's not locked."

"Well done," said Lawrence, admiringly when they were safely inside.

"We wouldn't have got in any other way," said Violet.

"You'll have to take the room now."

Violet ignored him, walked towards the shabby wardrobe and pulled it open. Inside, were two pairs of shoes, a coat and a dress. She picked up the shoes and examined them."

"I don't know what you think you'll find," said Lawrence. "Are you looking for a name tag?"

"Don't be silly. But I would like to know why they're two different sizes."

"Two different makers?" Lawrence suggested.

Violet shook her head. "No. There's a difference of at least two shoe sizes."

She returned the shoes to the wardrobe and opened the chest of drawers to the side. "I thought so," she said, removing two petticoats which she laid on the bed. "Look."

"They're petticoats," said Lawrence.

"Obviously, but look closely."

"Sorry, but they look the same to me."

"They're different sizes," said Violet, snatching the garments and replacing them in the drawer. "These clothes belong to two different women."

"Perhaps she's been wearing a disguise."

"Hardly. She'd look ridiculous wearing the wrong sized clothes. Have a look around."

Violet continued her search of the wardrobe and dresser while Lawrence examined the nightstand. Neither found anything of note.

"There's a case under the bed," said Lawrence, pulling it out. He coughed as a trail of dust followed behind. "Damn. It's empty," he continued as he looked inside. "Hello, there's a pocket on the outside." Lawrence inserted his hand and rummaged, blindly.

"Ah-ha! What's this?" He pulled out a handful of paper.

Violet peered over his shoulder. "Oh. A letter from her mother," she said, reading the closing signature.

"The letter is addressed to Dorothy," said Lawrence.

"So it is. Then we are on the right track." Violet eyes sparkled with renewed interest.

"It says she's on her way to London," said Lawrence, scanning the sheet. "Mrs Harmon has given Dorothy's mother the letter, and she's coming to find her. What's this?" he continued, turning to the final page. It was written in a different hand and was not part of the letter.

"It's an address," said Violet, needlessly. "Muller Homes, Ashley Downs, Bristol. That must be where they've gone."

"But what an odd address," said Lawrence. "It sounds more like an institution than a residence."

"I have never heard of it."

"Nor have I. Right. Is there anything else to look at?" asked Lawrence, sliding the letter into his breast pocket.

"No. We've checked everywhere."

Lawrence opened the door of the room and listened.

"All clear," he said.

"She'll see us."

"Not if you're quick."

They tiptoed down the stairs and stole a glance towards the open parlour where the landlady was comforting a crying baby on her shoulder.

"Excellent timing," said Lawrence, unlatching the door and walking silently into the street.

CHAPTER TWENTY-SIX

Pest Control

These days I use traps to stop the rats. I ceased laying rat cake after Dante died – too much risk to other felines. But there is more than one way to get rid of pests, Morty Eagles will tell you that.

Morty is an old work friend of mine. He lives on a farm in Beckenham where I visit him occasionally. Morty keeps a terrier for rat catching. A mangy cur with half an ear missing, but a good, solid animal that shakes his prey senseless, then bites their throats out leaving piles of corpses in the barn for the cats to feast on – a fitting end to the loathsome creatures. Morty keeps a small crow rifle for his other pests and shoots them out of the sky for sport. Bang, bang, bang. He rarely misses, exterminating the hateful birds before they wreak unnecessary havoc across his newly planted fields. Later in the year, he watches packs of baying hounds and sweat-flanked horses surge across the farmland in pursuit of the vermin fox, spilling its blood into the hard earth.

Some call cats vermin. They are wrong. One man's pest is another man's pet. Some love dogs, some loathe them. Some tolerate children, but I cannot abide them. They make me physically sick. Nasty, dirty, noisy, parasites. I detest them almost as much as the rats whose disgusting habits they so closely mimic. I would like another cat. I am lonely, and as I can expect to be on this earth a while longer, I want more reliable companionship than a fickle woman can give. A cat will be constant, not here one moment and gone the next. But how can I protect it? How can I be sure that it won't end up dead in a ditch like the loyal Dante? Here's how. I set a trap. A rat trap. Many traps.

Isn't it strange that the minute a thought comes into your head, the means to achieve it arrives almost magically before you can change your mind? I wonder if I would have bothered, had it not come into my possession so readily. After years of using rat cake before Dante, I would have recognised it anywhere, even with the red colouring which, despite what they say, is not always added. It lay on the counter, just propped against a bottle as if it had been waiting for me, and it was the work of a moment to grasp it and shove it into my pocket. Once I had it, I ached to use it – to purge the streets of those wicked creatures posing as young human beings. As I closed my hand over the wrapping paper, a thrill shot from my fingertips to my groin. A profoundly sensual, bottomless ache of pleasure at the thought of the power I held, and I could not wait to use it. I left the shop to seek a suitable victim.

#

The first time is always the most satisfying. None of the other poisonings has ever quite lived up the satisfaction of watching that stupid girl refuse the rat cake only to discover that she did precisely what I intended later that day. The little bitch bit me as I handed her the cake. I don't know why. I only held her arm briefly, and that was enough to make me feel ill at the thought of the nasty pale flesh beneath. I only chose her because she was there, brashly leading a group of children, commanding the unholy brood as if she was the Pied Piper of Hamelin. Arrogant, she was. I'm a good judge of character. I could tell at a glance that they would do as she asked, and they did – eleven of them. Only one died, which was a pity, but it was a close-run thing. I could so easily have had four or five more vermin souls that day. It was a good feeling and one which I was in a hurry to repeat.

I attended the Yeo boy's inquest. It was risky, I suppose, but I felt no more in danger there than I do today. The verdict was satisfying.

The judge ruled that the deceased died from the effects of some irritant poison, but how or from what source the evidence did not show. In other words, I had got away with it, and there was no reason why I shouldn't continue, so I did.

The first challenge was where to acquire more poison. The rat cake had worked as well on the human vermin as it did on the rodents. And it seemed quite fitting that the greedy little children should learn a lesson from eating cake that did not belong to them. I decided not to seek another means of poison, but to procure the same. I couldn't rely on the Tullises to be quite so obliging this time, and with a few gentle enquiries, I soon learned that they used rat poison extensively at the docks. It was no difficulty at all to move among the dock men and the gangers. A small adaptation to my working garb and I had a legitimate reason to be there, but it was February, and several visits later before the poison was safely in my grasp.

It happened almost by accident. After two abortive visits, I had gone by foot and was making my way towards Custom House when I spied a man ahead of me who was carrying a weather-beaten leather satchel with a broken strap. As he walked, he leaned over to tie his lace, and a single glove fell to the floor. He rose and waved towards another man in the distance. I nearly hailed him to tell him about the missing glove but thought the better of it and watched as several other items dropped from the unstable satchel as he ran towards his friend. He did not notice, so great was his hurry. I waited until he was a safe distance away and examined the items. He had dropped the second glove, a pouch of tobacco and a small object wrapped in greaseproof paper. I opened it to find a circle of rat cake. This slice of good fortune allowed two other fatalistic decisions. As soon as I realised what he had been carrying, I lost no time in tracking him down and following him back to the docks, keeping a safe distance behind. One docker would have been fair game, but I could not hold my own against two and fighting was not my way. I hoped he would lead me to a stash of poison cakes, but instead, he dropped his bag in a dirty room with a feeble fire and two long benches. The two men lingered for a while before making their way towards a warehouse, and I made a split-second decision not to follow them, but to investigate the room instead. It was a wise decision. Who knows what I might have found in the warehouse? I may or may not have laid my hands on poison, but the bag turned out to contain more than one rat cake. There were at least twelve. Not entirely content, I rummaged around the second man's satchel. He also carried a substantial amount of poisoned cake, and I took every last item. It was a good night's work, and I left with the best part of two dozen vermin-destroying objects for my future pleasure.

Everything takes practice, and murder is no exception. I wasted several precious poison cakes perfecting my craft. I left them in plain sight, but the creatures either wouldn't take them or did not eat them. I was reluctant to show my face again so soon after the Yeo boy died, which ruled out persuasion but not for long. It's addictive, you see, just like smoking a pipe or chewing tobacco. All my life, I have been ruled by rats, both while awake and in my dreams. But since I have learned to control the human vermin, I am not quite so troubled. Destroying the Yeo boy cleared my mind, defogged it, if you will. I slept through the night without being disturbed by scratches and squeaks, not just once but for several weeks. But as the bait failed to trap the prey, so the rats returned. They even intruded into my place of employment which had never happened before. Desperation made me act, and I directed a girl child to the cake on the road, but I was careful and wore a scarf over the lower part of my face. She would not have recognised me.

It took a day or two to find out whether I had been successful, and though I managed to exterminate two children on that occasion, it did not bring the same degree of pleasure. Whether it was because one child lived, or whether it was because the dead girls were so young, I cannot say. On reflection, though, I prevented them from reaching the age at which children become wicked and cruel, so it served the purpose.

The path to realising my objective has not always run smoothly, and there was one particular failure that I couldn't have anticipated. One bright evening in July, I laid a cake, red side down, near the Seamen's Hospital. It was a balmy evening marred by the number of shrieking children polluting the streets but, for the same reason, an excellent evening to hunt. I retreated into an alley and watched, fully expecting a young rat to spring the trap, but it did not happen that way. From my excellent vantage point, I saw, instead, a man of my age approach, stoop and remove the cake from the ledge upon which I had left it. Without looking at the underside, he devoured it, wiping the crumbs from his hands with an air of satisfaction. My first inclination was to help him, but I quickly dismissed it and followed him instead. The effects of the poison were rapid. Within ten minutes he was leaning against a post, clutching his stomach and within another five he had doubled back towards the Seamen's Hospital doors through which he staggered just after seven o'clock. I kept an eye on the newspapers and it did not take long for reports of his death to reach the press. My conscience was troubled for a while, but it did not last, and I surrendered to the urge to poison whenever it manifested itself. Surprisingly, at least three other deaths went unreported – vermin children who were so unloved that their demise did not come to the attention of the authorities.

And now we are in September with the year's end rapidly approaching, and I am minded to lay my traps again. It has been too long since my last kill. Yet strange reports emerge of a girl child who has died from the effects of poisoned rat cake. The police have attributed her death to the killer of Joseph Yeo and the Cochlin girls. But they are wrong. I did not poison Edith Eliza Beard and cannot lay claim to her death, as much as it would please me to do so. Was she poisoned at all, or do I have company? Surely, there cannot be another like me?

CHAPTER TWENTY-SEVEN

Deborah Lister

Thursday, September 24, 1896

"Violet, where are you going?"

Violet pulled her hat over her ears as the wind whipped through her hair. For a moment she thought she had heard something, but a quick glance to her side showed an empty street. She ploughed on, battling the wind as she passed the farm gates and slowed down a few yards beyond.

"Violet!"

This time there was no mistaking the bellow of a male voice. Violet turned full circle and found herself facing Francis Farrow's Arnold Benz.

"What are you doing here?" she asked in surprise.

"I could ask you the same," said Francis.

"You first."

"I've just collected a mantel clock from old Tom Gould in Thorpe Morieux. The man's a marvel. The clockmaker in Bury said it would never run again. Well, he was wrong. Tom showed me. It's running better than ever."

Violet smiled. "I'm pleased to hear it," she said.

"Well. Why are you here? You've only just returned from London."

"I've got one more person left to speak to."

"Who?"

"Deborah Lister. She sold Julia the cakes."

"Really. And that's why you're in Felsham? How did you get here?" asked Francis without waiting for Violet to answer the first question. "And why didn't you ask me for a ride?"

"By cart," said Violet. "And I didn't want to bother you again. It's been kind of you to ferry me around, but I really didn't want to impose any further."

"We're friends," said Francis quietly, his usual bombastic tone replaced by humility. "You can ask anything of me."

"Thank you." Violet pulled out her notebook in a bid to change the conversation, which was heading into dangerous territory again. "The Hall," she said under her breath.

"Over there," said Francis, pointing left.

Violet did not ask how he knew, choosing instead to return the notebook to her bag. "Lovely to see you, Francis," she said. "But I must press on."

"I'll wait," said Francis. "You'll have a more comfortable return journey."

"That won't be necessary."

"It's my pleasure," he continued.

"Very well. I won't take long."

Violet ventured up the windy path to The Hall and proceeded down the side of the building towards the tradesmen's entrance. While she did not know Deborah Lister's connection to the property, she assumed it was more likely to be as a servant than an owner. The back door was held open by a basket containing a selection of vegetables. Violet knocked and called out.

"Hello, miss," said a young girl, craning her head around the door to the left. "What do you want?"

"I'm looking for Deborah Lister."

"She's in the scullery," said the girl, nodding towards the right-hand door.

Violet thanked her and went inside to see a plump, red-faced woman heaving an oversized pan from the stove onto the draining board. The pan sloshed as the woman set it down. Just in time, thought

Violet, watching as it teetered unsteadily. The woman took a cloth from a fold in her apron and wiped her forehead.

"I'm getting too old for this," she complained, as she sat down heavily on a wooden stool.

"Are you Deborah Lister?"

"I might be. Who's asking?"

"Violet Smith. I'm an acquaintance of Anna Fisher."

"Anna Fisher. I haven't seen much of her since she moved to Hitcham. What does she want?"

"Nothing. I've been investigating an old case. Well, a new case to me, but something that happened a long time ago, and Anna mentioned your name."

"What case?"

"The death of Freddy Brown."

Deborah's piggy eyes glinted. "That was thirty years ago. What can you hope to achieve?"

"My client would like to clear Julia's name."

"Don't you think it would have happened by now if it were possible?"

"It's beginning to look that way. I've exhausted all suggestions."

"And how do you think I could help?"

"I hoped you could tell me what mood Julia was in when you met her that day. Does your memory go back that far?"

"For this, then yes," said Deborah. "It's not the sort of occurrence easily forgotten. I've just finished baking. Stay here and I'll fetch something to eat. I've been up since five and I'm peckish."

Violet watched as Deborah leaned against the tabletop and heaved herself up. She plodded through the door, returning a few minutes later with a plate laden with thickly cut slices of gingerbread.

"Take a piece," said Deborah, sliding the plate towards Violet.

Though not hungry, Violet obliged. The gingerbread was moist and tasty, and Violet finished it quickly.

"Have another," said Deborah, helping herself to a second slice. Violet shook her head and waited for Deborah to finish.

"Happy," said Deborah, through a mouthful of crumbs.

"Sorry?"

"Julia was happy when I met her. She was in a good mood, and I can remember watching her swinging her basket as clear as day. She was singing a ditty as I walked towards her."

"Did you know her?"

"Yes, reasonably well. Enough to enquire after her doings."

"Did she tell you where she was going?"

"Oh yes. Julia said she was going to see her boy and was looking forward to it, except that she'd hoped to take him a present. She always liked to take him something, but that week she'd been too busy to look. I said I could help her and that I had just the thing."

"Then you gave her the cakes?"

"I sold her the cakes," Deborah corrected. "That's why I was going to Brettenham, to sell them at the village fayre."

"I see," said Violet. "Were all the cakes the same?"

"As far as I could tell," said Deborah. "And the boy didn't die because of the cakes. The doctor tested them."

"He only tested one," said Violet.

"I didn't do anything to the cakes," Deborah snapped defensively.

"Of course, you didn't. Please don't feel that you need to explain yourself. If I've said anything to imply otherwise, then I'm sorry, but I don't believe for one moment that you've done anything wrong. I'm just trying to understand everything that happened that day."

"Good," said Deborah, "because I didn't interfere with the cakes, and Julia isn't the only one who has had to deal with underhand suggestions over the years."

"You too?"

Deborah nodded.

"I'm sorry. It can't have been easy."

"Neither Julia nor I ever married," said Deborah, bitterly. "What man would want a wife that he couldn't trust."

Violet opened her mouth to placate Deborah but changed her mind fearing she would make the situation worse. She sat silently for a moment.

Deborah helped herself to a third slice of gingerbread. "Who engaged you?" she asked.

"Drucilla Brown."

"I like Drucilla."

"Everyone seems to," Violet agreed. "She is a kind woman."

"Is there anything else?" asked Deborah. "I need to prepare the evening meal."

"Not really," said Violet, "except that it might help to know where you purchased the cakes."

"I had an arrangement with Jimmy Gladwell," said Deborah. "The village baker didn't trade from his premises and sold his wares through the grocers."

"Both of them?"

Deborah nodded. "Yes. They didn't get on, you know. What one sold, the other insisted on selling too. So, they both stocked the baker's goods. Anyway, Jimmy always bought more than he needed, so his stock looked bigger, and I would take what he didn't sell and hawk it to the local villagers. I kept half the profits and Jimmy had the other half. It worked well for both of us until we fell out."

"And you sold baked goods this way on the day that Freddy died?"

"Yes. Jimmy wasn't at his shop when I arrived, and I couldn't wait for him without missing the start of the fayre, so I took half the cakes from the counter and some more from a tray on the window ledge."

"Which Julia purchased. Were there any left?"

"Several dozen," said Deborah. "They sold well at the fayre, and nobody took ill." She glared at Violet and smiled insincerely.

"Jimmy must have been pleased," said Violet.

"He should have been," said Deborah. "I sold more that day than ever before, especially as Julia gave me a little extra for helping her out. But Jimmy snatched the money from me and barely spoke. I asked him what was wrong, and he snapped at me and said never to take things from his shop when he wasn't there. I suppose he thought he would have made more money selling them himself and not cutting me in. But he knew I was coming for the cakes and it wasn't my fault that he was out."

"Quite," said Violet watching Deborah's hands which were shaking with silent rage. Even after all these years, she felt the unfairness keenly.

"That was the last time I bothered," she continued. "I found another way to make a living, and not long after, Jimmy sold his shop. So, I can't help you. I wish I could. Julia is a good person."

"You've been very helpful," said Violet, rising to her feet. She walked towards the door, then turned back. "I'm not married, Deborah. Sometimes it's just not in life's plan."

Deborah stared mutely and did not acknowledge her words. Violet walked towards the automobile, wondering whether she should have stayed quiet.

"Finished?" asked Francis, who was napping in the front seat and had just woken, bleary-eyed, at the sound of Violet's footsteps.

"Yes," she said, reaching for the passenger door.

Francis jumped down and rushed to open it. "Any good?"

"Not really," said Violet, reaching for her journal. She scribbled a few notes as Francis started the engine. They moved off and continued through Felsham and were proceeding down Cockfield Road when Francis took the corner too quickly and almost collided with a horse and cart on the other side. The horse bolted, and Violet's notebook slid across the vehicle. They heard a loud clunk as the clock bounced from the back seat and landed on the floor.

"Blast it," said Francis. "Are you hurt?"

"No." Violet recovered her journal and stuffed it in her bag.

"I hope the clock's not damaged."

"I'll have a look." Violet turned and retrieved it from the floor. She placed it on her lap and unwrapped the layers of newspaper covering the timepiece. "It's still ticking," she said.

"Thank God," said Francis relieved.

Violet took the newspaper and smoothed it across her lap, ready to rewrap the clock. As she did so, she saw an advertisement for lachrymatory bottles.

Francis craned his neck to see what she was reading. "Damn silly idea," he said.

"Hmmm?"

"Some antique dealers are like snake oil sellers," he continued, nodding towards drawings of tiny glass vials on the page. "It's all a myth."

"What is?"

"Those objects are lachrymatory bottles, so called because they are supposed to contain tears," said Francis. "It's fanciful and just another way to get the rich to part with their money."

But Violet wasn't listening. Her mind wandered back to Deborah Lister's words.

"I need to send a telegram," she said urgently. "I think I know how Freddy died."

CHAPTER TWENTY-EIGHT

What Nance Said

"You're lucky I'm still here," said Isabel Smith, looking at the wall clock. She stuffed a sheaf of papers into a leather case and walked towards the door."

"I'm sorry," said Lawrence. "I'm only here on the off chance and know perfectly well that I've been pushing my luck. I'll look in to say goodbye before I leave London. I have a lot to thank you for."

"It's nothing," said Isabel. "And I have faith that your information will be useful. Where are you going?"

"The usual place."

"Silvertown?"

"Yes. I want to drop in on Louisa Tullis one last time. Don't worry. I'll get the train."

"There's no need. I'm on my way to Thrawl Street."

"Whitechapel?"

Isabel nodded.

"Grim," said Lawrence. "And not very safe."

"It's safer for me than you," said Isabel. "I've nurtured relationships with many of the women. It's the only way to offer some protection to their poor children. Follow me. Jennings can take you to Silvertown, while I'm in Whitechapel."

"Are you sure?"

"Perfectly. It will be nice to have your company."

"Thank you, Isabel."

Lawrence opened the door of the carriage before Jennings got there, and held out his hand to assist. Isabel took her seat and smiled as Lawrence joined her.

"Thrawl Street, please," said Isabel, placing her bag by her feet. She relaxed into the hard leather and watched as the carriage navigated the busy roads towards the East End. "How are you getting on, Mr Harpham?" she asked, after a few minutes of thoughtful silence.

"I don't know," said Lawrence honestly. "Every time I run out of ideas they're replaced by a glimmer of hope – a nebulous glimmer of hope. Nothing certain."

"But enough to send you back to Silvertown?"

"In desperation," said Lawrence.

"What are you looking for?"

"Apart from inspiration, a quick name count on who was definitely in the shop on the day the poison went missing. I know roughly, but not exactly and I'm going to make a list of names."

"Haven't the police already done it?"

"Probably. But I don't have that information myself."

"It can't do any harm."

"Quite. There is one other thing you can help me with."

"Name it."

"Have you ever heard of Muller Homes?"

Isabel stared at Lawrence. "Haven't you?"

"No. Should I have?"

"Probably not. Naturally, I know all about Muller Homes, given my occupation. I take it you are talking about the institution in Ashley Downs?"

"Exactly. Is it a workhouse or prison?"

"Neither," said Isabel. "It's an orphanage."

"Good Lord."

"Where did you come across it?"

225

"In the rented house of a woman called Jane Venables, who I believe might be Dorothy Jones."

"So many names," murmured Isabel. "I wonder why?"

"She's on the run from justice, I should think."

"Do you? I'm not so sure. Anyway, as you will see from the change in scenery, we're nearly here."

Lawrence recognised the shabby terraces of Commercial Road, which were a considerable improvement on the filth and wretchedness of Thrawl Street. He watched in dismay as grubby urchins swarmed over the mud-strewn road, filled with debris and animal waste. There had been little change since his foray into the East End while investigating the doss house in White's Row. Women lined the streets dressed in rags while their menfolk loitered in separate groups smoking pipes and chewing tobacco. They eyed passers-by with suspicion.

"Stop here," called Isabel, as Jennings reined in the horses.

"I can't leave you alone in a place like this," said Lawrence. "Look at them."

"Don't worry."

"No, Isabel."

She ignored him, opened the carriage door and alighted. Lawrence watched in horror as she approached a group of women.

"Maggie, Flo. How are you?"

The women smiled as she walked towards them, and one of the men raised his hand in greeting. Isabel had been right. The relationships she had courted allowed her to move where others could not safely go.

Lawrence spent the rest of the journey recollecting his time in the East End, and when he arrived in the malodorous, crowded streets of Silvertown, he appreciated the vast improvement from Thrawl Street. Lawrence found himself unexpectedly relieved to be in familiar surroundings, but his reception at the corner shop was less than welcoming.

"Oh, for goodness' sake, what do you want now?" Louisa Tullis scowled as he approached the counter. "You've been here more often than the police. There's nothing left to say."

"I will only take up a minute of your time," said Lawrence. "I just need an address."

"Whose?"

"Your friend's."

"Nance?"

"Yes."

"Why?"

"Does it matter?"

"You're not getting it if you don't tell me." Louisa put her hands on her hips and stared.

"Very well. I know some of the people who visited your shop and a few facts about those you didn't recognise. But I don't know many of their names."

"I'm not surprised. I can't remember half of the people who were here that day."

"I know. But Nance's brother came in. I would like to speak to him, at least."

"He was only in for a moment."

"It might have been long enough to see something."

Louisa tutted. "I suppose so. She won't thank me for it," she continued, scribbling on a wrapper. "She's not keen on the police."

"I don't suppose you know where her brother lives? It will save me having to bother her."

"No, I don't," said Louisa, passing the slip of paper. "Is that everything?"

"Absolutely everything. I will never darken your doors again," said Lawrence affably, doffing his hat. He whistled as he left the shop and quickly scanned the piece of paper while he walked back to the cab.

"Back to Poplar," said Lawrence, as he approached the cab driver. "How long do you think?"

"Twenty minutes. Fifteen at a push. Where are we going?"

Lawrence read out the address and returned to the cab. His excellent mood lasted precisely nineteen minutes until he realised that no amount of knocking would cause Nance to be at home. Both front and back doors were locked, and there was no sign of Nance or anyone else in the house. He decided to wait and checked his watch to see how long he could reasonably stay. His visit to Silvertown had been shorter than anticipated. He could afford another thirty minutes delay and still be back in Whitechapel as arranged with Isabel. Lawrence returned to the carriage to advise the driver of his intentions. Jennings was happy

227

to wait and keen to feed himself and his horse, agreeing to meet at the same spot within the half-hour. Lawrence returned to the cottage and sat on the low wall. Ten minutes passed, then ten minutes more and just as Lawrence was about to give up, a middle-aged woman carrying a large shopping basket appeared.

"I know you," she said, pointing to Lawrence.

"That's right. We've met. You've got a good memory for faces."

"I know. What can I do for you?"

"I need your help Mrs...? Oh, sorry. I only know you as Nance, and I can't really call you that."

"Of course, you can, but if you insist on formalities, then I'm Mrs Nancy Masters, although that is not my given name."

"Well, I'm Mr Lawrence Harpham, and I also have an alias."

"Is it because you're an investigator?"

"Yes. It's a bit of silliness. Violet, my business partner, tells me off for using it. She says nobody will believe it, but it's surprising how many do."

"What do you call yourself?"

"Alistair Blatworthy," said Lawrence with a rueful grin.

"It's a better name than mine," said Nance. "Stupid to give a girl a boy's name. I can't imagine what she was thinking of when she christened me Noel."

"I know a Noel," said Lawrence. "Admittedly, a male, but in my humble opinion, it's as good for a woman as a man and either spelling works. I think it's a pretty name."

"Really? Do you think so?"

"Yes, I do."

"Then how can I help you. Ask me anything you like." Nance beamed at Lawrence and flicked back her greying hair coquettishly.

"I'd like to speak to your brother. Can I have his address?"

"Well, yes," she said doubtfully. "But why?"

"I'd like to know if he saw anything the day the poison went missing. That's all."

"I doubt it. He was in a horrible mood and in and out of the shop in no time, but feel free to ask him. My brother lives in Wapping." She reeled off directions, and Lawrence wrote them down before waving and striding back to the carriage.

Jennings was waiting when he arrived. "Where to now?" he asked, somewhat impatiently.

"Wapping," said Lawrence, reading back the address.

"I see," said Jennings, slowly. "We will need to be quick. I don't like the look of Byron. He's a bit off-colour."

"I'm sorry," said Lawrence, eyeing the sweaty withers of the black horse. "I'll go another time. It's more important that Miss Smith gets home safely."

Jennings nodded, and they set off towards the East End.

The return journey to Thrawl Street seemed to take longer than the outgoing trip, and the further they travelled, the slower the carriage went. Eventually, Jennings veered away from the main thoroughfare, pulled on the reins and the horse stopped. Lawrence opened the window and leaned out.

"What's wrong?" he asked.

Jennings shook his head. "He's lame," he said, running a hand down the horse's dark foreleg. I was afraid this would happen."

"Oh dear. Poor Isabel will be waiting. Where are we?"

"We've made it as far as Wapping, so not much further to go." Jennings picked up the other foreleg and examined the hoof. "He's only limping on one leg," he said. "And he'll probably make it if we give him ten minutes rest and some water. Byron's hot and tired and no longer young. A bit like me."

Lawrence smiled, but Jennings was searching for something in a box at the front of the carriage. "I just need to strap his leg," said Jennings. "Can you fetch him some water?"

"Where from?" asked Lawrence, looking around for a bucket.

"There's a yard at the rear of that house," said the cabman, pointing ahead. "Down the alleyway and to the right."

Lawrence shuffled down the tiny passage which led to a walled yard about twenty feet square. Squeezed into a corner was a rusting metal trough half full of stagnant water. Someone had set a wooden bucket which had seen better days by the side. As Lawrence squatted to retrieve it, he wondered how Jennings had known about the yard. Then he felt a slight movement and a crack of pain on the back of his scalp before the world went black.

CHAPTER TWENTY-NINE

Rat in a Trap

Friday, September 25, 1896

Lawrence woke with a start and opened his eyes as he tried to make
sense of his surroundings. It was dark, and his cheek was icy cold.
Why? He raised his head a few inches and winced as a jag of pain
flashed from the back of his skull to his temple and throbbed angrily.
Where was he? Why couldn't he see? Lawrence blinked and raised his
head again, wiping his cheek with a trembling hand. His fingers
smelled of blood and earth. A chink of light appeared beneath a
shadowy void, and Lawrence realised that it was night time and his
eyes were slowly growing accustomed to the darkness. He hoisted
himself up to a sitting position, leaning heavily on his hand which was
gritty with dirt, racking his memories for some clue about where he
was and how he'd got there. Water – it was something to do with water.
Yes, he'd been about to fill a bucket before his world filled with pain.
Someone must have hit him on the head. He touched the back of his
scalp and his fingers settled on crusty, matted hair and a large painful

lump. Lawrence groaned and patted his jacket pocket, surprised to find the familiar bulge of his wallet still there. Not a robbery then, so why had he been hit? He tried the other pocket finding his trusty tin in its usual place. Lawrence struck a match with trembling hands and lit the candle stub he kept for emergencies, setting it in the upturned lid while he surveyed his surroundings.

Lawrence was sitting on the earthen floor of a cellar beneath a large barred window through which he could just make out a sprinkling of stars in the clear night sky. The tiny flicker of the candle cast scant light over the room, but enough for Lawrence to make out a succession of battered wire cages. He picked up the candle and peered at the nearest, narrowly missing a spring-loaded trap by his left hand.

'What on earth...?" he said aloud as the light settled on the wooden block. Lawrence took a pencil from his pocket and pushed it against the treadle activating sprung metal which snapped vice-like over the pencil, splitting it in two. Lawrence jumped, even though he had been expecting it. He'd seen a working prototype of a newly invented mousetrap while on a visit to Yorkshire the previous year but had hardly expected to be encountering another quite so soon. He reached for one of the wire cages and held it to the candle which cast just enough light to see a mouldy piece of cheese. Lawrence gingerly stood, reaching for the candle with one hand and holding his head with the other. He took a step and clattered against another trap, then another. The floor was littered with cages and traps as far as the eye could see. Lawrence shook his head, hoping he was dreaming, but when he opened his eyes again, he was still in the dark, in a cellar full of baited traps.

Lawrence shuffled towards the window, then inched around the room, clinging to the safety of the wall. He navigated the cellar, feeling his way until his fingers found a wooden door architrave. With a sigh of relief, he held the flickering candle aloft and yanked at the door handle. It did not move. He pulled it again, rattling the round metal doorknob that hung loosely from the door – nothing. The handle spun uselessly while the door stayed firmly locked. Lawrence kicked it in frustration, but without the key, he was imprisoned in the cellar. He groaned, then pulling himself together, inched beyond the door and further into the room before kicking something soft on the floor. Lawrence started as a sound like a deflating balloon rose softly by his feet. He stopped still and listened. There it was again – a faint sigh. Lawrence knelt, heart thumping, and cast his candle over the ragged bundle of cloth. – except that it wasn't cloth. And it wasn't one bundle – it was two. And the bundles had faces.

Lawrence stepped back in alarm, almost dropping his candle with the shock of the discovery as the tin top clattered across the floor. Taking a deep breath, he recovered the tin from the rubble-strewn corner and looked again. The faint flame settled on the pallid skin of a woman in her late sixties. Her mouth hung open, and her eyes rolled back in her sockets. He reached a hand towards her face, and his fingertips kissed cold dead skin. Lawrence turned away in horror, almost losing the contents of his stomach as he battled a sudden bout of nausea. He recovered himself and turned to the second body. The woman was younger, perhaps in her thirties and her lips, though tinged blue with cold, trembled as she struggled to speak. Lawrence set the candle beside her, grasped her hand and rubbed it in his. "Wake up," he said. "I can help you. Wake up."

She moved her lips but was too weak to speak. Lawrence stood, removed his coat and pulled her off the floor as he wrestled the jacket around her shivering body. Then he put his arm around her and held her tightly, using his body heat to warm her. He continued to talk, murmuring nonsense to keep her awake and alive and after half an hour he was rewarded by a half-smile and a croak of thanks. They must have fallen asleep but not for long, as it was still dark when Lawrence woke. He shook his companion in panic, cursing himself for not keeping her awake and alive, but when she opened her eyes and whispered, "What's your name?" he knew she would be safe.

"My name is Lawrence," he said. "Who are you?"

The woman gulped, then stared at Lawrence through frightened eyes. "Dorothy Jones," she said.

#

Lawrence shuffled back as if her words had burned him. "Dorothy Jones? Then what the hell have you done with the boy?" he yelled.

"What boy?" asked Dorothy through half-open, anxious eyes. She rocked back and forth, staring at the ground and rubbing a gaping wound in her leg.

232

"And who is she?" asked Lawrence, pointing to the dead woman. He had avoided mentioning the body while comforting the wounded girl, but now he knew who she was and what she'd done, he was in no mood to spare her feelings.

"My mother," said Dorothy, before putting her head in her hands. She cried silently with her head on her knees, shoulders shaking in anguish. "Oh, Mother, what have I done? This is all my fault."

Lawrence eyed her from a distance, mellowing but not ready to offer comfort.

"What did you do to her?"

"Me? Nothing. I loved her. She came to help me?"

"Help you steal children?"

"No. Why would you say that?"

"You took Bertie Johns."

"I minded Bertie Johns. I cared for him while his mother worked."

"You stole him."

"I saved him."

"He didn't need saving. Flora is a good mother."

"I know she is. I wasn't saving Bertie from her."

"Then who?"

Dorothy shuddered. "From him," she whispered. "The man who owns this house. Oh God." Dorothy cowered against the wall as the doorknob rattled. "He's here. God help me."

Lawrence moved towards her and held her hand as a key slid into the lock and the door swung open.

CHAPTER THIRTY

The Ratman Returns

Light flooded in from the opened door, glinting on the metal butcher's knife, as a chair scraped against the passageway floor. Lawrence squinted, shielding his face from the light while trying to see the man who stood silently in the doorway, but a scarf covered the man's mouth, making identification impossible.

"What do you want?" asked Lawrence, trying to mask the fear in his voice.

"Stay where you are," hissed the man, waving the knife towards Lawrence. "Don't move an inch or I'll cut her face."

Dorothy Jones shrank into Lawrence and trembled against his body.

"Who are you?"

"Be quiet." Their captor backed towards the window carrying the chair, which he positioned to face the outside of the building. He rummaged in his jacket and untied a length of rope from his waist. Lawrence peered at the chair. The back was unusually high.

"Over there," said the man, pointing to Lawrence.

"Why?"

"Get on that chair now or so help me, I'll show you what I can do with this knife."

Lawrence glanced at Dorothy. If imprisoned alone, he would take a chance. Apart from a head wound, he was uninjured, but the man was too close to Dorothy, and if Lawrence tackled him, it would be at considerable risk given her leg wound. She might be able to stand, but Lawrence doubted she could walk. He sighed and prepared to obey.

"Slowly, and on your hands and knees."

"Is that really necessary?"

"This is your last chance."

Lawrence crawled towards the chair and sat facing the window, fighting the urge to hurl the chair at his captor. He listened as the man crossed the room, wondering if it would be possible to immobilise him while seated. But the opportunity did not present itself, and Lawrence was shocked at the sudden sensation of a rope whipping across his chest as it was lowered from above and pulled tight. The rope, fashioned into a lasso, was simple to secure, leaving Lawrence bound and helpless.

"Dirty little boy," muttered the man.

"What?" Lawrence stared ahead, contemplating the prospect that he was in the presence of a lunatic.

"As for you..." The man had wandered across the room and was standing over Dorothy.

"Don't," she whispered.

"I told you what would happen."

"You know I could never harm them."

"You didn't love me." He kicked viciously towards the wound on her leg.

Dorothy screamed as his heavy boots dug into the exposed flesh and blood spurted down her leg.

"What's going on?" yelled Lawrence, unable to see past the high-backed chair.

"Just deserts," spat the man. "Disloyal little strumpet."

"Leave her alone."

The words were barely out of his mouth before a knife blade flashed before his eyes, then rested on his neck. The man leaned against Lawrence putting his mouth to his ear as he pushed the sharpened edge into his skin.

"She's mine," hissed the man. "To do with as I please. And if I tell her to do something, I expect her to do it."

"What's this got to do with me?" asked Lawrence

"Nothing," said the man bitterly. "If you'd left well alone, you could have lived a long and happy life. But you couldn't stop prying into matters that don't concern you."

"I know your voice," said Lawrence, screwing up his eyes in frustration.

"You should," said the man, stowing the knife and walking to Lawrence's side, before pulling the scarf from his face. "We were only travelling together a few hours ago."

#

"Valentine Jennings," said Lawrence, as the cab driver edged forwards until the shaft of light from the door fully illuminated his face. "Why?"

"You know why."

"No, I don't," said Lawrence.

"Don't be ridiculous," snapped Jennings. "You gave me directions to my own house."

"You're Nance's brother?"

"Certainly, I am, as you very well know."

Lawrence sighed and lowered his head. "Of course, you are. I'm every kind of fool. Valentine and Noel. I should have guessed."

"You did."

"I didn't," said Lawrence. "I had no idea. Visiting Nance was a last resort. I would have left London tomorrow."

"Damn you," cursed Jennings, thrusting the knife towards Lawrence's face. "You'll pay for this. It's only a question of whether I cut you up or leave you here to starve. The way I feel now, cutting is looking preferable." He stared menacingly into Lawrence's face.

"Won't Isabel have missed you yet?" asked Lawrence.

"I'm not stupid," snapped Jennings. "I collected her as soon as I knocked you out. She's none the wiser, and when you don't turn up to say goodbye, she'll think nothing of it."

"Are we in Wapping?"

"Yes. At my house. You very obligingly collected a water bucket from the yard by my basement. You could have hardly made it any easier."

"So, if you're Nance's brother, then you must have taken the rat cake?"

Jennings clapped his hands slowly. "Finally, you understand."

"Then how did the children get hold of it?"

"You are a stupid man, Mr Harpham."

"It's a reasonable question."

"Yes, I suppose it is. And as you're going to die anyway, then I'll tell you everything. Wait here," Jennings continued, smirking as he left the room, as if Lawrence could do anything but wait. The lock turned as the door slammed and for a moment, Lawrence sat in silence.

"Are you alright?" he whispered.

"Yes," Dorothy gulped as she momentarily stopped sobbing, and clutched the raw wound on her leg.

"Can you walk?"

She shook her head. "I don't think so."

"Try."

But it was too late. Lawrence could already hear another item scraping against the passage floor. The door opened further, and Jennings emerged with a stool which he placed in the corner of the room between the window and door, just in Lawrence's eyeline.

"It's her fault," said Jennings, settling on the stool and jabbing a dirty finger in Dorothy's direction. "All I wanted was someone to love me."

"I thought I did love you for a while," said Dorothy, her thin voice barely audible.

"And do you love her?" Lawrence interjected.

"Not now. She's just like all the others. No loyalty."

"If you ever loved her, let her go."

"What? And let her lead the police to my door? Never. She will die, and so will you."

"No one needs to die."

"Well, they're going to."

"Did you hurt her?" asked Lawrence, pointing to Dorothy's mother.

237

Dorothy's voice rose in an anguished wail from the corner of the room.

"No. The old woman was perfectly well when I took her."

"She had a weak heart," sobbed Dorothy, clutching her brow. "How dare you talk of love, when you're responsible for Mother's death."

"She shouldn't have interfered."

"I still don't understand," said Lawrence.

Jennings stood up and walked towards Dorothy. She cringed in fear as he approached.

"Why don't you explain?" he said, fingering the blade.

"You'll hurt me," Dorothy whispered.

"I'll hurt you more if you don't. You see, I don't understand either. You said you loved me and then you betrayed me. So, you explain, and I'll listen. And if at any stage, I don't believe you, I'll cut off your ears."

#

"We met five years ago," said Dorothy in a quavering voice. "My occupation brought me to London from Surrey, and I needed somewhere to lodge, so I moved in with Jennings."

"Mr Jennings," glared Valentine. There was a momentary pause, then he slashed the knife through the air, narrowly missing Dorothy's ear. "Mind your manners," he snarled.

"Sorry, Mr Jennings," whispered Dorothy.

Lawrence continued, oblivious to the near miss. "Were you living in his house?"

"Yes. We had a formal arrangement. I paid for my keep."

"And you were happy, dear, weren't you?" said Jennings, insincerely.

Dorothy faltered.

"Weren't you?" Jenning's voice was louder, insistent.

"I was content for the most. I enjoyed my job, and it was nice having company. And I liked your cat. We couldn't have one at home because they made my father sneeze. But Dante was a good companion."

"Did you live here long?" Lawrence risked another question, and Jennings didn't react.

"For a year," said Dorothy.

"Why did you leave?"

"Her employer made her live-in," snapped Jennings.

Lawrence wished he could see Dorothy's face. He could tell from the tone of her voice that there was more to the story. "Is that right?" he asked.

Dorothy gulped. "I told my employer that I was worried about my living arrangements, and she offered me a room at the asylum where I worked."

"Liar." Jennings' voice thundered through the cellar as he jumped to his feet.

"Steady on," yelled Lawrence. "You insisted that she told the truth, so listen."

Jennings shot him a glare, but returned to his seat, muttering under his breath.

"You frightened me," said Dorothy, "just like that outburst. Yes, I cared for you, but I didn't like it when you lost your temper, and I didn't like your house. All the traps and the constant talk of rats. I've never seen a rat in this house."

"But you were friends when you left?" asked Lawrence.

"Yes. And Valentine was kind to me when my situation changed. I thought it would be nice living with the other nurses, but one of them was hateful. She took an immediate dislike to me and made my life miserable. Valentine sympathised and suggested that I came back to live with him – he was lonely after Dante died and longed for company. I didn't immediately agree and waited to see if he would slip back into his bad-tempered ways. But he didn't. He was even-tempered and solicitous of my needs, so I came back and moved into my old room."

"Where you would have stayed if you'd known what was good for you."

Lawrence ignored the angry words. "Obviously, something did change?"

"Yes, but so gradually that I didn't realise what was happening at first." Dorothy sighed as if the weight of the world was upon her. "I don't know how to say this."

"Don't start peddling your lies," snarled Jennings.

"Either you want to hear her side of the story or you don't," said Lawrence.

"I don't want her to say it."

Lawrence stopped talking, and Dorothy waited. The room fell silent again. Lawrence circled his ankles. His leg was seizing with cramp, and he could feel the familiar prick of pins and needles. His foot scraped against the chair leg.

"What was that?"

Jennings darted out of his seat, a tremor in his voice.

"Nothing," said Lawrence.

"Oh, for God's sake, get it over with," said the cabman. "Say whatever you want. You're both going to die."

Dorothy moaned in abject terror. "It's a trick," she said. "If you're going to kill me anyway, then why should I say anything."

Jennings stood and walked towards Dorothy. She cowered as he lunged forward and grabbed her by the hair. He twisted her towards him and pulled her down until she was lying face up in his lap. He held her head with one hand and traced the knife across her neck with the other. "I think I'll cut your tongue out," he mused calmly.

"Damn you," cried Lawrence straining against the ropes. The chair clattered as he flexed every muscle in his body.

"Hah. It's no good," laughed Jennings.

"For God's sake, man. You go to work every day, taking Isabel to see the worst of humanity. How can you be as monstrous as they are, when I know you have intervened to save children's lives?"

"Only where it was unavoidable," said Jennings coldly.

"He hates children," whispered Dorothy. "In a way you could never understand."

"Try me," said Lawrence

"He'll hurt me."

"I'll only hurt you if you don't cooperate. I want to know exactly why you promised to help me and then went back on your word," Jennings snarled at Dorothy, sending flecks of spittle across her face.

"Because it was unreasonable, cruel. How could you expect me to do such a thing – or think I was capable?" Dorothy was crying now. Rivulets of tears ran down her dirt-covered cheeks, and she gulped as if in pain.

"You said you would do anything for me," said Jennings. "You said you would prove that you loved me."

"Dorothy, stop crying." Lawrence issued the instruction kindly but firmly. "Tell me exactly what you mean. I'm not following."

Dorothy bit her lip and tried to stem the tears. "When I left the asylum, Valentine helped set me up with the means to work as a childminder. He didn't want the children here and gave me the money to rent rooms in Battersea to mind the children on a short-term basis. I would look after them for six months and then we would get married."

"And have children of your own," said Lawrence.

"No. Valentine made it perfectly clear that could never happen. It was one of the reasons why I chose to care for children while I still could."

"So, there was a proposal?"

"Yes. I offered to marry Dorothy," said Jennings. "On condition that she demonstrated her loyalty to me."

"How?"

"He wouldn't tell me at first," said Dorothy. "He called on me several times at Gideon Road, but I had to leave the children in the room as he wouldn't tolerate them. The first child I took in did not stay long. Her mother collected her after only a few weeks. She had left her position for the sake of the child and said she would rather go into the workhouse than be parted from her again. Valentine asked if I would miss little June and I said I would, and he flew into an awful rage."

"It was a business proposition, Dora," spat Jennings. "That's why you took another name. You weren't supposed to become fond of the little rats."

"I couldn't help it," murmured Dorothy. "Unlike you, I love children. Anyway, other children came and went, and by the time I left Gideon Road, little Molly and Bertie were the only children in my care."

"And you stole them away?"

"Not the way you think."

"You stole them from me," hissed Jennings.

"I thought you didn't like children?" Lawrence was fast losing track of the conversation.

"He doesn't, Mr Harpham. He asked me to prove I loved him, and when I asked how, he told me to choose between him and the children."

"All you had to do was give them back," said Lawrence. "You didn't have to take them."

"You don't understand. Valentine wanted me to kill them to prove how much I loved him."

The room fell silent. Lawrence lowered his head. "Oh my God," he said. "How?"

"He wanted me to give them some poisoned cake. At first, I said I wouldn't, and he tried to take Bertie from me and said I could watch him do it if I preferred."

"Monstrous," said Lawrence.

"Shut up, or I'll cut her."

Dorothy ploughed on, ignoring the knife at her throat. She sounded resigned but relieved to tell the tale. "I begged him to give Bertie back and said I would do what he asked, but I needed time to make a plan to get away as Bertie's mother still called on him at Gideon Road. Valentine agreed. He said he would find me another room and would return the next day to get me."

"And you weren't there when I called. Where did you go, as a matter of interest?" asked Jennings. "I'm burning to know."

"Clapham Orphanage," said Dorothy. "It was all I could think of, but they wouldn't take them, so I brought them back, packed, and left with no idea of where to go. I found myself in Silvertown and was lucky enough to come across an untenanted house with a landlord prepared to accept low rent. I had an address for Molly's mother and wrote to her as soon as I could. She sent for the child after a few days, but I didn't know how to reach Flora Johns. She'd insisted on visiting us and would not give her address away so I kept Bertie as safely as I could. I didn't dare return to Gideon Road for fear that Valentine would find me."

"Disloyal bitch," said Jennings, jabbing the knife into Dorothy's chin.

"I went to your address in Silvertown," said Lawrence. "You'd already gone. Why did you leave so quickly?"

"Yes, why?" asked Jennings.

"Because I saw you, of course."

242

"Saw me?"

"Yes. I was in the corner shop picking up a few bits, and as I walked back to Albert Road, I saw your carriage on the other side and recognised it immediately. I pushed the perambulator behind a bush and watched until you left, not daring to go home. I thought you must have found me but probably didn't know the number of the house, so I took Bertie and fled."

"Where did you take him?" asked Lawrence. "On second thoughts, don't answer. You've kept him safe, and I wouldn't want him to be in danger just because we are."

"You will tell me," said Jennings, slowly and in a voice dripping with malice. "You chose the child above me, and you can now decide between your life and his."

"Leave her alone," thundered Lawrence, kicking against the window ledge. His chair teetered precariously, then settled back on the floor.

Jennings laughed. "You're a rat in a trap," he said," and you're going nowhere. Now, where was I?"

Dorothy whimpered, and Lawrence changed tack. "I got your address from Isabel Smith," said Lawrence. "How did she know it?"

"My income suffered when Molly left, and I took another child to pay for the next week's rent," murmured Dorothy. "It was only for a few days, but the mother was particular about seeing my certificate and not happy about the difference in the address. Perhaps she checked with the council."

Jennings groaned. "I could have found out where you were just by asking. You are such a disappointment. And just so you know, I was in Silvertown visiting my sister. She may live in Wapping, but she's gossiping with the Tullis woman, more often than not."

"I found a newspaper clipping in your house," said Lawrence. "with a drawing of a rat on it. Did you leave it as a clue?"

"No. I cut the article from the *Essex County Standard*," said Dorothy. "The poisonings were uncomfortably similar to the method Valentine suggested, and I wondered whether he got the idea from the newspaper. I don't remember drawing the rat, but perhaps I scribbled it without thinking."

"It was you, though, wasn't it, Jennings?" said Lawrence. "You killed the children?"

"Pests," said Jennings. "Vermin. Yes, I exterminated them, all but the last girl."

"Why?"

"I don't like children. Sorry if you're looking for something more profound, but I just can't bear the dirty, feral creatures."

Valentine Jennings tightened his arm around Dorothy's throat and shifted from a sitting to a kneeling position. "I think that's everything," he said.

Lawrence, still facing forwards, surveyed his restricted part of the room, looking for something to use as a weapon. There was nothing in sight but a sea of rat traps, and he was bound so tightly that he couldn't reach them if he tried. Dorothy whimpered again, and Lawrence closed his eyes, searching for a solution. Rat traps, rats, why so many? Fear of rats. Dirty, noisy, scrabbling rats. Lawrence clawed his nails against the hard wooden back of the chair and waited.

"What was that?" Jennings spat the words like bullets.

"What?"

"That noise?"

"I can't hear anything." Lawrence scratched again.

"Is that you?"

"Is what me? Don't be ridiculous."

Jennings jumped to his feet, hurling Dorothy from his lap. "Move and you die."

He inched towards Lawrence, peering from a distance. Lawrence scratched once more.

"It was you." Jennings's voice trembled unconvincingly.

"Oh my God!" Lawrence exclaimed at the top of his voice, nodding his head towards the corner of the room. "Over there. A dirty great rat."

Jennings rushed for the door and clung to the handle, holding the knife with trembling fingers. Two seconds later, he felt a crack on his temple and fell to the floor with a sickening thud as Dorothy wiped a rubble coated hand on her skirt.

#

"What's happened?" yelled Lawrence, straining but failing to peer past the high-backed chair.

"Dear God. I think I've killed him."

"Good. I hope so."

"Shall I check?"

"No. Don't risk it. Come and release me first."

"I don't know if I can walk."

"Try. Take it easy." Lawrence was panting as he contemplated freedom for the first time. He had been in many scrapes before, but this had seemed so final. He heard a low moan as Dorothy got to her feet.

"The pain in my ankle is excruciating," she said, gingerly tiptoeing forwards, then collapsing in a heap. "It's no good. I can't do it." Tears trickled down her face as she whimpered in pain.

"You must," said Lawrence firmly.

"I can't."

"Look at Jennings. Is he dead?"

"I don't know," Dorothy breathed. "He's very still."

"That's something, I suppose. Now crawl towards me."

"But I'll have to pass him."

Lawrence sighed. "You will be no closer than you would have been if you were walking."

"I'm frightened."

"I am too, but I'm also worried about what will happen if he wakes up and I'm still trussed to this chair. You must get a grip, Dorothy. Come on."

Dorothy didn't reply, but Lawrence could hear her moan as she inched across the floorboards on her elbows, dragging her body behind.

"Good girl," muttered Lawrence, waiting with bated breath.

Dorothy finally reached him, and got to her knees, wincing as a sickening jolt of pain flashed through her damaged leg. Her fingers trembled as she untied the knots around his ankles.

"Thank you," said Lawrence, flexing his feet.

Dorothy began working at the knot that pinned his arms to the back of the chair. The rope was thick and coarse, and the lasso arrangement had made an almost impenetrable bond.

Dorothy's head jerked as Jennings groaned. "He's awake," she cried.

"Ignore him. Keep working," Lawrence commanded.

"My fingers are shaking."

"Don't worry. Jennings will be unconscious for a while."

But he wasn't. Moments later, Jennings groaned again and raised a stubby hand to his temple. "What...?" he asked, gazing at his bloodied hand through half-open eyes.

Lawrence strained against the ropes. "Any progress?" he asked.

"I can't do it."

"Then you'll have to incapacitate him again."

"What?"

"Throw another brick at his head."

"No. I'll have to crawl past him to reach one."

"Then do it," hissed Lawrence as Dorothy let out a terrible screech.

"Get off me," she screamed. Jennings' hand had snaked out and grabbed her by the ankle. He was trying to raise himself while dragging her towards him in confused fury.

"Did you do this?" he yelled, wiping the blood from his head onto her skirts. "You'll live to regret it, but not for much longer."

Dorothy screamed again as he gained purchase higher up her leg and hauled her close to his still prone body. Jennings scrambled to his knees and straddled Dorothy, pinning her to the floor. "Where's the bloody knife?" he yelled, scrabbling on the floor for his weapon. "There it is."

Jennings lunged for the knife, but Lawrence was quicker. Spinning around, still bound to the chair, he launched himself at Jennings who fell to the ground, winded. This time, Dorothy held her nerve. Freed from the weight of Jennings' body, she grabbed the knife and plunged it into his neck. Blood spurted across the room in a gruesome scarlet arc as Lawrence watched with satisfaction knowing that the Ratman was finally trapped.

CHAPTER THIRTY-ONE

Telegram

Saturday, September 26, 1896

In the pigeonhole of Room 14 at Gray's Hotel:

From: Smith, The Butter Market, Bury St Edmunds
To: Harpham, Gray's Hotel, Battersea
24 September 1896, 4.45 pm
Come as soon as you can. I think I know how Freddy Brown died. I'm going to Felsham to test my theory.

Letter postmarked September 25, 1896

Lawrence, old chap. I have enclosed a clipping from the local rag.
They found Jimmy Gladwell hanging from a tree on Thursday night.
His name kept cropping up when Vi and I were in Felsham – it's a rum
old thing, don't you think? Have you heard from Violet? I haven't seen
her for a few days.
Pop by for a swift one when you're home next.

Francis

CHAPTER THIRTY-TWO

Reunited

Wednesday, September 30, 1896

"Is she here?" Lawrence was standing at the front door to Netherwood House, while Alfred Floss stood uncertainly in the doorway.

"Yes, Mr Harpham. Just as you asked. I do hope it's not bad news."

"Are they in the drawing room?"

Floss nodded.

"Then hurry along and tell them I've arrived. I'll catch you up in a minute."

Lawrence turned to his companion in the carriage and passed over a purse of coins. "Thank you," he said. "I wouldn't have managed without you." He scooped the squirming bundle from the woman's arms, entered the hallway and opened the drawing room door with his foot.

"Master Bertie Johns," he announced, thrusting the sleeping baby towards his mother.

Flora's hands flew to her mouth as she trembled, eyes wide, hardly daring to look. "Bertie – is it truly you?"

Lawrence pulled the covering away from the baby and handed him over.

"Oh, Bertie." Tears streamed down Flora's face as she recognised her son. "I can't believe it. How did you find him?" She sobbed and smiled in turn as she ran her finger down his soft cheek. The child's eyes flickered open, and he focused on his mother and smiled.

"It's a long story," said Lawrence. "But I must tell you that Dorothy Jones did not kidnap Bertie. She saved his life."

"Why didn't she tell me?"

"She couldn't find you, and she couldn't stay where she was without endangering him."

"Where was he?" Albert Floss watched his niece with a beaming smile on his face. "He doesn't look any the worse for wear, Flora dear," he continued.

"Bertie was cared for very well," said Lawrence, "in the Muller House orphanage."

"An orphanage. How horrible," exclaimed Flora.

"Not at all. I've just left Ashton Downs. Muller House is the most remarkable place and runs solely on donations. The orphans are treated kindly and with love and care."

"But Bertie isn't an orphan."

"I know. And even had he been so, and forgive my frankness, your unmarried status would debar him from entry. But Bertie was in danger, and Dorothy Jones was desperate to help him. By luck, she encountered a Christian missionary while she was inside Clapham Orphanage. The Clapham overseer declined to take Bertie, but the missionary gave her a pamphlet about Muller Homes orphanage and told her to contact him in Islington if her situation became intolerable. When it did, she tracked him down and handed over Bertie. It was a risk, but not as great as the one he would have suffered had she kept him. He was transported to Ashley Down and was only there for a short time before I collected him yesterday."

"But I don't understand why Bertie was in danger."

"Because Dorothy cared about him. She was fond of all the children in her care. Dorothy was due to marry a man who she thought she knew, but who turned out to be unhinged. He wanted her to prove her love by destroying something she cared for – your son, Bertie."

"Then I owe her my thanks."

"You do," said Lawrence. "And I hope one day you can give them in person. Now, it just remains for me to find Violet and give her the good news. I'm surprised she's not here."

Francis Farrow cleared his throat and stepped forward. "About that, Harpham."

"Yes?"

"There's no easy way to say this. She's put her cottage on the market. Violet has gone, and I don't think she's coming back.

CHAPTER THIRTY-THREE

Vanished

Lawrence didn't stop to ask for details and flew to thirty-three The Butter Market with indecent haste. His hands trembled as he unlocked the office door, hoping against hope that he would find Violet inside. The office was cold and empty and Violet's desk was clear, which was out of the ordinary. Tidiness was not one of her strengths. Lawrence strode across the room and yanked her desk drawers open. Apart from some sundry pieces of stationery, Violet's effects had gone, and nothing personal remained. Lawrence sat down at his desk with his head in his hands, then glanced at the mantlepiece above the fire. A single letter written in Violet's hand and bearing his name leaned against the carriage clock. Lawrence returned to his desk and set the envelope down in front of him, fearful of the contents. Prevaricating, he opened his desk drawer and searched for the bottle of whisky that he kept for visitors. He emptied a jumble of drawing pins from an old teacup on his desk, sloshed in a slug of alcohol and drank it in one swift gulp. Lawrence wiped his mouth, then stared at the letter before screwing up his courage and slitting it open.

Saturday, September 26, 1896

Dear Lawrence,

By the time you read this, I will have left Bury. Aunt Floss has died, and I must now take charge of a matter that I should have dealt with last year. It is high time that I faced up to my responsibilities and accepted that my time in Suffolk is over. I am leaving you my share in our partnership as a wedding gift and wish you every happiness in your forthcoming nuptials. I do hope that this will make things easier for you. All the necessary legal documents are in the hands of my solicitor and you will receive a communication from him shortly. You will also notice some transactions in our bank account. Drucilla Brown has paid our fee, and I have taken my share.

I expect you would like to know what happened to Freddy Brown. After all these years, Julia's name is clear at last, and it is mainly because of a clock repairer's choice of wrapping paper. But for that, I would never have heard of lachrymatory bottles which were a vital component in Freddy's death. Bear with me, Lawrence. I am short of time and beginning to ramble, so I'll take a few moments to re-organise my thoughts and write more clearly.

Now, it's important to note that Julia Brown purchased some cakes on her way back from Brettenham. You will also remember the shards of glass located near Freddy's bed. One of the cakes was tested and declared to be perfectly safe. The doctor, therefore, assumed that all the cakes were uncontaminated, but it was not the case. Somebody had tampered with one and inserted a tiny vial of sulphuric acid. You may wonder who would have wanted to harm a young child, or indeed any member of the Brown family. They had no known enemies. Well, the answer, of course, is nobody. That was never the intent. The cakes had come from a batch sold at the grocer's store, but Deborah took the wrong ones. The cakes she removed had been placed in a side window, to set them apart from those due for sale. But the grocer was unexpectedly detained when Deborah Lister arrived, and she took both batches of cakes.

I should have worked out what happened far sooner. The clues were there right from the start. I'd heard that there were two grocers in Felsham, both during Freddy's lifetime and now. By sad coincidence, neither set of grocers could tolerate the other. But the disagreement between Alfred Chipperfield and Jimmy Gladwell was much more serious than the harmless antipathy between their recent counterparts. Alfred and Jimmy hated each other, were unhealthily competitive and profoundly resented any trading success by their rival. Their relationship became so bitter that Jimmy Gladwell deliberately poisoned a cake intending to put it in Chipperfield's shop. They both sold the same products from the same baker, and it would have been a simple matter to make a switch or persuade someone else to do it. There was no glass in little Freddy's stomach, and I can only assume that he bit into the vial, picked it out and finished the cake. The sulphuric acid would have leaked into the sponge cake the moment the glass shattered.

I went to see Jimmy after I sent you the telegram and I told him what I suspected. He did not deny it and walked away without saying a word. He must have killed himself soon after and they found him hanging from a tree the next day. A policeman brought a note over yesterday which they removed from Jimmy's jacket pocket. It was addressed to me and contained only three words – 'you were right'. He must have lived with the guilt for years. I know he suffered because he sold the grocer's shop not long after for a fraction of what it was worth. I suppose he couldn't bear to keep it, knowing what he had done.

So, that was it, Lawrence. A simple mistake – a stupid vengeful act that he might not have gone through with had he given it more thought, but fate took it out of his hands.

I received your telegram just before I packed, and I am thrilled that you have located Bertie Johns. It has made me feel so much better about leaving. I want you to know that I have enjoyed every moment of our business relationship and I will look back fondly on our times together. But all good things must come to an end, and this is the right moment for our lives to diverge. I wish you luck and good fortune in everything you do.

Your friend always, Violet.

Lawrence turned the letter over, searching for a forwarding address, but the back was empty. He put his head in his hands and sat silently for a while. When he finally turned the key in the office door, his face was still wet with tears.

THE END

Note: The Infant Protection Act of 1872 made it necessary to register all houses in which more than one child was taken for reward for longer than twenty-four hours.

Thank you for reading The Felsham Affair. I hope you liked it. If you want to find out more about my books, here are some ways to stay updated:

Join my mailing list or visit my website
https://jacquelinebeardwriter.com/

Like my Facebook page
https://www.facebook.com/LawrenceHarpham/

If you have a moment, I would be grateful if you could leave a quick review of The Felsham Affair online. Honest reviews are very much appreciated and are useful to other readers.

Printed in Great Britain
by Amazon

78145272R00149